SABLE PEAK

SABLE PEAK

USA TODAY BESTSELLING AUTHOR

DEVNEY PERRY

Entangled Publishing, LLC
644 Shrewsbury Commons Ave., STE 181
Shrewsbury, PA 17361
rights@entangledpublishing.com

Amara is an imprint of Entangled Publishing, LLC.

Visit our website at www.entangledpublishing.com.

Edited by Elizabeth Nover
Cover art and design by Sarah Hansen at OkayCreations
Stock art by OSTILL is Franck Camhi/Shutterstock,
otenko Oleksandr/Shutterstock,and nighty-stock/DeviantArt
Interior design by Toni Kerr

ISBN 978-1-64937-673-2

Manufactured in the United States of America

First Edition December 2023

10 9 8 7 6 5 4 3 2

ALSO BY DEVNEY PERRY

PART I

Before

CHAPTER 1

VERA

DECEMBER

I was surrounded by Edens.

"Can I get you something to drink, Vera?" *Anne.* The mother. Her name was Anne, right?

"Um... sure. Water, please."

"You got it." Anne—I was ninety percent sure that was her name—quickly filled a glass from the sink. She delivered it to my seat at the kitchen island with a smile, then returned to the stove to stir the spaghetti sauce.

A large pot of water was boiling for the pasta. Steam coiled up into the overhead fan. The scents of garlic, tomatoes and herbs infused the room, mingling with the voices.

There was so much talking in this kitchen. So many people. So many Edens.

I used to love being in the middle of a crowd.

Before.

Now? I wasn't sure yet. Maybe I hated them. Maybe I liked them. Considering this evening was my first foray into a social life, it was too soon to tell.

"You okay?" Uncle Vance leaned in close to speak quietly in my ear.

"There's a lot of them," I whispered.

He put his hand on my shoulder, giving it a squeeze. "Just breathe."

Lyla, his girlfriend, scooted her stool a little closer to mine.

Vance and Lyla were the only people I knew here tonight. This was Lyla's childhood home and her parents had invited us out for a family dinner.

She'd warned me on the drive that it would be loud. An understatement. There were at least five different conversations overlapping each other. Pockets of laughter bubbled up from every corner of the room. This wasn't loud.

This was chaos.

Did I like it? Sort of.

I drew in a long breath, holding it in my lungs until it burned, then blew it out. Then I sipped my water, letting it clear the scratch in my throat while I listened.

"What does Drake want for Christmas?" Lyla asked a blond woman.

What was her name? Madison? No, Memphis.

Memphis. Memphis. Memphis.

Her husband was Knox, the tattooed, bearded one. Or was she married to the cowboy? What was his name again? Garth? No, Griffin.

There were too many Edens.

"Anything dinosaur," Memphis told Lyla just as a string of kids rushed into the kitchen.

They blew in like a wild breeze, sweeping in, then out, disappearing back into whatever room they were playing in. Not a chance I'd figure out the kids' names tonight. My goal was to get their parents sorted first.

"Did you enjoy your time at the hotel, Vera?" Eloise asked.

"Yes, it was lovely." I was one hundred percent certain her name was Eloise because it was written on the hotel where I'd spent the past week.

But who was her husband? Jasper or Foster? Both men were sitting at the table in the adjoining dining room. One had a beard, and I was pretty sure that he was Foster.

Foster was the UFC fighter and he was married to Talia. Talia was Lyla's twin. So that meant that Jasper was Eloise's husband, right? Maybe?

Oh, God. I had a headache.

This dinner was a bad idea. It was too much, too soon. But I hadn't had the heart to tell Lyla no. She'd been so excited for me to meet her family, something she'd told me no less than five times as we'd moved my things out of The Eloise Inn.

I'd spent the past week sequestered in my hotel room, enjoying the solitude and endless hours of TV. If I could have stayed for a month, I would have, except the hotel was booked for the holidays. From now until January, every room was taken, including mine.

Besides, I'd spent enough of Uncle Vance's money. He didn't need to be wasting anything extra on a hotel charge. So this morning, with a heavy heart, I'd packed my suitcases and checked out.

For the time being, the upstairs guest bedroom at Lyla's farmhouse would be mine. It was a lovely room, and her house was the epitome of cozy. I had privacy. Down pillows. A mattress. Hot water. Flushing toilets. Electricity.

There was nothing for me to complain about.

But at the moment, I really wanted to be in the mountains, in a cold, drafty shelter where the only person around was Dad. Where I didn't have to worry about the noise or the names or being that awkward outsider at a family dinner.

I really missed my dad. I missed him so much it hurt to breathe.

Maybe I shouldn't have left him. Here I was, surrounded by Edens, and he was out there alone.

Was he okay? Was he still in Montana? Was he angry at

me for leaving? It felt like a lifetime ago, not seven weeks, since we'd said goodbye.

My gaze drifted to the window over the sink and the darkness beyond. White snowflakes tickled the glass. Every morning this week I'd woken up to find two or three more inches of fluffy white covering Quincy, Montana. And mountains were buried beneath the snow and ice.

Had Dad found a safe, warm place to stay this winter? Maybe he'd hiked south to Arizona or Nevada to spend a few months in the desert. Maybe he'd trekked north to Canada, where it would be easier to avoid the FBI. Without me along, slowing his pace, how far could he have traveled on foot in seven weeks?

"Are you heading back to Idaho before Christmas?" Harrison asked Vance.

Harrison was Lyla's father. There was a kid, a small one, named Harrison too. Because why make it easy for newcomers.

"I'm not sure when we'll head back." Vance looked to me with a silent reminder that it was my choice.

Sooner or later, we needed to return to his house in Coeur d'Alene. He had belongings to pack. He had a life to finish relocating to Montana. Except I hated Coeur d'Alene. I hated that it was my hometown.

But as much as I wanted to pretend it didn't exist, we had to go back. One last time.

"Before Christmas." When the new year began, I wanted to start fresh. Here, in Quincy.

Vance nodded. "Before Christmas."

He'd given me as much freedom and choice as possible over the past seven weeks. Not that I'd wanted much freedom. I'd stuck to him like glue, especially in the early days right after leaving Dad.

This past week at The Eloise had been the most time I'd spent alone in four years. It was weird not to have Dad. When was it going to stop being weird?

But as much as I missed him, as weird as it was, I sort of liked being alone too. In high school, I'd loathed being by myself with nothing to do. Dad had always called me his bouncy ball, in perpetual motion. But that was *before*.

The quiet and stillness weren't so bad.

I liked late nights, when the stars were bright. I liked early mornings, when the world was asleep. I liked TV. I liked hot coffee. I liked shaving my legs every day so that when I slept, my skin was smooth.

I was rediscovering what I liked. And what I didn't.

"Veggies?" Lyla slid the tray of veggies and ranch dip closer.

"Um, sure." There were toothpicks on the counter. Were those for the veggies? Or just the cheese cubes and black olives and mini pickles?

No one had touched the veggies. Everyone had used toothpicks.

I snagged one from the glass dish, hovering the tip over the vegetables. I didn't like celery or broccoli, so I skipped over those and opted for a baby carrot.

The toothpick wouldn't pierce it. Stab. Stab. Stab. It kept rolling away. I stabbed harder.

My toothpick broke.

I was surrounded by Edens. And everyone was staring at me.

Winslow—Winn—snagged a carrot from the tray, using her fingers. She dunked it in the ranch and popped it in her mouth.

Everyone descended on the tray. With their fingers.

I tucked mine in my lap.

"So Vance," Winn said. "I know you're not settled yet. But if you're interested in a job, I'd love a visit. Come down to the station anytime."

His eyebrows lifted. "Yeah?"

"Yeah." Winn was married to either the cowboy or the chef. And she was Quincy's chief of police.

"Thanks, Winn," Vance said, sharing a look with Lyla. "I'd like that."

For his sake, I hoped Winn could find a place for him in her department. It would be strange to see him work construction or in an office. He was meant to carry a badge. He was a great cop, like Dad had been once. *Before.*

"What can I help with, Anne?" Harrison moved to stand behind his wife at the stove, placing his hands on her shoulders as he bent and kissed her temple. "Put me to work, darlin'."

Anne. Her name was Anne.

Anne. Anne. Anne.

She smiled up at him. "Would you call your son and find out if he's on his way?"

Wait. There was another one?

I scanned the room. Lyla's brothers and sisters all had rich, brown hair and sapphire-blue eyes.

One. Two. Three. Four. Five.

There were six siblings. We were missing an Eden. Damn it. Who? Whose name was I going to forget next?

Harrison had just dug his phone from a pocket of his Wrangler jeans when the front door closed and boots stomped down the hallway. "There he is."

He strode into the room wearing a pair of faded jeans and a black plaid shirt with its sleeves rolled up his forearms. It hung open, revealing a white T-shirt underneath that pulled tight across his broad chest. A silver and gold belt buckle gleamed beneath a flat stomach. His brown cowboy boots were scuffed and faded. Like the other Edens, he had dark hair and sapphire eyes.

It was the playful grin that set him apart. The mischievous smirk on his soft lips. The sharp corners of his stubbled jaw and the twinkle in his blue gaze.

This kitchen was full of beautiful people.

He put them all to shame.

My heart pounded. My face flushed. I was staring like a fool but couldn't stop. I couldn't blink. My body was having a whole reaction with or without my brain's permission.

"Finally," Eloise groaned. "I'm starving."

"Sorry I'm late."

God, his voice was incredible. Deep and rugged and smooth. A shiver raced down my spine.

Everyone drew closer to him, like he was a magnet and they were metal. That pull was so tempting but I kept my seat, clutching the stool's edge so I wouldn't topple over.

He shook his brothers' hands. They talked and laughed. When Lyla moved closer, he pulled her into a sideways hug, his tall frame towering over hers.

A flutter stirred in my belly, whirling and falling and lifting and spinning, like the snowflakes blowing outside.

He was…

I couldn't think of the right word. Perfect? Handsome? Mesmerizing?

Yes. Mesmerizing.

"Come meet Vera." Lyla tugged him over, smiling as they shuffled toward the island.

"Hey." He dipped his chin, like he was tipping an invisible hat. "I'm Mateo."

That name locked into place for all time.

Mateo.

CHAPTER 2

I liked carrot cake muffins with cream cheese frosting. I liked turkey sandwiches more than ham. And I loved Eden Coffee.

Lyla's cafe had become my favorite spot in Quincy. It made working here feel like a treat. For the past week, she'd taught me how to make espressos and lattes. I'd learned how to use the sales system to ring up customers and which switches controlled each light. I'd washed dishes and mopped floors and bussed tables.

Was it my dream job? No. But it was a good job and it accommodated my study schedule. If I wanted a dream job someday, I was going to need my GED first.

Since we'd moved to Quincy—since I'd left Dad—I'd been set on taking everything in stride. In making small, deliberate steps. I'd set out to discover things I liked. Things I didn't. Small steps to building a normal life.

Were small steps enough? Was it time to take a leap?

Maybe. But not today.

"What can I help with next?" I asked Lyla. We'd just finished restocking the counter with her latest batch of pastries.

"Want to do a sweep of the tables?"

"Sure." I smiled and snagged a damp rag, taking it with me to clean one of the recently vacated chairs.

The lunch rush was over, and like the previous days this week, we were in an afternoon lull. It gave us time to catch up on dishes and cleaning. The only people in the cafe were the teenage girls who'd come inside ten minutes ago.

School in Quincy ended around three, and each afternoon, students would pop in for food and coffee.

I went to the table beside theirs, picking up an empty mug and plate with a wadded-up napkin.

"My acceptance letter came today from MSU," one of the girls said.

"Yay," another girl cheered as a third clapped. "Oh my God, it's going to be so fun. I'm glad we're all going to Bozeman together."

"Me too."

"What dorm do you think we'll be in?"

My heart twisted, just a little.

A lifetime ago, I'd been a seventeen-year-old girl excited about college acceptance letters. A girl who'd been ready to leave home on a new adventure. A girl who'd just assumed *home* would be there when she was ready to return.

But that girl hadn't graduated high school. She hadn't needed to worry about roommates or professors or what party to hit on a Saturday night.

That girl was gone.

Maybe, if I put my life together, if I found some semblance of normal, I'd find that girl again. The girl from *before*.

It didn't bother me like it used to that I'd missed so much. There were better things to mourn. But it still pinched sometimes. So I gave myself a few seconds of self-pity, then I put it away.

That pity, along with anger and resentment and grief, was tucked away into a box. A box that lived down deep, where it stayed shut. Where it *had* to stay locked up tight.

If I let its lid so much as crack, the emotions in that box

would swallow me whole.

One of the girls glanced my direction. I smiled when her eyes met mine, then whisked the dirty dishes away.

Lyla was standing beside the stainless steel prep table, smiling at her phone, when I walked into the kitchen. It was a beaming smile, one she reserved for Vance.

"Flirting with Uncle Vance?" I teased.

"Always." She giggled. "He's on his way over from the station to hang out until we close."

"You know, I could close up the shop tonight. You guys could go home."

Though Vance would have to come back to town to get me later. Driving practice was going... not great. Yesterday, I'd nearly decimated a mailbox with Vance's truck.

It wasn't the mechanics of driving. I could steer and hit the gas and brake pedals. It was just... hard.

Driving reminded me of Dad. He'd been the one to teach me when I was fifteen. And while I loved Vance, I wanted Dad in the passenger seat.

I missed my dad. Was he okay?

"Vera?"

My gaze whipped to Lyla. "Huh?"

"I asked if you were sure. About tonight."

"Of course," I said, too brightly. "Maybe you guys could go out on a date. Celebrate Vance's new job."

"Maybe. I'll ask him." Lyla studied me for a long moment, probably to make sure I was okay.

Was I okay? Sort of.

Day by day, I was inching toward okay.

"You guys, um, didn't tell Winn anything. Right?" I asked, my voice low. "About Dad?"

"No. We trust her. But..."

The fewer people who knew my real story, the better. Everyone here, including the Edens, could go on believing what they read in the newspapers. "Thanks."

"No thanks needed. I'm going to do a quick inventory of the walk-in," she said.

"All right. I've got the counter."

The high school girls were still at their table, gossiping and talking, when I returned to the front of the shop. I went to work, making myself a hazelnut latte. Did I like it more than caramel?

"Nope." I sighed after the first sip. Caramel was still the front-runner, but the hazelnut wasn't awful.

The bell above the coffee shop's door jingled. I almost dropped my coffee as Mateo strode inside carrying a box. Would my heart ever not do cartwheels when he was around?

His broad shoulders were covered in a thick, tan canvas coat with the Eden Ranch brand embroidered in white beneath the corduroy collar. The lining was a soft sherpa.

Anne and Harrison had gifted everyone in their family those coats at Christmas.

Me included.

I'd almost cried when I'd had a package under their tree. The last time I'd had a real Christmas was *before*.

Mateo's dark hair was trapped beneath a black beanie. His stubble was nearly a beard these days, and every time I thought he'd let it grow, he'd come into the shop freshly shaven. I wasn't sure which version I liked best.

But in every way, he was beautiful.

Mateo's broad, six-three frame was corded with muscle and strength. He moved effortlessly, his strides fluid and sure. Maybe it was the confidence that radiated off his body that unnerved me so wholly.

Don't stare. The effort it took to force my gaze away made me break out into a sweat. My cheeks were on fire. When he was around, blushing was involuntary.

"Hey, Vera." Mateo set the box down on the counter.

"Hi." My voice was soft and weak. It was so freaking hard to breathe when he was around.

"Did you get a haircut?"

My hand flew to the end of my ponytail. Oh my God, he'd noticed. Not even Lyla had noticed. Granted, I'd only cut an inch off the ends, but he'd noticed. "Just a trim. I did it myself in the bathroom. It's probably choppy." Why was I still talking?

"Looks nice."

Nice as in pretty? Or nice as in I should pay a professional from now on?

"This is for Lyla." He splayed his hand on top of the box. "Is she here?"

"Um, yeah." I nodded so wildly that a lock of my red hair escaped the tie. "I'll go get her."

I turned and almost slammed my face into the espresso machine. But I righted my feet and hurried into the kitchen.

Ugh. Freaking get it together, Vera.

The last time I'd had a crush on a guy had been four years ago. Maybe I was just out of practice, but this crush had only seemed to double in the past month. What would happen in two or three?

Mateo was too perfect. That was the problem. It had taken me a month to nail it down in my head. He was a dream personified. It was like he'd been plucked from my mind and crafted just for me. And apparently finding my dream guy meant turning into a bumbling idiot whenever he looked in my direction.

I was almost to the kitchen when Lyla came through the door, the two of us nearly colliding.

"Sorry," we said in unison, then both laughed.

"Mateo is here for you." I pointed down the hallway. "He brought a box."

"Yay." Her face lit up. "My Christmas present."

She hurried to the counter, sharing a smile with Mateo as she went straight for the gift.

I lingered a few feet away, not wanting to intrude while Lyla opened the box's lid and pulled out a ceramic, mint-green mixing bowl.

"I love it." She skimmed her fingertips across the flower details on the rim, then set it down to stretch across the counter and haul him in for a hug.

He wrapped her up, grinning. "Sorry it's late."

"Oh, I don't care." She let him go and motioned to the display case. "Want something to eat or drink?"

Before he could answer, the group of high school girls giggled so loudly we all looked to their table. The second they realized Mateo was watching, they huddled closer together, attempting to hide their flushed cheeks.

He groaned. "And that's my cue to leave."

"They're just harmless girls," Lyla said. "Ignore them."

But the giggling only got louder. One girl pressed a hand to her heart. Another batted her eyelashes.

"I'll see you later," Mateo said.

"Okay. Bye, Matty." She swept up the bowl, heading to the kitchen to put it away. "Thanks for my present."

"Welcome." He smiled as she disappeared, then winked at me. "Bye, Vera."

He winked. At. Me. The girls at the table didn't get winks. Lyla didn't get a wink. Just me. What did that mean? Did he wink at everyone? Or just girls with *nice* home haircuts?

One of the girls blew a kiss at Mateo's back.

I scrunched up my nose.

Something flickered in Mateo's expression. But before I could figure it out, he turned and headed for the door.

Every pair of eyes at the girls' table was glued to his ass as he walked across the room.

It was a perfect ass. I knew, because I'd ogled it plenty of times myself.

I'd fit in with those high school girls, wouldn't I? We weren't all that different. I didn't have a diploma yet. I was working part-time and living rent-free with Vance and Lyla. I blushed and babbled when Mateo Eden came around.

I was twenty-one years old, not seventeen. Twenty-one.

But I'd fit right in at that table.

A sour taste spread across my mouth.

CHAPTER 3

With the car parked beside the barn on the Eden ranch, I unleashed the breath I'd been holding for miles. Driving on icy Montana roads had frayed my nerves, but at least I hadn't been alone.

"Thanks, Mr. Eden." I smiled at my passenger.

"How many driving lessons do you think we'll need until you call me Harrison?"

I smiled and turned off the engine. "At least one more."

"Then how about we cross that off the list tomorrow?"

"Okay."

"It's a date." He grinned. "Pop the trunk. I'll help you carry up your groceries."

"Oh, that's okay. I can get them." I pointed to the vase that rested between his feet. "You'd better take those flowers in to your valentine before they freeze."

"Good thinking." He bent to pick up the two dozen red roses he'd bought for Anne. "See you tomorrow?"

"Tomorrow. Bye."

A rush of frigid air blew inside as he opened his door, chasing away the warmth. We'd had the heat cranked the entire drive from town because the high today was two below.

My nostrils stung with that first icy inhale as I stepped out of my door. The bitter cold seeped through my jeans and bit into my skin as I hurried to the trunk. At least the ice cream I'd bought wouldn't melt.

With four bags looped over my forearms, I tucked my chin into the collar of my Eden Ranch coat and hurried for the barn.

It wasn't much warmer as I stepped inside but at least the wind didn't cut straight to my bones. I flipped on the overhead light and climbed the stairwell to my loft.

The scents of hay and dirt were replaced with crisp green apple from the candle I'd burned this morning after my shower. I plopped the groceries on the kitchen's small counter, then jogged downstairs again, bracing for the cold.

Winter had started off relatively mild, but it was finishing with a bang. Three days ago, a massive storm had covered the area. There were two feet of fresh snow and counting. An icy snowflake cut across my cheek as I pushed through the exterior door, pausing only long enough to glance at the mountains. The peaks were obscured by thick clouds, all dumping snow.

Was he up there? Did he have a shelter? Was he huddled close to a fire? Was he warm enough? Did he have food?

My heart squeezed. It would be *cold* tonight. But it wasn't the first winter Dad had spent in Montana. And this cold snap was only supposed to last a week. By next Sunday, it was forecast to be well above freezing.

Even if the cold lingered, Dad had always made sure I had a fire to keep warm. He'd do the same for himself, right? He wouldn't do anything stupid, would he? Was his mind okay?

Yes. He was fine. There was no other option I'd consider. He'd stay alive. *He is alive.*

The assurances didn't do much to quiet the turmoil in my heart. The worry for my father was a constant these days, as automatic as breathing. Some days, the fear screamed so loud that it took everything I had not to rush into the mountains to track him down. But that would be reckless and stupid, so I worried instead.

My boots crunched on the snow as I hustled to the trunk. The bag with cooking spray and an array of spices clinked as I grabbed it with one hand and hauled out a gallon of milk with the other. I was about to snag the case of toilet paper to tuck under my arm when a deep voice startled me.

"I'll help."

I stood and turned so fast I banged my head on the trunk's lid. "Ow."

"Sorry." Mateo held up a hand clad in a tan leather glove. "Didn't mean to scare you."

"It's fine." Heat crept into my cheeks just like it did every time he was around. Every. Freaking. Time.

Hopefully today he'd think the pink was from the cold.

"Um, what's up?" God, that sounded stupid. My voice was too breathy and that was actually the dumbest question of all time. What's up? *The sky, Vera. Your hopes. Your delusions.*

"Had some work to do for Griffin today. One of the hired hands quit, and there's no point finding someone new when I can do the work, so I came down to feed the cows."

"Oh. That's nice of you."

"Yeah, I guess." A crease formed between his eyebrows.

"Do you not like it? Working on the ranch?"

"It's great."

It didn't sound great, but it didn't sound bad either. He sounded... blah. I'd never heard blah Mateo before.

"I've been thinking about maybe going back to Alaska," he said. "I used to fly planes up there. The people I used to work for asked if I'd come back. I might."

What? My heart landed with a muffled thud in the snow. No. He couldn't move.

"I don't know." He sighed, moving for the trunk to lift out two grocery bags. "Do me a favor and don't mention it to

Lyla? I haven't decided yet and don't want to stress my sisters out. Mom and Dad know, in case they mention it. It's pretty unlikely I'll go, but it's something I've been thinking about."

I managed a nod.

"Anyway, after I was done with the cows, I stopped by to say hi and give Mom her Valentine's Day chocolate. Dad said you guys hit the store, so I thought I'd come help you carry stuff up."

"You got your mom Valentine's chocolates?" That was the most adorable thing in the entire world.

"Tradition. Keep her on my good side so she'll bake my favorite cookies."

Yep, he was perfect. Funny. Charming. Sexy. This crush was going nowhere fast.

He couldn't move to Alaska. Not when I had to stay in Montana to find Dad and make sure he was okay. Who would buy Anne chocolates if he moved? He really, *really* couldn't move.

"That's, um—"

Before I could finish my thought, Mateo grabbed my package of toilet paper.

Oh, hell. This wasn't happening. The man I was completely infatuated with was *not* carrying my toilet paper. Except he so was. The heat in my cheeks melted the next snowflake that tried to attack.

Mateo made a move for another bag but I snagged it first, a certain blue box showing through the thin white plastic. The toilet paper was bad enough. I didn't need him scoping out my tampons too.

"You can head on in." He jerked his chin for the door. "I'll grab the rest."

"Okay. Thanks." I backed away, taking one second to appreciate the thick stubble on his jaw before I scurried inside and out of the cold.

I piled the bags on the counter once I made it upstairs and stripped out of my coat. Then I smoothed down the front of my green turtleneck as Mateo's footsteps echoed in the stairwell. Between the stress of winter driving practice and the cold wind blowing everything into disarray, my hair was a mess.

He had my toilet paper under one arm and paper towels under the other with three bags in each hand. "Stocking up?"

"Yeah." I tucked a lock of hair behind an ear and untucked it just as quickly. What was wrong with me? I hated having my hair tucked behind my ears. Why couldn't I just relax around Mateo? *Gah!*

"Where do you want these?"

"The counter is great. Thanks."

He deposited everything on the space. "So you and Dad have been doing driving lessons?"

"Yep." I started putting groceries away to hide my face. For once, the flush of my cheeks wasn't only from this crush. Mortification crept through my veins, turning my face from pink to red.

I was twenty-one years old and needed driving lessons like a teenager.

Harrison had volunteered to help. Just like Anne was going to give me cooking lessons. And while I was so grateful to the Edens, my incompetence wasn't exactly something I'd wanted to broadcast, especially to Mateo. Though of course he'd know. This family was as close-knit as the threads of my sweater.

"It's kind of embarrassing," I admitted.

"There's nothing to be embarrassed about, Vera." Even the sound of my name in his deep voice couldn't chase the humiliation away. "So you're out of practice driving. Who cares? Dad said you're doing great. Just needed to knock the rust off."

"I guess." I shrugged and put the milk in the fridge.

Part of me had wanted to avoid driving forever. Except now that I was living on the ranch, it was much too far to walk to Quincy, so I'd had no choice but to start learning again.

Vance and Lyla had offered to buy me a car but I'd insisted on buying it myself—or paying them back. Without savings or credit, I'd borrowed from Uncle Vance to buy my older-model Honda Civic with its dented bumper and nearly one hundred thousand miles.

But at least it was mine. And as of this week, I was living on my own.

I was taking leaps. Not many, but leaps, nonetheless.

"You doing okay out here?" Mateo asked.

"Yes." Sort of. "I love the loft."

"It's a great place."

The footprint of my new home was only a third of the actual barn, and it was still more space than I needed. The stairs led to the back of the apartment, where my bedroom shared a wall with the kitchen and bathroom. Then the rest of the space was open living space.

The walls were covered in varying shades of gray and brown barnwood. The furniture was plush and comfortable in charcoal and cream and white. It was welcoming. Simple, yet fancy.

Not that I needed fancy. I was ecstatic to sleep on a pillow each night and to shower with hot water in the morning.

My favorite place to relax was on the enormous U-shaped sectional that took up the bulk of the living room. I'd camped out every night this week buried under thick blankets to watch movie after movie when I couldn't sleep.

New home, new sounds and that ever-present anxiety for my dad to keep me awake.

He was alive. He'd survive this winter just like all the rest.

I was stubborn enough to will it into reality.

"Whack your head yet?" Mateo asked, pointing to the slanted ceilings. They were tall enough that I only had to duck at the very edges of each room.

"A couple times getting into bed I banged it."

The words registered, and I cringed. Getting into bed I banged it? What the hell was wrong with me? What did that even mean? Why couldn't I speak correctly around this man?

Mateo rubbed the back of his neck, looking anywhere but at me. Great, now I'd made him uncomfortable. As if the toilet paper weren't bad enough.

"Did you, uh, get everything moved out of Lyla's farmhouse?" he asked.

"Yeah. I didn't have much." Thank God the loft had come furnished.

"We all know you're going through a lot of change. We're here to help." His gaze met mine and my tummy fluttered. Gah, those eyes. "Whatever you need."

It wasn't the first time a member of the Eden family had said as much. Though unlike the rest, there was no pity on Mateo's handsome face. He was just stating the truth. Making a sincere offer.

"Thank you."

He dipped his chin. "Welcome."

All of the Edens, Mateo included, knew that I'd spent the past four years living in the wilderness with Dad. They knew he was guilty of murder and hiding from the authorities. They knew that for years, the world had assumed I'd been dead. That I'd been one of Dad's victims.

They knew the story.

Not the truth.

It was better that way. Secrets only stayed secrets through silence.

My dad might not be with me, but I'd do anything in my power to keep him safe.

"Did you know I used to live here?" Mateo took a step deeper into the loft, surveying the space.

"Lyla told me."

Whenever anyone mentioned Mateo's name, whatever tidbit they shared, was instantly committed to memory. I would have liked this loft had he not lived here, but knowing this had been his home too made me love it that much more.

When I'd declared last month that it was time to find a place of my own to live, Lyla and Vance had balked, insisting I stay in the guest bedroom for a while longer. Except I'd refused to budge.

Maybe I needed driving and cooking lessons, but I could take them while I was living on my own. My idea had been to find a place in Quincy, but apparently rentals weren't exactly easy to find.

The loft had been empty since Lyla's uncle Briggs had moved into an assisted living facility in town for help with his dementia, and since the place was empty, Anne and Harrison had offered it to me.

Vance was happy that I had the Edens nearby, and being out here on the ranch meant the mountains were just beyond my door.

It had been impossible to do much hiking with the winter weather, but soon, the season would change. Out here, I'd have a better chance at some freedom. Once this snow stopped and melted a bit, I'd head out to the mountains and see what I could find.

Who I could find.

Mateo's boots thudded on the wooden floor as he walked past the sectional to the windows. Beyond Anne and Harrison's house, the world was white. Snow blanketed the meadows and dusted every tree.

As he stared at the landscape, I stared at him. Faded jeans molded to strong thighs. Scuffed boots and his heavy Carhartt coat. A beanie with the Eden Ranch brand embroidered on the rim. Dark hair that escaped that hat, curling at his nape.

He fit perfectly in this loft, rugged but beautiful.

"This is a great place to find your footing," Mateo said.

I cocked my head to the side. "That's exactly what Lyla said. Word for word."

"Hazard of hanging out with your siblings too often. We start to sound alike." He turned, the corner of his mouth turning up. Wow, he was cute. His gaze shifted to the coffee table, taking in the books and laptop strewn over its surface. "Did you finish your tests?"

"Yeah." If I wasn't working at Eden Coffee, I'd been studying for my GED.

"And?"

A smile spread across my mouth. "Passed all five."

"Nice." He grinned. "Not at all surprised."

"Thanks." I dropped my gaze to my boots as my smile widened under his praise.

"What's next?"

"I don't know. Keep working at the coffee shop. Maybe enroll in some college courses? I like school."

I'd always liked school. Even *before*.

Studying for my GED had been refreshing. It was the mental challenge I hadn't even known I'd needed. I wasn't ready to enroll full-time at a university, but a couple of classes would be nice to keep my mind occupied. And with spring coming, two or three classes wouldn't be all-consuming.

I'd need a flexible schedule. I'd need free days to head into the mountains.

"I'll get out of your hair." Mateo crossed the loft for the door. As he passed, his spicy scent caught my nose. Leather and spice. Wind and earth.

It was perfectly male and delicious and... Mateo.

"Thanks for helping with the groceries."

"Anytime." He winked.

A wink, and my heart did a handspring.

That wink didn't mean anything. He didn't—couldn't—like me. Not that like. Right?

I squashed that budding hope before it could bloom. "See ya."

He disappeared, closing up behind him, and marched down the stairs.

I waited until the door downstairs closed with a thud, then I rushed to the loft's front windows.

Mateo's long legs made short work of the distance to his truck. It was parked around the side of the house where I hadn't noticed it earlier, probably because I'd been too busy death-gripping the steering wheel.

The snow around him stopped blowing. A sunbeam tore through the clouds to touch his shoulders.

He was the light. My light. The shining star that chased away the dark.

Please don't move to Alaska. I pressed my palm to the glass.

"Happy Valentine's Day, Mateo."

CHAPTER 4

MARCH

I was surrounded by Edens. Again.

It was fun. Sort of. Definitely overwhelming. But... fun. There was so much happiness in Anne and Harrison's kitchen it was hard not to get swept up by the smiles and laughter.

It reminded me of the barbeques we'd had growing up. When Dad would flip burgers and kids would chase around and we'd go out on the—

I dropped a mental guillotine on that memory, chopping off its head. Nothing good came from revisiting the past, so I shoved it away. I tucked those happy moments from *before* back into their box and secured the lock.

Tonight was not the night to replay old times. Tonight, we were celebrating. Lyla and Vance had just announced their engagement.

I was so happy for them, especially Uncle Vance. The way he looked at Lyla made my heart melt. He deserved her. He'd gone through hard times recently, but now that he had Lyla, the bad was in the rearview mirror. And he'd move mountains to make her dreams come true.

Someday, I wanted a man to see me the way Vance saw Lyla. To love me with his whole heart.

I'd made a thousand wishes on a million stars for that man to be Mateo. I didn't put a lot of faith into wishing, not anymore. But there was always hope.

"Where's Mateo?" Eloise asked, popping a carrot from the veggie tray into her mouth.

Just the mention of his name made my heart skip.

Since I'd moved into the loft, our paths had crossed at least twice a week. So far, I'd seen him three times since Sunday. And all of those times, he would talk to me about school or driving or the loft. Not once had he mentioned returning to Alaska. Thank God. Then before he left to go home or to work, he'd give me a wink.

Winks meant something. Harrison winked at Anne, and every time, I felt like there was an underlying meaning. He winked to say *I love you. I'd die without you in my life. You're the reason I breathe.*

Mateo winked at me. I wanted it to mean something. Desperately. It probably didn't. My crush overshadowed all reasonable thought.

"I don't know." Anne checked her phone. "He said he was coming."

"Well, I'm getting hungry." Harrison patted his stomach. "I'll start the grill. We can cook his burger when he gets here."

Griffin and Knox followed their dad outside to the deck. Foster and Jasper followed closely behind. Uncle Vance gave me a soft smile, then slipped out of the kitchen too.

"So where do you want the wedding?" Anne asked Lyla as she took the burger patties she'd prepped earlier from the fridge.

I'd helped make those patties. Anne had been teaching me how to cook and tonight, I'd been her sous chef, taking orders and following instructions on how to season the meat and make homemade potato salad.

"I was thinking the barn," Lyla said. "If that's okay with you guys."

"Of course." Anne clapped, giddy with excitement. "What

about the ceremony?"

"The weather is always a risk, but maybe we could have it outside."

"We could set up tents just in case of rain," Winn said.

The women all clustered around the island while the kids played in the other room. It had taken a while, but I'd finally learned everyone's names, the children included. And I knew which kids belonged to which adults.

The framed photos in the living room had been hugely helpful. That, and how often Anne and Harrison talked about their grandchildren.

Since moving to the ranch, I'd been a regular in this kitchen. Anne and Harrison were generous with their dinner invitations, either because they missed having their own kids around or because they pitied me and didn't want me to be alone.

I was determined to learn how to cook, but between the meals eaten here and the others I had with Vance and Lyla, I fended for myself only once or twice a week.

Breakfast was on my own at least, and I was perfecting my omelet skills. Dad would be proud. He loved breakfast.

Maybe, when I found him, when I made sure he was okay, we could eat an omelet together.

As the discussion at the island revolved around wedding planning, I glanced to the window. It was dark outside, but that never stopped me from looking. Searching. Wondering if I might catch the distant flicker of a campfire.

Dad would never come this close to civilization. I knew that down to my bones. But hope was a funny thing. It chased away all logic. So I looked for those tiny campfires, even though I knew I would only find a black night beyond the glass.

The weather had shifted in the past month. February's storm had been short-lived and the snow had melted off the roads shortly after Valentine's Day. It had cleared enough that I'd risked a few hikes.

On the days when I wasn't working at the coffee shop or taking my online classes, I'd venture into the foothills. The snow was still too deep to go far, but it had cleared enough for me to traverse into the woods. To a few places where Dad had once set snares or hunted for deer.

There'd been no sign of him. Yet.

"How are your classes going, Vera?" Talia's question snapped me out of my thoughts.

"I really like them," I told her. "I still have no idea what I want to do, but for right now, I like having options."

I was currently enrolled in a psychology course and a nutrition class. They'd seemed like good choices. Maybe with psychology, I'd learn more about the human mind. How it worked. How it broke.

And if that failed, then I'd have nutrition as a fallback. In the four years we'd lived off the wilderness, Dad had taught me a lot about food. How to forage. How to hunt. It was interesting blending that knowledge with more conventional teaching.

He wouldn't stop eating, would he? He wouldn't just give up and starve himself?

No. He was alive. He was fine. Soon enough, I'd find him and see for myself.

The door to the deck opened and the men returned to the kitchen. Vance immediately went to Lyla and pulled her close.

They started talking about the local sheriff and his pending retirement. Vance had been working for Winn and had told me at lunch the other day how much he was enjoying it. While they talked, I checked the clock on the microwave, then glanced toward the hallway.

Where was Mateo? Yeah, he was normally the last to arrive. He seemed perpetually five minutes late for most gatherings. But he was never this late.

Like my thoughts had conjured him from thin air, the front door opened and bootsteps thudded down the hall.

The moment he appeared in the kitchen, my stomach dropped. Something was wrong. The color was gone from his face. His dark brown hair was sticking up at odd angles, like he'd been raking his fingers through it over and over.

"There you—" Anne's eyes widened. "What's wrong?"

The room went quiet.

"I, um…" Mateo blinked. Then he shook his head, disbelief plain in his features. "I have to go to Alaska. Tonight."

No one noticed my quiet gasp, probably because there were plenty of others to drown it out. Alaska. What? Why? Already?

"Tonight?" Harrison asked. "Why? What's going on?"

Mateo swallowed hard. If his face had been pale before, it was ghost white now. "I think… I think I have a daughter?"

Wait. *What did he say?*

The room erupted in questions. All of them went unanswered because Mateo was already gone, having dropped the bomb.

He had a daughter? With who?

Was that the reason he was considering Alaska?

Because he was in love with someone else?

CHAPTER 5

*A*laina.

Her name was Alaina.

The day Mateo brought her to Montana I knew I'd never win his heart. Because he'd given it to Alaina.

With silky dark hair and eyes the color of sapphires, he called her Allie.

Alaina.

His daughter.

CHAPTER 6

MAY

"Anne?" I called into her house from the front door.

"Come on in!"

I toed off my shoes and padded down the hallway, finding her in the kitchen.

Nothing was on the stove or in the oven. She had her hands braced on the island as the sound of a wailing baby girl echoed from the living room.

"Um, everything okay?"

"It's been a day." She pinched the bridge of her nose, then forced a smile. "How are you?"

"Good." That tiny scream got louder. It was so startling and heartbreaking, I forgot for a moment why I was here. "I brought you those strawberries."

"Thanks. I hope it wasn't too much trouble."

"Not at all."

Lyla had ordered an extra flat from her distributor so that Anne could make strawberry jam.

"Where do you want me to put them?"

"I'll get them." She rounded the island and pulled me into a quick hug. "You've been working since four. I'll take care of the strawberries. And I need just a minute out of the house."

"Are you sure?"

"Definitely." She steered me toward a stool at the island. "Sit."

"All right. The flat is in my backseat. Doors are unlocked."

She patted my shoulder, then disappeared outside.

Alaina's cries seemed to get louder every second.

What was happening? I pressed a hand to my heart and slipped out of the kitchen, toward two male voices attempting to battle a baby's scream.

Mateo was lapping the living room with his red-faced daughter in the crook of his arm. With every step, he bounced and swayed, trying to get her to settle down.

Harrison sat on a leather couch, his elbows on his knees as he gave his son a sad smile. "Want me to take her?"

"No, I've got her." Mateo blew out a long, exasperated breath, then squished her bottom. "Her diaper is dry. I tried to feed her but she's not hungry. I'm walking her around, which is the only way to get her to sleep, but she's not sleeping. I just... I don't know what's wrong with her."

"There's nothing wrong with her," Harrison said. "Babies cry."

"It's constant, Dad. Day and night." Mateo's voice cracked. With it, so did my heart. "I feel like I'm losing my fucking mind."

"Talia said there was nothing to worry about. Colic is normal. Griffin had it something fierce when he was that age."

Mateo made another three laps. "Or maybe it's me."

"What do you mean?"

"Maybe what she really needs is a mother."

"Oh, son. You're doing fine. It'll get easier."

There was nothing but exhaustion, desperation, on Mateo's face. He looked like a man who had a newborn baby, and who'd been caring for that baby on his own since the day he'd brought her home from Alaska.

I'd only heard bits and pieces of the story. Anne or

Harrison would tell me if I asked. So would Lyla or Vance. But for some reason, it felt like a betrayal. It was Mateo's story to tell and it was something I wanted to hear directly from him.

But I hadn't asked.

All I knew was that Alaina's mother had died in childbirth. A friend had called Mateo the night of that dinner in March when he'd announced he had a daughter.

So he'd flown to Alaska. And he'd brought Allie home two weeks later.

"This is so messed up, Dad." Mateo swallowed hard. "What am I doing?"

Harrison stood and walked to his side, putting a hand on Mateo's shoulder. "Being a father."

Mateo nodded and blew out a long breath. "I'm just tired."

"Why don't you plan to stay here tonight? Your mom and I will take a midnight shift so you can get some rest."

Relief flooded Mateo's features. "You don't mind?"

"Not a bit."

Was that the first time he'd let them help? No wonder he was exhausted. He'd been trying to do it all himself.

Harrison clapped him on the shoulder, then walked out of the living room, finding me waiting. He came right into my space and hauled me in for a hug, whispering, "Hi."

"Hi."

He let me go and walked down the hall, probably to search for Anne and tell her that they'd just volunteered to babysit.

I stepped into the living room. "Hey."

"Hey." His eyes met mine and the sorrow in them seemed endless.

Was that sorrow for Allie's mother? Had he loved her? What was her name? Did he say it often? Or did he keep that name locked inside because it was too hard to speak aloud?

"Are you doing okay?" I asked.

He lifted a shoulder and stopped walking.

The minute his feet halted, so did Alaina's crying.

The silence was deafening. I held my breath, not wanting to startle her again. But her eyelids fluttered, her lips pursed, and then she fell asleep. As quickly as I could snap my fingers, she was out.

Mateo's eyes widened, but otherwise, he didn't so much as breathe. He stood statue still for a full minute before finally risking a step. He shuffled to the couch, slowly and deliberately bending until he was seated. Then his gaze roved over his daughter's face, tracing over the little eyelashes that formed crescents against her smooth cheeks.

He gave it a few more moments, making sure she wasn't going to wake, then sagged into the cushions. "Can I do this?"

That question seemed more like one he was asking himself, but I answered it anyway. "You can do this."

As our eyes locked, he gave me a sad smile. Then he let his head rest against the back of the couch. Just like his daughter, one moment he was awake. The next, he was out. *Snap.*

But his hold on that baby never faltered, even as he slept.

CHAPTER 7

JULY

I loved fireworks.

But raucous, crowded fairgrounds? Not so much.

Sixteen-year-old me would have come alive at the Quincy Fourth of July Rodeo. Sixteen-year-old me would have been all toothy smiles and unending laughs. Sixteen-year-old me had lived for events like this. *Before.*

The fireworks were tempting. I loved them so much that it was almost enough for me to endure the noise. To put up with the jostling and nudging as people milled around the fairgrounds. But I'd been at the rodeo for hours already, and I couldn't stop yawning.

"Tired?" Harrison asked.

I nodded. "It's been a long day."

Starting at four o'clock in the morning, when I'd met Lyla at the coffee shop to open and prepare for the onslaught of preparade customers. It was the busiest workday in my time at Eden Coffee. Even Anne and Talia had come in to help.

Meanwhile, the rest of the Edens had been at The Eloise Inn, either assisting Eloise with the hotel or Knox at his restaurant, Knuckles. Everyone had pitched in, working tirelessly, to help make sure the day had gone smoothly for every Eden-owned business on Main.

But once six o'clock had rolled around, the coffee shop and

restaurant had closed, so the Eden family had all congregated for the rodeo. There were a few noticeable absences.

Uncle Vance and Winn were here at the fairgrounds, but working. The entire staff at the police department was on duty through the night.

Eloise and Jasper had decided to skip the festivities and spend the night at home with their one-month-old daughter, Ophelia.

And Mateo was gone.

He'd brought Alaina to the rodeo for an hour but had left shortly after inhaling a cheeseburger for dinner. Allie had gotten fussy—she'd had a long day being strapped to Mateo's chest while he'd helped at the hotel to keep guests happy.

Quincy was brimming with tourists and visitors. Lyla had warned me that summers were hectic. At the moment, squished on a bleacher in a grandstand with hundreds and hundreds of people, hectic was an understatement.

How had I not noticed just how many people flocked to Quincy each summer? It wasn't like I'd never come to town during the summers.

Dad and I had lived in these mountains for two years. We'd spent most of that time close to the shelter he'd built out of small trees and saplings. But once a month, I'd ventured to town for supplies.

Batteries for our flashlights. Tampons for my period. First-aid items like bandages and antibiotic ointment because one or both of us usually had a cut or scrape.

Two summers, and the sheer volume of people in Quincy had escaped my notice. Maybe because those visits had always been such a torrent of stress and worry.

It had always felt like I was holding my breath during those trips to town. I'd do everything in my power to go unnoticed as I stopped by the grocery and hardware stores. Then as quickly as I came, I left, hiking to our mountain rendezvous point.

I wasn't hiding anymore. I wasn't walking with my chin tucked to avoid eye contact. I wasn't the girl everyone had assumed was dead.

This summer, from my spot behind the counter at Eden Coffee, I had a front-row seat to the madness that was a Quincy summer.

It was exhilarating and exhausting.

With the back of my hand, I covered another yawn, glancing to the sky. The evening light was fading. The jagged mountain horizon in the distance glowed yellow and orange, but overhead, there wasn't a star in sight. Nightfall was a wait.

"What time do the fireworks start?"

Harrison checked his watch. "Oh, probably in another hour and a half."

I groaned. Ninety minutes? I'd never make it.

"It's a clear night." He cast his blue eyes heavenward. "The mayor was bragging to me the other day that they've gone all out this year. I bet, if you hurry home, you'll be able to see them from the ranch. Your windows in the loft have a great view. Can't promise it, but there's a chance."

I perked up. "Really?"

He chuckled. "Drive safely. Watch out for other drivers. People are out drinking tonight."

"Okay." I scrambled to get my purse from beneath my feet, slinging it over a shoulder. Then I spun, about to shuffle past knees and dodge beer cups, but stopped and turned back, bending to drop a kiss to Harrison's cheek. "Good night."

His eyes crinkled at the sides as he smiled up at me. "Night, Vera."

After more goodbye hugs and waves, I made it to the stairs and jogged to the walkway at the bottom of the stands. Then I took the nearest exit and hurried through the dirt and grass parking lot to my Honda.

The drive out was quiet except for the blast of air that rushed through my open windows—the Civic's air conditioning had gone out last week, something I hadn't mentioned to Vance because if I decided to get it fixed, I wanted to pay for it on my own.

By the time I pulled off the highway and drove beneath the log archway that marked the entrance to the ranch, the stars were beginning to pop and that yellow glow on the horizon had faded to pinks and purples.

Beside the gravel lane were twin barbed-wire fences. Beyond them were meadows, evergreens and cows. The scents of grass and cattle filled the cab and I breathed it in deep.

Over the past five months, that smell had started to mean *home*.

Anne and Harrison's house was dark, other than the porch light. During the day, there was always activity at the ranch, hired hands coming and going from the shop or stables or barn. Griffin stopped by at least once a day, though according to Lyla, he was running more and more ranch business from his own house these days.

Tonight, it was peaceful and still. Only a lone white truck was parked outside. The Eden Ranch brand—an *E* with a curve beneath—was painted on its door.

Mateo's truck.

My heart skipped. He must be spending the night. Maybe I'd get to see him in the morning.

I parked in my usual spot beside the barn and climbed out, about to head upstairs to camp beside the window and hopefully spy the fireworks. But the crunch of gravel startled me, and I whirled as Mateo walked my direction.

"Hey."

"H-hi." I pressed a hand to my racing heart.

"Sorry to scare you."

Not the reason my heart was trying to beat out of my

chest. It was him. It was always him. "That's all right. What are you guys doing?"

Mateo glanced to Alaina in his arms.

She stared up at him with bright eyes as she sucked on a pacifier.

"We had a long day." He sighed. "The cabin was too hot tonight so we snuck down to crash at Mom and Dad's. But since her nap schedule was all messed up today, she's wide awake. You just missed an epic screaming fit."

"Sorry." I winced. "She looks happy now."

"Some nights, she wants to sit. Others, she wants to walk around." He shook his head, staring down at his daughter. "We're still trying to figure each other out, aren't we, Allie?"

She didn't look confused at all.

Alaina Eden knew exactly who was wrapped around her tiny fingers.

"Skipped out early tonight?" he asked.

"Yeah, I was over the crowd."

"Same." He jerked his chin toward the open gravel lot. "We're walking laps. Knox suggested I give it a try on the nights when she won't sleep. Drake's a night owl, and I guess Knox used to spend night after night walking around with him until he'd finally conk out. You're welcome to join us."

"Okay." As we fell in step, our shoes crunching on gravel, I ducked my chin. A curtain of my hair hid the smile that stretched across my mouth.

"Did you have fun tonight? Despite the crowd?"

"I did." I nodded. "I've never been to a rodeo before. Your dad took it upon himself to teach me all about the events and scoring."

Mateo chuckled. "He's a good teacher."

"He is." Almost as good as my own dad, who would have loved the rodeo and the crowd and never would have let me leave before seeing the fireworks.

Allie squirmed, nestling deeper into Mateo's chest.

"I like her name."

Alaina Anne Eden.

"I don't think I ever told you that." For a reason I couldn't explain, it felt important that he knew I liked Allie's name. "Did you pick it out?" Or had Alaina's mother?

"Yeah." Mateo stared into the distance as he nodded. "In the hospital, after she was born, I was struggling to wrap my head around everything. I think the staff knew that and took pity on me. They let Allie stay an extra day when normally they would have sent us home. One of the nurses told me I should give her a name. That maybe it would help with the grief. They all thought I was together with..."

Alaina's mother.

He didn't say her name.

I didn't say the names of those I'd loved and lost either.

"Anyway, I needed a name for her birth certificate so I pulled up Google on my phone and thought the best place to start was with *A*. Scrolled until I found one I liked."

"You made a good choice."

"Thanks."

We turned a corner, walking the width of the parking area, then turned again, this time heading back toward the house and barn.

"Have you thought any more about moving back to Alaska?"

He shook his head. "No. Not with Allie. We belong here."

The relief was staggering. "I was born in Alaska." Another random fact I wasn't sure why I was sharing but did anyway.

"You were?"

I nodded. "Before my parents moved to Idaho."

Mateo hummed.

He didn't ask questions. Maybe because he knew I'd share about my life but it had to be on my terms. And right now, my terms were limited. Random facts. Harmless details.

Anything more and that was where the sharing stopped.

We walked five more laps—until Alaina was sound asleep in his arms.

Mateo ran a thumb over his daughter's cheek. Maybe they were still figuring each other out, but he was so in love with his baby girl. "I'd better take her inside."

"Okay. Good night, Mateo."

"Good night, Vera." He winked, and I learned in that very moment what it was to swoon.

I waited until he disappeared into Anne and Harrison's house before heading to the barn and climbing the stairs.

When I made it to my loft, I looked out the window just in time to see a final stream of sparks in the distance. Smoke disguised as clouds floated into the sky.

I'd missed the fireworks.

Worth it.

CHAPTER 8

Uncle Vance was happier than I'd ever seen him. He spun Lyla in a slow circle as they danced together as husband and wife. The hem of her strapless lace gown skimmed the temporary floor Griffin and Mateo had installed in the barn.

True love. That was the name of the smile they shared.

He'd earned this happiness and more.

Vance had done everything in his power to help me in the past year. He'd handled all of the logistics to bring me back from the presumed dead. He'd helped me get a reinstated social security card and a driver's license. When I'd needed a checking account and credit card, he'd taken me to the bank. And when I'd asked him to leave Idaho for Montana, he'd agreed without hesitation. Granted, that was mostly because of Lyla, but partly for me too.

He'd lied for me.

He'd lied to the police and to the media. He'd invented a story that meant I could have a life and Dad could remain free.

It had been Vance's idea to tell the authorities that I'd left Dad. That it had been my choice to escape. And when I'd broken free from my father's clutches, I'd run to our family's closest friend.

Uncle Vance.

He hated lying, but he'd done it for me. For that, I'd be forever grateful.

Almost everything else we'd told the FBI and police was true. Or a version of the truth.

Dad *had* taken me that night. The night they'd died. He'd killed my mother. And for four years, we'd lived off the grid. Did I know where Dad was now? No.

I wished that last truth was a lie. I wished I had my father. That he could be here to see Vance on his happiest of days. That we could dance and be a family again.

Sometimes, it stung to be so happy when I was surrounded by Edens. They'd pulled me into their fold, embraced me into their family, and I was grateful for their love.

And felt guilty for it, all at the same time.

Because while I was living with this large, chaotic, happy family, Dad was alone.

Yes, he'd insisted I go with Uncle Vance. He hadn't wanted me to live on the run forever. But maybe that decision had been too hasty. Maybe we should have talked through it more. Maybe I should have stuck it out for a few more years until we'd come up with a plan to meet from time to time.

Instead, I'd just left. He had no one to talk to. No one to care for. No one to make sure he was all right.

I'd left him.

The guilt gnawed, but even as it crawled through my veins, I wouldn't have wanted to miss this wedding.

It was magical.

The barn had been transformed over the past two weeks. Lighted strings hung from the rafters and beams. Tables and chairs covered with crisp white linens filled most of the space. The dance floor at the far end of the building was positioned in front of a stage where a live band was playing a slow country song.

The Edens had gone all out. Somehow, they'd even

managed to erase the smell of animals and hay. Roses and lilies and draping greenery hung from the posts. Along with the luscious bouquets on each table, they filled the barn with a sweet scent.

Smiling guests sipped champagne. Laughter and conversation mingled with the music. A group of kids clustered in the center of the dance floor as adults skirted around them.

I watched from my seat at the Edens' table. I'd told Uncle Vance it was fine to put me anywhere, but he'd insisted I sit with family. Not even Vance's sisters and parents had been gifted this table. Instead, they'd gotten their own a couple rows over.

"Want to dance?" Foster stood from his chair across from mine.

I waited for Talia to stand from her seat beside his, but then he extended his hand my direction.

"Me?" I pointed to my chest.

He grinned. "Yeah. What do you say? Fair warning, Talia says I'm a hopeless dancer."

"It's true." She smiled up at her husband. "Though last night we were dancing in the kitchen and he only stepped on my foot once."

"Not exactly selling me on this dance," I teased and stood.

Foster chuckled and bent to brush a kiss to Talia's forehead. Then he waited for me to round the table and held out an elbow to escort me toward the stage. "Having fun?"

"I am." I nodded, searching the crowd on the dance floor.

Vance and Lyla were still together, locked in a quiet conversation as they moved. The world beyond their bubble didn't exist. Mateo was close, dancing with Anne.

As one of the groomsmen, he was in a tux tonight. So was Foster. And I was dressed in a black satin gown and strappy heeled sandals, just like the rest of Lyla's bridesmaids.

My hair had been curled and pinned into an elaborate updo at the Quincy salon this morning. I hadn't worn this much makeup since my last high-school prom. But I felt pretty.

It had been a long time since I'd felt pretty.

Foster spun me into his arms and began to sway. It was on the fourth count that his foot landed on my toes. "Damn it. Sorry."

"You did warn me." I giggled. "Don't worry. I have tough feet."

"That, and you're a brave soul, Vera."

He'd told me the same when I'd offered to let his eight-year-old daughter, Kadence, paint my nails last weekend at the coffee shop. Kaddie was a doll but not exactly the steadiest hand with the nail polish brush. It had taken a solid soak in acetone to remove the rainbow shades from my cuticles.

Foster and Talia were regulars at Eden Coffee. I saw them nearly as much as Anne and Harrison. Probably because Talia and Lyla were close as twins.

My sisters had been that way too. *Before.*

Talia took Fridays off from working as a doctor at the hospital to spend them with their eight-month-old son, Jude, and she'd bring him in for a lunchtime visit. Foster would bring Kaddie in after school some days for a daddy-daughter date. And at least once a month, he would come in to buy Talia's favorite cookie to take to her while she was at work.

All of the men in the Eden family adored their wives, but there was something special about the way Foster looked at Talia. Like she was the very reason he breathed.

Dad used to look at *her* that way.

"Ooof." I let out a grunt as Foster's foot crunched mine again. The French pedicure I'd gotten this morning wasn't going to survive this dance.

"Shit. I'm sorry, Vera."

"It's o—"

"I think you'd better let me cut in." Anne appeared at our sides, pointing to her closed-toe pumps.

"I think maybe that's a good idea." Foster gave me an apologetic frown. "Sorry."

"It's okay. Really." But before I could leave the dance floor and retreat to my chair, a large hand appeared in front of me. A hand belonging to the man I'd been stealing chaste glances of all night.

"May I?" Mateo asked.

"Sure." My voice was as wobbly as my knees. This dance was going to be a disaster, but I took Mateo's hand, his palm warm and calloused and big enough to envelop mine.

It was the first time we'd touched.

He probably had no idea. Why would he keep track?

But I remembered. We'd never hugged. We'd never shaken hands. We'd never so much as accidentally bumped into each other.

I drew in a shaky breath as he stepped close, his hand coming to my hip. It was a stretch to put my hand on his shoulder. God, he was tall. I tilted up my chin to keep his gaze as his spicy cologne filled my nose. Leather and spice. Wind and earth.

This was just a dance. Just. A. Dance. *Breathe.*

"Having a good time?" he asked as we moved with the music.

"Yep," I squeaked.

His Adam's apple bobbed as he spoke. How had I never really noticed that before? Maybe because I'd been so fixed on his face and arms and legs and ass. But damn that Adam's apple. It was just so... manly. So different from the boys I'd crushed on in high school who'd barely crested puberty.

"Are you? Having fun?" I asked.

"I like weddings." He nodded. "But I love wedding cake. I've already had four pieces."

"Four?"

"There's a chance I'll go into a sugar coma soon."

"I promise to bring Alaina to visit your body in the hospital."

A low, deep chuckle escaped his chest. Again, that Adam's apple moved.

Never in my life had I wanted to lick a man's throat. Until now.

Heat crept into my face so I dropped my chin, staring at a pearl button on his shirt. "Where is Allie?"

"At the house with the babysitters. Hopefully asleep, but I'm not holding my breath."

Anne had wanted all of her children to enjoy the wedding, so she'd hired two babysitters to come to the ranch and watch the little ones so their parents could have a night off.

"You look pretty tonight."

This was the best wedding of my life. "Thanks."

He didn't mean it as an advance. It wasn't a pickup line or attempt to woo me into his bed. Mateo's compliment sounded a lot like those I'd gotten from Griffin and Knox and Jasper.

Still, it was impossible to hide my smile. I tried anyway, ducking my chin so low that I had the perfect view of my stiletto heel landing on Mateo's foot.

He grunted.

I gasped. "Oh my God. I'm so sorry."

"It's all good."

"Sorry."

What the hell was wrong with me? Why couldn't I just relax around Mateo? I was a confident woman. I was coordinated. But when Mateo was around, I became this clumsy, shy girl.

She was pissing me off.

Dad and I used to dance. We didn't have music but there would be nights when he'd spin me around our campfire, humming a tune to the stars. Not once had I stepped on his foot. Not once.

Foster's hopeless dancing skills had rubbed off.

I squeezed my eyes shut. "Sorry."

"Vera, it's fine. Stop apologizing." His grip on my waist tightened. "Doesn't even hurt."

He might be uninjured but my pride was running through a meat grinder. Before I recovered, the song was over. Time to sneak upstairs to the loft, bury my face in a pillow and cry.

"Would you dance with me again?" he asked.

"Oh." My. God. Yes. A thousand times yes.

Except before I could say one of those yesses, Vance's voice was at my back. "My turn."

No. Damn it.

Mateo let me go and took a step away. Then he held up his hands in surrender so Vance could step in. "Thanks for the dance, Vera."

I sighed. "Sure."

He tapped me on the shoulder, then weaved through the crowd toward the cake table.

My skin tingled from where he'd touched me.

No, not touched. Patted. He'd patted my shoulder.

Like he'd do to a friend. Or a sister.

He saw me as a sister, didn't he? The Edens had embraced me fully, and I was an honorary member of the family.

Would Mateo ever touch me the way I wanted to be touched? Would he ever kiss me?

Not if he saw me as a sister. As just a friend.

My heart sank to my scuffed toenails as Vance pulled me close. And later that night, when I disappeared into the loft after the wedding, instead of crying into my pillow, I screamed.

CHAPTER 9

NOVEMBER

Thanksgiving. Dad's favorite holiday.

Was he eating turkey tonight? Last year, he'd killed one to cook over the fire. Did he even know it was Thanksgiving?

The days and months and years tended to blend together when you lived without phones or calendars or jobs or schedules. But Dad had always kept track of the date by his automatic watch. What if it had stopped working? What if he'd decided tracking time was pointless? Did he know how long it had been since I'd left?

It had been over a year since I'd seen my father.

The day I'd left, he'd told me he loved me. *Never forget how much I love you.* When I asked if I'd see him again, he'd said, "Of course."

That was a promise, right? Dad kept his promises.

Where was he? I'd spent the spring, summer and fall in the mountains outside Quincy. I'd searched and searched and searched for any sign.

Either there wasn't one to be found. Or…

He was alive. *He's alive.*

"Vera?" Lyla's fingers touched my wrist.

I jerked, startled, and my fork clattered to my plate.

"Are you okay?" Her eyebrows knitted together.

"Great." I forced a smile and picked up my fork. "Just

really full. Dinner was delicious."

She didn't buy the act. Neither did Vance.

He stretched an arm past the back of her chair toward mine to put his hand on my shoulder.

I stabbed the last bite of turkey on my plate and popped it in my mouth, smiling as I chewed.

Vance and Lyla shared a look—they knew my smile was a fake—but they didn't push it, not with so many people crammed around the Edens' dining room table.

It wasn't fair that I was here, sharing a feast with this lovely family, while Dad was alone. Because I'd left him alone.

And I was surrounded by Edens.

There were so many overlapping conversations happening at once, I couldn't keep up. Or maybe I just wasn't in the mood to try.

The only voice I never missed was Mateo's.

He sat directly across the table, though his chair was angled so he could feed Alaina.

I wished I had been seated beside him. He'd pulled out a chair for me earlier, offering it up. But then Vance had told me to come around the table and sit beside Lyla.

I should have taken the chair beside Mateo anyway. If I was sitting beside him, I would have been so worried about saying the right thing, doing the right thing, that I wouldn't have even started thinking about Dad. I would have been too busy trying to not sound ridiculous when I offered to take the tomatoes from Mateo's salad.

He hated raw tomatoes. Cooked was fine. Ketchup was his favorite condiment, and he loved marinara sauce. But his lip curled at the cherry tomatoes Anne had cut up for the green salad.

I liked tomatoes, in any size, shape or form.

But I didn't offer to take them. I was sitting too far away.

We never sat by each other. Why was that? Because of the

high chair? Even though Anne had offered to feed Alaina tonight, he'd insisted on doing it himself.

He wasn't a good dad, he was a great dad. He loved that girl with his entire heart.

It was hard to stop crushing on Mateo Eden. Impossible, actually.

Over the past three months, I'd done everything in my power to forget about that wedding dance. To banish these feelings and forget about him. I'd even gone on one—and only one—date.

The guy had been a regular at the coffee shop. He'd shown up thirty minutes later than the time we'd arranged to meet at Knuckles, and after our meal, he'd told me he'd forgotten his wallet, so I'd had to pay.

Wasn't crushing on a good man, a great father, better? Even if he didn't know I existed? Sure. Sort of.

Maybe Mateo would only ever see me as a sister slash friend. Maybe I was okay with that.

If I was being honest with myself, I was in no place for a relationship. I had more small steps to take. More leaps. I was still discovering what I liked and what I didn't.

So while I worked on me, I'd hold him in my heart. He'd be my ray of sunshine to chase away the rain.

"Bzzzz." He made an airplane noise as he flew a spoon of sweet potatoes over Allie's tray.

It was addicting, watching them together. Watching that bond grow stronger and stronger. Every day, he seemed to fall deeper and deeper in love with his daughter. And the affection was returned.

Alaina's blue eyes sparkled as she opened wide for that airplane spoon.

I smiled, the first real smile of the meal.

Allie kicked her chubby legs as she pinched a green bean with her little fingers and shoved it into her mouth. Her

Gobble Gobble bib was smeared with mashed potatoes. There were even some in her hair.

Mateo used the spoon to clean up her chin. "You're a mess, Sprout."

He'd started calling her Sprout not long after Vance and Lyla's wedding. The first time I'd heard him, at a family dinner at this very table, I'd had to excuse myself to the bathroom to hide the tears.

Vance had snuck away to check on me two minutes later.

Dad had called Elsie Sprout. And he'd called Hadley Jellybean.

Vance had offered to talk to Mateo, ask him to pick a different nickname. But I'd told him to leave it alone. My sister would have loved sharing a nickname with Alaina.

And because I wouldn't want Hadley to be left out, I'd started calling Allie Jellybean.

Sometimes it hurt less. Sometimes it hurt more.

Tonight... tonight was a bad night.

I missed my sisters.

I missed my dad.

I didn't like Thanksgiving.

CHAPTER 10

"Happy Birthday, Jellybean." I scooped Alaina into my arms and smooched her cheek.

She giggled when I tickled her side, then gave me a string of babble as she showed me the toy car in her fist.

"Car," I said.

"Ca."

"Close enough." I kissed her cheek again. "Look how cute you are today."

Her hair was in two short pigtails, each clipped with a white bow. *ONE* was printed on her lavender hoodie.

Chatter drifted from deeper inside the house, and given the line of vehicles parked out front, I was likely the last to arrive at the birthday party. But I'd worked most of the day at the coffee shop so Lyla could take the weekend off.

On Talia's orders, she was supposed to be slowing down during her last month of pregnancy. Though instead of resting, I was guessing that Lyla had spent her Saturday putting the finishing touches on the nursery. It wouldn't be long now until there was another Sutter. A baby boy that Uncle Vance and Lyla were naming Trey.

I loved him already.

"Let's go find everyone," I told Allie, carrying her down the hall.

The kitchen was empty but the island was crowded with glasses. The birthday cake was beneath a glass dome on the counter. It was decorated with colorful rainbow swirls—Lyla's creation, no doubt. More evidence of her not taking it easy.

The gifts were all on the dining room table, including the stuffed unicorn I'd brought over from the loft. I'd added it to the pile two minutes ago, then slipped back outside to the porch to ring the doorbell.

No one used the doorbell at Anne and Harrison's place. Visitors on the ranch knew to just knock, poke your head inside and holler. Especially since most visitors were their children.

But Allie loved the doorbell. Pushing it. Answering it. Any time I knew she was here, I'd ring the doorbell, wait for her little pitter-patter of hands and knees, then ease the door open and find her crawling toward the entryway.

"You're here." Anne poked her head out from the living room and smiled, waving me toward the noise. "We're in here, sweetie."

The entire family had crowded into the room. All eyes were locked on the television and a basketball game playing. Jasper had organized a family bracket pool for March Madness and the first round of games was in full swing. Considering I'd chosen my teams based on school colors, I wasn't holding my breath that I'd win.

Mateo was seated on the couch beside Harrison and Vance. All three men were on the edge of their seats as the game clock wound down to less than a minute.

"Shoot it," Harrison yelled.

"Where's the foul call?" Knox huffed, dragging a hand over his beard.

"Come on, Timmy." Mateo sighed. "Make those."

I leaned in closer to Anne. "They do realize that the players can't hear them, right?"

She laughed and put her arm around my shoulders. "How was work?"

"Good. Where's Lyla?" She trusted me to run the shop, but I also knew her well enough to know she liked a full report on the day.

"She was tired so I sent her to lie down. Though I doubt she'll get any sleep with these guys shouting at the television." Anne rolled her eyes. "Shushing them is pointless. Trust me, I've tried."

I laughed. "What about dinner? Can I help with anything?"

Nearly a year of cooking lessons from Anne and I was no longer hopeless in the kitchen.

"You can help me with the salad later. But I just put the lasagnas in the oven. We'll eat in about an hour."

"Perfect." I shifted Allie on my hip, surprised she hadn't squirmed to be put down yet. But she just rested her head on my shoulder, her attention fixed on the toy car's wheels.

"She didn't get a nap today," Anne said. "Mateo said she just wouldn't fall asleep."

"Early bedtime." I kissed her forehead and swayed with her in my arms.

There were days when it felt like a minute ago that Mateo had walked into that family dinner and announced he had a daughter. And other days, like today, I couldn't remember what life was like before Allie.

Before the Edens.

The memories of years spent with Dad in the mountains seemed to get fuzzier with each passing day. It scared me, the thought of losing him. Of forgetting.

But spring was coming, and with the warm weather, my search would resume. It had been a long, cold winter of worry. This year, I'd find him.

This year, I'd make sure he was okay and he wouldn't be alone.

Alaina yawned a big, gaping yawn that stretched her tiny mouth.

Mateo caught it, stood from the couch and crossed the living room. "Need me to take her?"

"No." I shook my head. "I've got her."

His eyes softened as he ran a knuckle over her cheek. "She's tired."

"It's hard to be the birthday girl."

He hummed. "How was work today?"

"Good, thanks. How was—"

Something happened in the game and the room erupted in a mix of cheers and curses, stealing Mateo's focus as he whirled to the TV.

Alaina straightened at the noise, holding up her car as she squealed. Then the bigger kids came darting into the living room and she kicked her legs, wanting to be put down.

"Okay, fine." I sighed. Allie rarely cuddled with me, not with so many aunts and uncles vying for attention. "Go play."

She crawled faster than most toddlers walked, disappearing with her cousins into the adjoining playroom.

Anne and Harrison had converted a bedroom into an office and made the former office kid central before Christmas.

Mateo stood in front of me, eyes glued to the TV for the final seconds of the game.

With him standing there, I had no choice but to stare at those broad shoulders. At his dark hair trapped beneath a baseball hat, the ends curling at his nape. Every time he wore a hat, it made the corners of his jaw seem stronger. Sharper.

He put his hands on his narrow hips, and the movement lifted the hem of his T-shirt an inch. His jeans were frayed at the hems, the strings tickling the thick soles of his cowboy boots. One of his rear pockets had a slight tear and through the thinning denim, I could make out the black cotton of his underwear.

That man had the most perfect ass I'd seen in my life. My hands itched to slide into those pockets and *squeeze.*

My cheeks flushed and I tore my gaze away.

And found Anne's eyes, waiting.

Shit. Definitely did not need her knowing I was obsessed with her son. "I, um... I'm going to grab something to drink."

Without another word, I slipped out of the room, drawing in a shaking inhale when I reached the kitchen. My reprieve was short-lived. The game ended, and like always, the crowd shifted to the kitchen to snack on the ever-present veggie tray and visit while the scents of tomatoes and garlic and basil filled the house.

"So what time tomorrow night?" Winn asked Mateo.

"Can I drop her off at five?"

"Sure."

"Should be back around nine or ten to pick her up."

"Or," Griffin drawled, "bring stuff so she can spend the night. Just in case it goes well."

"In case what goes well?" Eloise asked, taking a stool beside mine at the island.

Mateo grinned. "I'm going on a date tomorrow night. Griff and Winn are babysitting."

*Ooh*s and *aah*s filled the room along with questions about the woman and where he was taking her. The noise masked the sound of my whimper.

A date.

He was going on a date.

It hurt. It hurt more than it should, considering he'd never once given me that sort of attention. Still, it hurt.

The world felt like it was spinning the wrong way, but I forced a smile. I made the salad for dinner. I visited over our meal. And I clapped when Alaina shoved a handful of birthday cake in her mouth.

It was just one date, right? He wasn't going to fall in love with her. He was allowed to date.

So was I. If I wanted to, which I didn't. But maybe I'd change my mind.

It just wasn't the time for Mateo and me. I had to wait a little longer. I was good at waiting.

I breathed through the ache in my chest. I locked away the hurt in that box down deep. Compared to the rest of the pain I kept in that box, this paled in comparison.

I just had to wait.

In the meantime, I'd keep working on me. I'd find Dad. And I'd wait.

A month. Six months. Twelve. Maybe in a year, he'd see me. Eventually he'd see me.

I just had to wait.

CHAPTER 11

"Jellybean!" I opened my arms wide as Alaina raced toward the front door at Anne and Harrison's. She launched herself into my chest, so I swept her off her bare feet, spinning her in a circle as I peppered her cheeks with kisses. "Hi."

"Hi."

"Are you having a birthday party today?"

Her birthday hoodie this year was violet with *TWO* in rainbow letters on its face. "Boon."

"Boon?" That was a new word in her exploding vocabulary.

She pointed down the hallway. "Go."

"Are you being bossy today?" I tickled her ribs and closed the door, toeing off my shoes, then headed for the noisy kitchen.

A chorus of hellos greeted me as I walked into the Eden fray with Alaina perched on my hip.

"Did you find Vera?" Mateo asked his daughter.

"Yep." Like always, whenever I rang the doorbell, Alaina came running. And I was still the only person to ring.

"Boon." Alaina pointed to the bouquet of balloons on the island.

"Ah." Boon. "Bal-loon," I enunciated, stressing each syllable.

"Boon."

I giggled. "Close enough."

"Dow." *Down.* Alaina squirmed but I held her tighter.

"Not without a smooch." I puckered up and made a kissing noise.

She took my cheeks in her little hands and squeezed, then her slobbery mouth landed on mine.

"Okay, go have fun." I pushed a small dark curl off her forehead, then set her on her feet so she could run to the playroom, already filled with the other kids' laughter.

"What can I help with?" I snatched a carrot from the veggie tray on the island.

"Nothing." Anne dried her hands with a towel beside the sink. "I think we're all set."

"Sorry I'm late."

She waved it off. "You're right on time."

My feet were killing me, so I slid into the last empty stool at the island beside Lyla, nudging my elbow with hers. "Hi."

"Hi." She smiled, glancing down at a sleeping Trey in her arms.

How that baby could sleep through the noise was beyond me, but this wasn't the first family gathering he'd snoozed through. His first birthday would be the next we celebrated, probably right here in this kitchen. Maybe he'd stay awake for that party.

"Hey, kiddo." Uncle Vance tossed an arm around my shoulders for a sideways hug. He must have caught the scent of wind and pine in my hair, and though he tried to hide it, a small frown tugged at his mouth. "You went hiking."

"You went hiking?" Mateo asked from the opposite side of the island. "Where?"

"Sable Peak."

"That's my favorite trail."

"I know."

He chuckled. "I've told you that before, haven't I?"

"Once or twice." I smiled as a blush crept into my cheeks.

The flush wasn't as fierce or fiery as it had been a year ago. Time and familiarity had made it easier to hide my crush on Mateo. That, or maybe my love for him didn't come roaring to the surface anymore whenever he was in the room—because it had seeped deep into my bones.

He snagged a snap pea from the veggie tray and dipped it in the ranch before popping it into his mouth. "Maybe I'll go up with you the next time you head out."

He'd told me that too. Once or twice.

"Sure. I'll let you know the next time I head that direction," I lied.

No matter how much I loved the idea of Mateo and me spending time alone together, he'd never get invited on my hikes. No one would. And I hadn't gone to Sable Peak today.

I'd been on the opposite end of the valley, traversing woods where the closest hiking trail was at least a mile away. March had been unseasonably warm this year, making it easier for me to get into the mountains.

Vance stiffened at my side, his arm falling away. His jaw flexed.

That flex meant I'd be getting a lecture the next time we were alone. I'd gotten to know that look well over the past year. The lectures too. But his concern stemmed from a good place.

"Are we still going to Willie's tonight?" Lyla asked, probably because her husband's rising tension was clouding the room and soon, people would start asking questions.

"We're in." Eloise leaned into Jasper's side. "Mom, you're still good to babysit?"

"Yes. I've been looking forward to it all week."

"Me too," Lyla said, meeting my gaze.

"Thank you," I mouthed.

Lyla had come to my rescue more often than not when it came to the hiking subject.

She knew, just like Vance, that I was searching for Dad. And she knew, just like Vance, that I wasn't going to stop.

Maybe he was still angry that Dad had attacked Lyla. I couldn't blame him for that.

Two years ago, Dad had gotten spooked when she'd stumbled upon him hunting and he'd... snapped. He'd choked her until she'd almost passed out, then let her go.

Vance had every right to be angry. So was I. Dad shouldn't have touched her. Why hadn't he just run away? What had been going on in his head that he'd do such a horrible thing?

If I hadn't left him so abruptly, I could have asked. I could have made sure he wasn't on the edge of a mental break.

But I had left him. Now I had to find him.

Lyla had accepted my hikes. Vance wanted me to move on.

He didn't give me enough credit for how far I'd already come. I was getting back to the person I'd been *before*. Living a normal life.

I had a job I loved at Eden Coffee. It paid my bills and allowed me a flexible schedule so that I had plenty of time to take my classes and study. I was doing what many twenty-three-year-old women were doing.

I drove my car. I spent too much time on my phone. I ate too much junk food and had a healthy obsession with Netflix.

In the past year, I liked to think I'd found constant.

I was chasing constant, at least.

But I wasn't giving up on Dad.

Maybe letting him go was the smartest decision. It would likely be the choice that saved myself heartache. In a way, the same could be said for my unending crush on Mateo. Was it reckless to love him even though he hadn't dropped a crumb of interest in my direction? Sort of.

Yet here I was, acting the fool.

Chances were, Mateo would never notice me. Chances were, I'd always feel damaged and broken. Maybe the past would always be something insurmountable for me to overcome.

Maybe no amount of waiting for Mateo would ever make a difference.

Deep in my heart, I knew it was time to let these feelings go. But forgetting Dad?

No. Never.

Dad was my family. He needed me. I was all he had left, and I'd abandoned him. Somehow, I'd fix that mistake. I'd figure out a way to stay in his life. To keep him in mine.

Even if the only place we could see each other was hidden beneath trees and a cloudless blue sky. Even if it took me ten years to find him. I would find him.

He was alive.

I wasn't giving up.

Even if down deep, I wondered if it was time to let both Mateo Eden and Cormac Gallagher go.

"Vera—"

"I heard you, Uncle Vance." I'd heard every word of the lecture he'd been giving me for the past five minutes outside of the ladies' bathroom at Willie's.

He sighed and rubbed a hand over his bearded jaw. "I'm worried about you."

"You don't need to worry." I gave him a sad smile. "I'm careful. I have my bear spray. I stay aware of my surroundings. I make noise when I'm in sketchy areas. I'm careful."

"It's not—" Another sigh. "I know you're careful. That's not what I'm worried about."

"Then what?"

"I'm worried..." He blew out a long breath. "I'm worried you won't find him."

We shared that worry. Not that I'd ever admit it out loud. To Vance or myself. "I'll find him."

"You might not."

"But I will."

"Kiddo—"

"He promised." My voice wobbled. "He said we'd see each other again. He promised."

I would find my father. I would be in his life. He needed me in his.

"I shouldn't have left him like that."

Vance blinked. "What? Do you want to go back?"

"No. Not to live out there. But it all happened so fast. You found me. We found Dad. And the next day, I left. It was hasty."

"Hasty. He wanted you to go, Vera."

"I know. And I'm not saying I regret it. But I just..." I sighed. "I'll find him."

Vance's eyes softened.

I hated the tender pity in his gaze. I hated his doubts. I hated that he could be right.

"I'll find him." My chin jutted as I spoke.

The expression on Vance's face didn't change. I couldn't stare at it for another minute, so I slid past him and stormed down the hallway, rejoining our group.

There were two bars on Main Street, Big Sam's Saloon and Old Mill. They bookended the touristy section of Quincy and catered to visitors who wanted the "authentic" Montana experience.

Big Sam's was decked out in over-the-top Western décor. Old Mill had a sports bar vibe. Willie's was a dive, and according to the locals, *it* was the authentic Montana bar.

The building itself was old, dark and dingy. The walls were crammed with neon lights and beer signs. Every table had an array of nicks and dings. No more than two chairs or stools matched, and the mirrored wall with shelves of liquor bottles probably hadn't been cleaned in a decade.

When I used the bathroom, despite years of peeing in the woods, I hovered over the toilet seat. Yet even with the stale scent of old beer, I liked these nights when the Edens would come into town for a night out.

I recognized nearly every face here tonight. Since the bar wasn't on Main, it didn't get the influx of tourists like the polished establishments.

Which seemed to suit Willie himself just fine. He stood behind the bar, looking about as pleased to have customers as he would to have a colonoscopy.

I walked to the bar and lifted a hand, signaling Willie from the end. I'd learned my first time here that smiles were wasted on the grumpy bartender so I didn't bother as he came my direction.

His white eyebrows seemed even bushier than they had been the last time we'd all come in for drinks, but his scraggly beard had gotten a slight trim.

"Coke, please."

Willie didn't nod or speak. He just filled a glass with ice and squirted my drink into it as I surveyed the room.

Griff and Winn always chose this as the hangout spot on these occasional outings. This was where they'd met years ago, and though he looked like a gruff cowboy, Griffin Eden was sentimental at heart.

At the moment, they were at the shuffleboard against the far wall, pretending to play when they were actually flirting between frequent kisses.

Memphis sat beside Knox, their chairs as close as possible so he could have one hand around her shoulders and his other hand splayed on her round belly. She was pregnant with their third, a girl this time.

Memphis was one of our designated drivers tonight.

Eloise was the other. She was sitting on Jasper's lap, his body cradling hers so naturally it was like they'd molded to each other.

Talia and Foster were holding hands, their fingers interlaced.

When Vance joined Lyla, they shared a silent conversation, his disappointment with me ripe from across the room. But when she put her hand on his thigh, he relaxed and kissed her temple.

The empty chairs at the table, Mateo's and mine, looked... lonely. Sad.

Where was he?

I scanned the room, finding him at the opposite end of the bar. He wasn't alone.

A blond woman was on the stool beside his. She was pressed so close that their shoulders nearly touched. A flirty smile toyed on her red lips.

My heart lurched.

Mateo swirled his whiskey on the rocks with a plastic straw before taking a sip from the tumbler.

The woman's gaze followed the movement and she licked her lips as he drank.

Oh, God. My stomach roiled just as Willie set my pop on the bar and held up one finger—the price.

"And rum," I blurted.

Willie's mouth pursed into a thin line, but he made me the cocktail while I watched Mateo.

Who was that woman? Did he know her? She hadn't been here when we'd come in. Besides our group, there were only a few other patrons tonight, a few older couples and three men with beer bellies sitting at the bar. I recognized all of them from the coffee shop.

But the blond. She was new. And she was beautiful.

Was he going to pick her up? Tonight?

When Willie held up three fingers this time, I dug a five-dollar bill from my jeans pocket, barely sparing him a glance as I slapped it on the sticky bar. "Keep the change."

My hand trembled as I took a long drink from my own glass, cringing at the burn of the alcohol. I took another sip. I stole another glance at the woman. Both hurt.

On shaking legs, I retreated to the table, sipping my drink as everyone else talked and laughed. My silence went unnoticed. It was overshadowed by the country music playing through the bar's speakers.

Mateo's empty chair was on the other side of the table. We still never sat beside each other, either at Anne and Harrison's or at Willie's. Somehow, I always landed beside Vance or Lyla. I wish I had taken that chair.

Mine was aimed directly at the bar where Mateo and the blond were talking. It was impossible not to watch them together.

She laughed. He grinned.

I fought a gag.

How many women had he picked up here? How many times had he taken a woman home from Willie's?

Mateo had dated on and off for the past year. I only knew about it because Anne was usually Alaina's babysitter. But it was all easier to ignore because none of his dates ever came to the ranch. To my knowledge, he hadn't introduced any woman to his daughter.

That had to mean something, right? That Allie knew *me*. That Allie loved *me*.

The woman leaned in close to say something into his ear.

I slammed the last of my drink, gulping it down until all that remained was ice. Then I shot out of my chair and went to the bar, flagging down Willie for a refill.

The rum didn't burn as much this time. My head felt lighter, my limbs looser, and when I sat in my seat, I tilted a bit too far to the side.

"Whoa." Vance steadied me with a hand on my shoulder.

"I'm fine." I batted him away.

Was this drunk? I'd never been drunk before.

I didn't like it.

What the hell was I doing? I didn't like drinking. If I went to a bar with the Edens or the friends I'd made this past year, I was a designated driver. Always.

But before I could shove my glass away and ignore it for the rest of the night, the blond put her hand on Mateo's thigh beneath the bar. Her nails dragged along the denim of his jeans.

There was a scream inside my chest. I clamped my lips together to keep it from escaping. When I was sure I'd swallowed it down, I lifted the glass and chugged the rest of my drink. The ice cubes clattered as I set it on the table with too much force.

"Vera." Vance put his hand on my wrist. "Enough."

Enough.

He was right, wasn't he? This was enough. This had to be enough.

Mateo was never going to think of me as anything other than an honorary member of the Eden family. He was never going to see me. He was never going to love me.

It wasn't fair.

I'd worked so hard these past two years. On the dark days, when I'd almost given up hope, I'd kept going. I'd come so far.

I'd waited for him.

I'd waited and waited and waited.

Why had I waited? Why had I convinced myself there was even a chance he'd be mine?

Dad would be so disappointed. He'd hate that I'd waited just to be entirely... overlooked.

Enough.

Yes. Yes, it was enough.

I was out of my chair before I knew what I was doing.

"Vera."

I ignored Vance and stalked to the bar. My head was fuzzy but my steps were surprisingly steady as I marched to that bombshell blond with red lips and matching nails.

Mateo noticed me first. He sat straighter, easing back from the woman.

She twisted on her stool, her smile dropping as she looked me over.

"Hey, Vera." Mateo's eyebrows came together. "You okay?"

"Don't say 'Hey.' And no. I'm not okay." I squared my shoulders. "I'm not your sister."

"My sister?" His forehead furrowed. "What are you talking about? Are you drunk?"

"I think so." I hated that I'd let myself get drunk. Hated that I'd done something like *her*. Hated that I'd lost him.

Mateo hadn't even been mine to start with, but I'd lost him anyway.

I'd lost all of them.

God, it hurt. When was it going to stop hurting?

"He's allergic to shellfish," I told the blond.

Her eyebrows came together. "Huh?"

"His favorite color is blue. He loves snap peas but only if there is ranch to dip them in. Almost everything he buys for his daughter is purple."

The woman glanced to Mateo. "You have a daughter?"

He ignored her, his stare fixed on me.

So I stared right back, holding his sapphire eyes as my own flooded. "He's a pilot but he doesn't fly anymore. I don't know why. He'll drop anything to help his sisters or brothers.

He wears brown boots with a black belt even though they don't match."

Mateo's throat bobbed and something flashed across his gaze, but I was too drunk to figure it out. Maybe he thought his brown boots and black belt did match.

"He's a morning person. He drinks black coffee. He's really good at math and can add numbers in his head faster than anyone I've ever met. He looks magical when he's riding a horse. And light follows him. It's always sunny when he's around."

Something wet dripped down my cheek. A tear. I let it splatter on the dirty bar floor and shifted my focus to the woman again.

The hardness and annoyance in her face was gone, replaced with that same tender pity Uncle Vance had given me earlier. It was excruciating to be pitied by this woman. This stranger who'd likely share Mateo's bed tonight.

"He won't treat you like you're broken, even when you are," I whispered as the tears streamed.

"Vera." Mateo's voice had a rasp, like he needed a drink of water.

He could have one when I was finished.

I rounded the woman's stool, sliding in between them. The blond tried to nudge me out of the way with her knee, but I ignored her, standing strong. And before Mateo could say another word, I pressed my lips to his, holding that soft mouth for two aching heartbeats before I pulled away.

He stared at me, his face unreadable.

"I'm done waiting for you to see me."

I flew from the bar. I ran. And as I raced down Quincy's sidewalks, I put my love for Mateo away.

I shoved it in that locked box.

And buried it down deep.

PART II

AFTER

CHAPTER 12

MATEO

I'm done waiting for you to see me.

That sentence was Vera's gut punch. Every time I replayed last night, it hit the hardest. Or maybe it had been the kiss that had nearly knocked me off my stool.

My fingers lifted, about to touch my mouth, before I pinned my arm at my side. How was it that I could still feel her lips, soft and sweet, on mine?

Vera. *Damn it.*

How long had she had these feelings for me? Where the hell did we go from here?

"Morning."

I jumped, the scalding black coffee in my mug sloshing over the rim and onto my hand.

"Sorry." Mom stepped out of the house as I wiped my skin dry. "Thought you heard me."

I couldn't hear a damn thing with Vera's voice so loud in my head.

His favorite color is blue.

He loves snap peas but only if there is ranch to dip them in.

Almost everything he buys for his daughter is purple.

"You're up early," Mom said, joining me at the railing on the porch.

"Yeah." I hadn't slept a minute and had finally given up lying in bed around three.

This morning was extreme, but I was usually up early. Like Vera had said last night, I was a morning person who drank black coffee and wore brown boots with a black belt, which apparently didn't match.

I leaned my forearms on the top rail, staring into the distance as I sipped more coffee. This was my third cup. Or maybe it was my fourth.

The trees and meadows were covered in silver frost. A layer of clouds obscured the mountains in the distance but the sun was rising. Another couple hours, it would be up to burn off the chill.

I'd been staring at the mountains since dawn, spinning over everything Vera had said last night.

I'm not your sister.

No, she wasn't my sister. I'd never seen her as a sister. She was… Vera.

"How was Willie's?" Mom asked.

Awful. Absolutely fucking awful.

Mom had been awake when we'd gotten home last night, but in the rush to collect sleeping kids, bundle them up and load them into car seats, she hadn't asked for details about the bar. Even if she had, I wouldn't have known what to say.

So I'd kissed her cheek good night and headed to the guest bedroom where Allie had been asleep in her portable crib. Since it was her birthday, we'd planned to crash at Mom and Dad's so they could spend time with her on her special day.

Not that I was in any mood to celebrate.

I'm done waiting for you to see me.

I saw Vera. I'd always seen Vera.

She was sweet. Strong. Her hair went wild sometimes and she'd get so annoyed she'd rake it into a ponytail with a huff that always made me chuckle. She loved cherry tomatoes. I hated them but always thought it would be weird to offer her food from my plate because that was something couples did and we weren't a couple.

"Mateo?"

"Yeah?"

She raised her eyebrows.

Right. Her question. "Willie's was, uh… Willie's. It was good."

Her eyes narrowed, no doubt smelling the lie—Mom was part bloodhound when it came to dishonesty in her children. She'd find out the whole truth soon enough. Not a soul at Willie's had missed the moment Vera kissed me.

The blond who'd been flirting with me had been forgotten as I'd tried to chase Vera out of the bar, but Vance had stopped me with a lethal glare before I could make it outside. He'd been the one to chase after her.

Probably smart. I wouldn't have known what to say anyway.

The party had died a quick death at that point. Without Lyla's car, we'd only had one designated driver, so we'd crammed into Memphis's SUV. No one had spoken on the drive to the ranch. Not to each other. Not to me.

The barn loft's windows were dark. Vera hadn't come home last night. She must have stayed at Vance and Lyla's place. Was she okay?

My temples throbbed. What a damn mess. Had everyone known that she had feelings for me? Or had we all been clueless?

Mom looked past me to the barn. "Did Vera have a nice time?"

"Not really."

She'd cried. I'd made her cry. And I couldn't stop seeing those tears track down her face.

"What—oh." Understanding widened Mom's blue eyes. "It finally happened, didn't it?"

So not everyone had been clueless. "You knew?"

"I've watched for years, wondering if and when you'd notice."

"Thanks for the warning." My voice sounded sharper than I'd intended.

"I'm sorry. I never knew what to say. I thought it would fade. Or that maybe you'd notice her too."

"I noticed her, Mom. It wasn't that I didn't notice her. But I didn't think… I didn't know she felt that way." Vera had been right. "I didn't see it."

Mom put her hand on my arm. "And now?"

I blew out a long exhale, my breath billowing in a white cloud. "Eyes wide open."

Maybe I'd missed it because of Alaina. My daughter had been my focus, and sure, I'd dated. But a relationship? I didn't want a relationship. Not while I was still trying to figure out how to be a single dad. Definitely not while I'd been sorting through everything that had happened with Madison.

Or maybe I hadn't caught on to Vera's feelings because she was… Vera.

No one had ever warned me away. Vance had never told me to keep my distance. But there'd been subtleties. At the wedding, Vera had looked so beautiful, and dancing with her had been the best five minutes of the night. I'd wanted to keep her in my arms—until Vance had cut in.

Every time I'd offered Vera a chair beside mine at family dinners, he'd asked her to sit beside him instead.

No warning. Not verbal, at least.

But I'd received the message, loud and clear.

Did he know how she felt?

Fuck. What the hell was I supposed to do now?

This wasn't just some woman I could walk away from if things fell apart. Vera was a part of this family. It was hard to remember life before she'd come into our lives.

She had a dry sense of humor and made quiet jokes no one appreciated enough. She liked milk and sugar in her coffee. She ate mashed potatoes plain.

She made the best latte at Eden Coffee, even better than Lyla. She'd stare out a window at the mountains and it looked so much like she wanted to be anywhere but indoors.

She had the sweetest laugh, second only to Alaina's.

She'd do anything for my parents.

She loved my daughter.

And she thought she was broken.

He won't treat you like you're broken, even when you are.

She wasn't broken. Not once had I thought she was anything but strong. A warrior.

"I'm not sure what to think or what to do," I told Mom. The last thing I wanted was to hurt Vera.

"That girl has been through hell, Mateo."

"I know," I murmured.

"I get the feeling we only know part of what all happened."

I nodded. "Same."

Mom stood straight, facing me as she raised her chin. "I love her like she's one of my own. She needs a mother, and I'm taking the job."

The reason Vera needed a mother was because her father had strangled her own after murdering her twin sisters. Then, Cormac Gallagher had kidnapped his oldest daughter into the wilderness and kept her there for four years until she'd finally broken free.

I was missing a lot of detail from the story, but after she'd left her father, she'd shown up on Vance's doorstep in Idaho. A woman brought back to life. Everyone had assumed she'd died with her sisters.

The years she'd been through. The nightmare she'd endured. To say she'd gone through hell was an understatement.

"Does she ever talk about it?" I asked.

Mom shook her head. "Not a word. In the beginning, I asked questions that she didn't answer. Every time I brought it up, she shut down. And she doesn't ever talk about her father."

That son of a bitch could suffer a slow death for all I cared.

Cormac had tried to kill Lyla a couple years ago. She'd gone out hiking and had stumbled across him beside a river. The motherfucker had nearly strangled her to death. It was nothing short of a miracle that he'd changed his mind about another murder and let her go.

We'd all searched for Cormac but he'd slipped away. Had Vera been with him then? Was the reason she'd left him because of what he'd done to Lyla?

Vance probably knew. Lyla too. But they weren't talking and neither was Vera.

Vera went hiking all the time. Why? Was she searching for her father? What would happen if she found him? Would she turn him in to the authorities?

"She's beautiful," Mom said, like she was letting me in on a secret.

"I might be oblivious, but I'm not blind."

Vera was beautiful. I'd thought so from the very first time she'd braved a family dinner. Any other woman and I would have chased her shamelessly.

Except she was Vera. When she'd moved to Quincy, the last thing she'd needed was a man drooling over her. So I'd just been there as a friend. The few times I'd flirted with her, she hadn't flirted back. Unless...

Vera knew I'd been flirting, right?

I rubbed my jaw, the stubble scraping my palm. "What a mess."

"You'll figure it out."

"I wish I had your confidence," I muttered.

"I love you, Mateo. And I love Vera. No matter what, just be gentle with her heart." She turned and headed into the house, leaving me alone on the cold porch.

Be gentle with her heart.

"Shit. What am I doing?" I dragged a hand through my hair

just as a tiny voice echoed from the baby monitor in my jeans pocket.

"Daddy. Wake."

I dumped the rest of my coffee over the porch rail, splattering it on the frozen gravel, then went inside to the guest bedroom. The moment I opened the door, a pair of little arms stretched in the air.

I picked Alaina up and settled her against my chest. "Happy Birthday, Sprout."

Allie nuzzled her face in my neck.

"Did you sleep good?" I kissed her dark hair and bent to get her stuffed unicorn from the crib.

It was a gift from Vera that Allie was rarely without.

Allie loved Vera. Vera loved Allie. It was as obvious as a full moon on a cloudless night. That, I'd seen. So why the fuck hadn't I noticed Vera's feelings for me?

Mom had said she'd watched for years. Since the beginning, then.

If I hadn't been so wrapped up in Alaina, would I have noticed too? What would I have done about it?

My stomach knotted, knowing exactly what I would have done. The man I'd been before my daughter was not the man I was today.

I would have wooed her into bed. I would have fucked it up at some point, and in the end, I would have broken her heart.

Funny how having a daughter made you think differently about the woman you were dating. About the kind of man I wanted for Alaina someday in the distant, distant future.

None of the women I'd met in the past two years had been good enough to even meet Allie. I hadn't planned to do anything with that blond at the bar but share a drink and let her flirt with me for a while. I'd always planned on coming home alone.

I'd been coming home alone for two years.

Vera had told that blond last night that I was good at math.

Yeah, I was good at math. At the moment, I'd rather be good at understanding women.

Especially Vera Gallagher.

"Go." Allie pointed to the door. She didn't give a damn about my internal crisis. She wanted to go.

The bed was a disheveled mess from my tossing and turning, but I ignored it to make later and headed for the kitchen.

"There's my birthday girl." Mom held out her arms, reaching for Allie.

Allie only snuggled deeper into my neck, her hand fisting my thermal. "Daddy."

In the mornings, she was my girl.

"Boo," Mom pouted, pretending to be hurt. "What if I made pancakes? Would you want me more than Daddy then?"

Allie loved Mom's pancakes.

"That should do the trick." I forced a smile and slid onto a stool at the island.

Mom went to work on breakfast, and I strained my ears past the clatter of pans and the sizzle of bacon.

With any luck, Vera would be home soon and we could talk. Not that I had a fucking clue what to say.

Maybe after my fourth or fifth cup of coffee, I'd figure it out.

Dad joined us a few minutes later, patting me on the shoulder on his way to kiss Mom. He filled a coffee mug and refilled mine, then played peek-a-boo with Alaina.

I'd just put her in a high chair when the crunch of gravel sounded outside.

"Be back." I felt Mom's gaze on my back as I rushed out.

Lyla's car was parked beside the barn when I opened the door. She hadn't said anything to me last night. She'd just sat in the middle row of Memphis's SUV with a worry line between her eyebrows.

If Lyla had known about Vera's crush, would she have warned me away?

Mom might not have missed it, but the rest of us...

Lyla would have told me, right? Talia or Eloise too. And I had to believe my brothers would have given me a heads-up.

I jogged down the steps, hustling toward the barn as the passenger side door opened and Vera stepped out.

She said something to Lyla, then closed the door.

Lyla reversed away from the barn, pausing when she saw me, but I kept on walking. So she kept on driving.

"Vera." I jogged a few steps as she walked toward the barn's side entrance. "Wait up."

The fresh air always cleared my head. It made me sharper. Maybe if we talked outside, I'd figure out what to say. How to fix this.

At my voice, Vera froze. Her hand hovered in midair above the door's handle. It took three of my long strides before she finally turned to face me.

She looked like hell. There was no flush to her cheeks. No sparkle in her pretty, brown eyes. She looked as cold as the morning air.

That look was entirely my fault.

I stopped in front of her, chest heaving as she stared past my shoulder. The sound of Lyla's car faded in the distance.

The breeze caught a tendril of Vera's red hair, floating it across her face. The strand skimmed her soft, pink lips. Normally, her cheeks were the same pink shade, but her skin had a white pallor today. The purple circles beneath her eyes meant we'd probably gotten the same amount of sleep last night.

She was dressed in a pair of black leggings that hugged her toned legs. The Eden Coffee sweatshirt was one she'd likely borrowed from Lyla's closet. It hung on her slender frame. She looked... small. Too small. Like a part of her had faded away.

My arms lifted slightly, the movement unconscious, like my limbs knew she needed a hug before it had even registered in my brain. But I dropped them to my sides, my muscles locking.

She wouldn't want me touching her, not after last night.

Her eyes flicked to mine for a second before darting away, falling to the dirt. "Can we not do this today?"

Her voice. It was as cold and lifeless as her eyes.

"You're not broken." That wasn't the right place to start. An apology or anything else would be better. "Everything you said last night was right. Except that. It's the one thing you got wrong."

Vera wrapped her arms around her waist, her shoulders curling forward.

"You're the most courageous person I've ever met, Vera. You're not broken. When I think about your strength... if Allie gets just a fraction of that when she's grown, I'll be grateful."

She squeezed her eyes shut as her chin quivered. "Please, Mateo."

Normally, I liked how she said my name. But that empty voice. I'd do just about anything to make it stop.

I opened my mouth to apologize but nothing came out. If I said *I'm sorry*, it would just sound like a rejection. I wasn't rejecting Vera.

I didn't know what I was doing, but I knew what I wasn't.

She stood, eyes closed, as the wind played with that tendril of hair. The morning light brought out the sprinkling of freckles across her nose.

She was beautiful. Vera had a beauty not a soul would miss.

"Will you give Allie a birthday kiss for me?" she asked.

Sad. Tired. Embarrassed. But she'd still remembered Allie's birthday.

Because Vera loved my daughter. My daughter loved Vera. That meant something. That meant everything.

I'm done waiting for you to see me.

Something shifted beneath my feet like moving sand. Things in my chest, around my brain, rearranged. It was like a deck of cards being shuffled.

There was before. This was after.

CHAPTER 13

VERA

My stomach pitched as I marched up the stairs to the loft. *Don't puke. Don't puke.*

Hot, humiliating tears streamed down my face and no amount of blinking would make them stop. At least I hadn't cried in front of Mateo. By some miracle, I'd managed to hold myself together until I'd slipped inside the barn.

The box. The lock was undone. The lid was opening.

The numbness from my sleepless night had worn off. Too many emotions were surging free. They tore up my throat, threatening to choke me to death.

Breathe.

I gulped the air as a sob hurdled from my throat. Oh, God. I was going to puke.

With my hands wrapped around my stomach, I jogged faster, bursting through the loft's door and running straight to the toilet. There was nothing in my stomach to retch, but the tears felt infinite.

Why was I so pathetic? How could I have been so stupid last night?

My head pounded and my muscles ached. Was this a hangover?

Never again. I was never drinking again.

I crawled from the toilet to the tub, twisting the knob until the water ran on the hottest setting. Then I stripped out of the clothes I'd borrowed from Lyla.

The spray was still cold when I clambered to my feet and stepped into the shower. I gritted my teeth through the sting. It wasn't the first time I'd washed in ice-cold water. This was just another frigid stream.

I missed my dad. I could really use a hug today.

He'd give me one even though he'd be *pissed* I'd gotten drunk. I grabbed the shampoo and squirted it into my hair, scrubbing too hard and too fast. What the fuck had I been thinking last night?

I didn't drink. I didn't want to drink. I didn't want to turn into *her*.

The memory of her slurring voice, of her swayed movements and gray, colorless face made my stomach lurch. The urge to vomit on my bare feet was so overpowering I had to clamp my mouth and eyes shut, breathing through the nausea until the water was so hot it nearly burned.

Never again. I was never drinking again.

I rinsed the shampoo away, my hair sluicing down my spine. Over the past year, I'd let it grow nearly to my waist. Maybe I should cut it all off. Go short.

Mateo's blond from last night had long hair. Did he prefer long hair? Why was I even curious?

It was over. I'd made a fool of myself last night with my drunken rambling. Then I'd kissed him.

"Ugh." My groan echoed off the cream stone walls.

Oh, God, that kiss. I'd lost my goddamn mind.

I buried my face in my hands, wishing I could hide from the world, Mateo included, from now until the end of time. I needed to apologize. I should have apologized already. I needed to figure out a way to make this not awkward because facing him this morning had been excruciating.

How was I ever going to survive a family dinner again? I couldn't even make eye contact with Vance this morning.

He'd found me after I'd raced out of the bar. He'd caught me running down Main and ordered me to get in the car. But other than that, he hadn't said much else. Granted, I'd been too busy crying in the passenger seat to chat about my fixation on his brother-in-law.

Vance hadn't spoken a word to me this morning. He didn't seem mad, at least not at me. When I'd asked for a ride to the ranch, Lyla had volunteered. The ride had been quiet. Uncomfortable. Mostly, I think she wasn't sure what to say. How to fix this.

But the only person who could fix it was me. And right now, that felt impossible.

One drunken night, and I'd ruined everything.

Maybe I was like her, after all.

Where was Dad? I needed him today. I needed to look at him and remember that I was *his* daughter. That I had *his* hair. *His* face. *His* eyes.

Not hers.

I needed Dad.

The pace of my shower changed from misery to mechanics. I quickly scrubbed the scent of Willie's from my body, then wrapped a towel around my waist and went to the closet. Dressed in my warmest base layer, fleece-lined pants and a thick sweater, I combed out my wet hair and twisted it into a knot at my nape. Then I donned a wool hat and headed out of the bedroom.

My keys were beside my textbooks and laptop on the kitchen counter. I'd planned to study for an upcoming test in my Personality Theory and Research class today. But I picked up my keys instead and swiped my coat from its hook. With my gloves in a pocket, my pack strapped to my shoulders, I stepped into my boots and jogged down the stairs.

The Honda's windshield had a thin sheen of ice, so I started the engine and scraped it enough to drive before sliding inside.

I gripped the wheel tight and refused to look at Anne and Harrison's house—at Mateo's truck—as I drove down the lane.

The highway was deserted, too early for traffic on a Sunday. I wound along three county roads to a parking area a few miles outside of Quincy. The moment my car was parked, I walked away without a backward glance, disappearing into the trees.

There was no trail off that parking area, but I followed a familiar path through the woods.

This was the path I'd taken on my once-a-month supply run to Quincy. Dad would wait for me at our meeting spot, hidden about half a mile off the road. Ready to run if we had to make a break for it. His pack had always been loaded with everything essential, including our dwindling stack of cash.

The money he'd taken from the ATM when we'd left Idaho hadn't lasted long enough. When we'd run out, he'd robbed a country gas station in Oregon.

I suppose that made me his accessory, didn't it? I was a criminal by association.

We'd been camping out in the Cascades at the time, and one day, he'd told me he was going hunting. Alone. Up until that point, we'd always gone together.

Dad was smart about nutrition. He always made sure we had enough fat in our protein-rich diet. Part of the reason I'd wanted to take a nutrition course last year was to compare notes with what he'd taught me.

But as hard as he tried to provide, it wasn't always easy. Having a can of beans came in handy when game was scarce and tummies were growling. So he'd give me a short list of necessities to snag whenever I snuck into a town.

The money from that night had dwindled too fast.

The day Dad had gone hunting in Oregon, he'd returned with pockets of cash. When I'd asked him how he got it, he'd confessed to robbing the gas station.

My father was a good man. I loved my dad. But he wasn't perfect. And his crimes, most of them, had kept me alive.

Was he out of supplies? Had he robbed another gas station, this time for food instead of money? If I could just find him, I could bring him anything he needed. It would actually be easier now than ever before. He wouldn't have to hunt or forage.

If I could just find him. He'd be okay if I could find him.

I trudged my way past tree trunks and through the underbrush toward our old rendezvous point. The snow hadn't melted here yet and a trail of footprints followed me as I hiked.

I breathed in the air, letting it chase away the hangover. When I made it to our meeting spot, I pulled off my gloves and cupped my hands over my mouth. The piercing whistle that came from my lips ricocheted in every direction off evergreens and rocks.

Then the forest stole it, leaving nothing but silence. Not a sound came in reply.

I whistled again. And again. And again.

Each time, I waited to hear a reply.

Was he out here somewhere? Was he watching me to make sure it was safe?

"Dad," I called, my voice hoarse. So I cleared my throat and shouted again. "Dad!"

The breeze rustled the branches above my head. Otherwise, nothing.

Of course there was nothing. How would he have known to be here? It was stupid to think I'd come out here and he'd just be waiting. It was dumb to think I'd find him today when

I'd spent months searching without luck.

The shelter we'd built as our home was gone. He'd dismantled it completely, from the walls to the ceiling to our beds and the table he'd made as a nightstand.

There wasn't a trace of where we'd lived.

It was just… gone.

He was gone.

I needed him today. And he was gone.

Because I'd left him alone.

"Dad!" I poured everything I had into my shout. I closed my eyes and balled my fists. And screamed. *"Dad!"*

Nothing.

"You said we'd see each other again."

Silence.

He was out there. He had to be out there. He'd promised we'd see each other again, and my dad kept his promises. Always.

He was alive. *He's alive.*

"Da-*ad*!" My voice broke as I yelled one last time, but there was no one to hear it crack.

There was no one to watch as I dropped to my knees and broke.

By the time I made it back to my car, most of the day had passed. Bone-deep exhaustion had stolen whatever sadness lingered in my heart. After hours of hiking and crying, the tears had run dry. A familiar numbness settled beneath my skin as I drove home.

My heart didn't give its normal trill when I spotted Mateo's truck still parked outside Anne and Harrison's house. They must still be celebrating Allie.

Would I be invited to the party for her third birthday? Or was everything so messed up now that they'd cut me out of their life?

Should I find a new place to live? The idea of moving out

of the loft made my insides twist.

It was never meant to be permanent. I'd always known that eventually, I'd have to leave. But I wasn't ready, not yet. That loft was the first place to feel like home, a real home, since *before.*

I had to fix this.

Tomorrow, I'd face Anne and Harrison. I'd suffer the consequences of my loud, drunken mouth. I'd call Uncle Vance. I'd go to work at Eden Coffee.

Tomorrow.

Tonight, I just wanted to be alone. I wanted to eat a peanut butter and jelly sandwich, then curl up in a ball on the couch and watch TV.

Except the moment I parked and opened my car's door, a rugged male voice thwarted my plans.

"Vera." Mateo strode from the house, his hands in his coat pockets. He looked gorgeous in the faded light. He hadn't shaved today. Mateo with a day of dark stubble was a favorite.

My heart trilled. *Damn it.*

Why did I have to love him? Why couldn't I want anyone other than Mateo Eden? It would be so much easier that way.

I sighed as he stopped in front of me. "Please, Mateo. I don't have it in me to—"

"You left. I don't want you to leave your home because of what happened. No matter what, this is your place, Vera. You don't have to leave."

He was so good at saying the right thing. Even when he couldn't have known I'd needed to hear it.

"Where did you go?" he asked.

"On a hike."

A muscle feathered in his jaw as he frowned, the same frown Uncle Vance gave me after my hikes. Except Mateo didn't know why I was going out there.

He believed Dad was a murderer who'd kept me captive

for years. That I'd escaped my father's clutches. From his perspective, why would I ever search for my father?

"You okay?" Mateo's forehead furrowed as he studied my face.

I shrugged and met his gaze.

He had the most amazing blue eyes. I was glad that Alaina had them too.

"Does Allie like her dragon?" For her birthday, I'd bought Allie a green plush rocking dragon. A musical tune played when you squeezed one of its ears.

He nodded. "She loves it. Been climbing on and off of it all day."

"Good." I'd brought it over after the party last night, but we'd been in a rush to head to Willie's so I hadn't seen her try it. If I asked, he'd probably let me see her tonight, but I didn't have it in me to face his parents.

Tomorrow. Once this embarrassment had faded a bit.

I took a step backward, ready to retreat to the loft, but he stopped me with a question.

"Why'd you pick a dragon instead of a horse?"

"She'll have real horses to ride her entire life. I wanted her to have something magical instead." The magic of childhood faded too soon.

Mateo rubbed a hand over his jaw. When it fell from his face, his shoulders dropped too. "At the bar—"

"Can we not talk about it? Please?"

"You said I was a pilot. That I don't fly anymore and you didn't know why."

I pulled my lower lip between my teeth, wishing there was a hole somewhere in the driveway I could crawl into and hide. "I'm sorry—"

"Don't." He held up a hand. "Don't apologize."

"For embarrassing you?"

"I'm not embarrassed, Vera."

"Well, that makes one of us," I muttered.

He blew out a long breath and took a step closer. Almost too close. He stood there and stared down at me with a look on his face I couldn't quite discern. He didn't look angry or upset. He just looked... serious.

"What?" I whispered.

He didn't answer. He just kept staring.

"I'm going to bed." I took a step away, scurrying to safety.

"Vera," he called.

Damn it. My frame sagged. My feet stopped. I'd waited a long time for Mateo to call to me. After months and months of pent-up desperation, I was powerless to resist.

"Yeah?"

"I love flying. I got my license while I was in college. Flew nearly the whole time I was there. I kept earning certificates until I became an instructor. I loved it so much that I almost dropped out of school just to be a pilot. But by that point, I'd spent a lot of Mom and Dad's money on my education. Everyone else had their degrees. So I stuck with school, graduated and came home. Didn't really have a passion for anything specific, so I helped out on the ranch and at the hotel to keep busy and make money. Figured I'd kill some time before I decided on my own career path."

Why did it feel like no one knew this? Why was he telling *me*?

"I realized after a while that I needed to forge my own path," he said. "Flying was the first thing that came to mind, so I started looking for jobs in Alaska. Got hired as a pilot to deliver supplies to remote areas of the state."

"Did you like it?"

"Loved it. Enjoyed living in Alaska too."

"Then why'd you leave?"

"I missed home."

It sounded true. But only partially true. There was more

to it, wasn't there? Missing home, missing his family, wasn't the whole reason he'd left a job he'd loved.

Was it Allie's mother? Was she the reason he'd returned to Montana?

"I went up there looking for something and came home when I realized I hadn't found it," he said.

"What were you looking for?"

"I don't know." He shook his head. "That's the hell of it. I don't even know what I was looking for. Everyone here has their passion. For Griffin, it's the ranch. Knox has Knuckles. Talia has only ever wanted to be a doctor, and Lyla has Eden Coffee. Eloise pours her heart and soul into the hotel. I guess I was just waiting for something to spark. For a time, flying was that spark. But it's different here. I don't have a reason to fly. And after I came back, I sort of fell into my old life."

A life where he supported everyone else in their dreams while forsaking his own.

"You don't have to be in Alaska to fly," I said. "Why did you stop?"

"I don't want to work for a commercial airline. Always traveling. Sleeping in hotels instead of my own bed. Living in a city because it's a hub. That's not the lifestyle for me. But there's not much demand for pilots in Quincy. Crop-dusting. Working for the forest service during fire season. It's not impossible but... flying is a hobby. It's easier that way."

Because of Allie. Because if he worked on the ranch and at the hotel, he could be with his daughter every day. She could live surrounded by grandparents, aunts, uncles and cousins.

He'd been considering moving back to Alaska a couple of years ago, but then Allie had been born. Mateo was a pilot. But first and foremost, he was a father.

"You should go fly," I said. "Even if it's just a hobby."

"Would you go with me?"

My jaw dropped. "W-what?"

"Go with me. Have you ever been in a small plane?"

"Um, no."

"Then we'll go tomorrow." He turned and walked away. Just declared we were flying, then walked away.

"Wait. I have to work tomorrow."

"Then Tuesday," he called over his shoulder, still walking.

No. Definitely not Tuesday. Why was he asking? Was this a pity thing? A way to make amends? For us to get past this, I needed some distance from Mateo, not to be trapped beside him in an airplane.

"I don't like flying." Maybe I liked flying. I'd never flown before.

He spun in a slow circle. Still walking. "You'll like this."

"Mateo—"

"Tuesday. I'll pick you up at eleven."

"Mateo," I called.

"Night, Vera."

Seriously? I wanted to puke again.

Instead, I stood, watching as he disappeared inside Anne and Harrison's house. Then I tilted my head to the stars. "Shit."

CHAPTER 14

MATEO

The alarm chimed on my phone. Ten thirty. Time to go. I had just enough time to put my tools away and drive from the hotel to the ranch.

"Mateo?" Eloise called.

"In here," I hollered back from room 309.

She found me in the bathroom, wiping down the mirror I'd just installed.

Over the past three months, I'd been replacing the bathroom mirrors in the guest rooms with larger, LED-lit pieces. We timed these update projects for the slow winter months, when the hotel wasn't packed. There were four rooms to go and then it was done.

"That looks so great." Eloise smiled as I closed my toolbox. "I love these mirrors."

"They're nice. It was a good call to swap them out. Give me until Friday, then I should have the rest finished."

"Excellent. Thank you."

"Welcome." I lifted my tools and followed her out to the elevators.

"I have this for you," she said, holding up a piece of paper.

"What is it?"

"The direct deposit form. I know I've always just written

you a check for your time, but since you're the official maintenance man, I was thinking this would be easier."

Wait. The *official* maintenance man? When had I become official?

Yeah, I did a lot of maintenance at the hotel. Before Allie was born, I used to cover the front desk whenever Eloise was short-staffed, but she'd lined up good clerks in the past couple of years and hadn't needed much help. These days, I mostly worked on building projects, like upgrading those mirrors. I was handy and didn't mind fixing the occasional broken dresser drawer or changing a florescent ballast bulb.

Dad helped too. Was he getting a direct deposit form and an *official* job title?

"Just fill that out whenever you can," she said.

I nodded. "You got it."

Official maintenance man. I grimaced as the elevator doors slid open. Eloise left for the desk, and I went to put my tools in the utility room.

What was I doing?

I was twenty-eight-years old working a job that was only supposed to be temporary. It had started as a way to pitch in, reduce my sister's stress and make a few bucks along the way.

Allie and I didn't need much to live on, so between the money I earned at The Eloise and what Griffin paid me for work on the ranch, I had plenty to pay for groceries, gas and whatever expenses came up. I'd even started a college savings account.

The hired-hand gig was supposed to be temporary too, except I'd been doing it for years. How long was I going to be Eloise's maintenance man? How long was I going to be Griffin's hired hand?

Was this really my future? Was I really wasting my college degree and the hours upon hours I'd spent flying?

Both jobs gave me a lot of flexibility to be with Allie. I

liked being home with her more often than not. The most important official title I had was *Dad*. And I wasn't just her dad. I was her mother too. I was filling both roles, and for that, I couldn't be strapped to a demanding career.

But what happened when she went to kindergarten? What happened when she moved and went to college? Would I still be doing maintenance at the hotel? Or fixing fence on the ranch?

"What am I doing?" I asked myself that question more often these days. Sure would be nice if I had an answer.

Griffin needed my help. Eloise did too. It seemed ridiculous to make them hire employees for jobs I had the skill set and time to do. Besides, it wasn't like I had anything else going on. I didn't want an eight-to-five job and a set schedule that would take me away from Allie. I had no desire to work as a bank teller or become a realtor or manage the hardware store.

Official maintenance man.

I wanted to crumple the direct deposit form and toss it in the trash. Instead, I folded it in thirds, tucked it in my pocket and walked out of the elevator.

A lot of people didn't love their jobs. Not my siblings, but a lot of other people in this world didn't love their jobs.

For now, until I figured out what I wanted to do, I'd be the official maintenance man.

And if I never figured out what I wanted to do, well...

The most important job I had was as Allie's father. That would be enough.

It would have to be enough.

Eloise was on the phone when I passed the reception desk. Jasper, seated at her side, lifted a hand as I strode through the lobby.

I jerked up my chin, about to leave, when the door opened.

Vance strode inside, dressed for work with his badge and

holstered gun on his belt.

Hell. Given the look on his face, I was going to be late picking up Vera.

"Hey," I said.

"Got a minute?"

"Just the one. I've got to get out to the ranch." As far as I was concerned, he could assume I was picking up Allie.

I wasn't sure what was happening with Vera, not yet. And I didn't need Vance in the middle.

"Then I'll be quick." He rubbed a hand over his beard. "I wanted to talk about what happened at Willie's."

"Did you know she had feelings for me?"

"No, I would have said something."

"What would you have said?"

He sighed. "Probably to stay away."

That was why he'd interrupted our dance at his wedding, wasn't it? And why he'd always made sure Vera was on his side of the table at family dinners.

"It's not about you," he said. "It's her. I wouldn't want her with anyone, right now. She's... different. She's not who she used to be. What happened changed her. She's fragile."

Nothing about Vera was fragile. Surviving the horrors inflicted by her father might have changed her. But she wasn't fragile. She wasn't broken.

"She's not, Vance. She's not fragile. And maybe she'd believe that herself if you stopped treating her like she's made of glass."

His jaw clenched. "You don't know everything she's been through."

"No, I guess I don't." When it came to Vera, there was a lot I'd missed.

It was time to catch up.

. . .

The Quincy airfield was fifteen miles from the ranch. For the past nine of those fifteen, Vera had been huddled so close to the passenger door that she looked like she was contemplating an emergency exit. Any minute now, she'd pull the handle, tuck and roll.

"How's school?" It was my fifth attempt to drum up conversation.

"Good."

Good. The same answer she'd given when I'd asked her how work was going and how she liked living in the loft. When I'd told her that Allie still loved the rocking dragon, she'd said, "Good." And when I'd promised she'd enjoy flying today, another "Good."

I was never saying *good* again.

"You're taking three classes, right?"

Vera nodded and shifted even closer to that door.

For fuck's sake. Was she scared of me now? Maybe this was a bad idea.

But I just... needed to spend time with her. Alone. Because Vera had kissed me, and I couldn't stop thinking about it. I couldn't stop thinking about her. It felt like someone had slipped glasses on my face. And that someone had given me permission to *see*.

Now I wanted to learn everything there was to learn about Vera. I wanted to see it all.

"Clear and a million."

Vera glanced over. "What?"

I pointed to the sky. "You have to know a lot about weather to be a pilot. There are different classifications of clouds, like overcast or broken or scattered. Then there's days like this. Not a cloud in sight. Unlimited visibility. Nothing but brilliant blue. Clear and a million. It's the best time to fly."

"Oh."

Even huddled against the door, she looked beautiful. Her

hair fell in silky strands around her shoulders, cascading to her waist. With the sunlight coming through the windshield, the freckles on her nose popped. I'd always liked freckles.

Vera's face wasn't covered in them like some redheads. There was just a scattering across her nose, like they'd been drawn by an artist, dotted with precision.

"Here." I took an extra pair of sunglasses from the console compartment and handed them over. "You'll want these today."

She eyed the aviators.

Was she going to make everything hard today? "They're just sunglasses, Vera. They won't bite."

She was careful not to let our fingers brush as she took them from my hand. Then she unfolded the temples, slid them onto her face and hid those pretty brown eyes.

A strange feeling stirred in my chest. What was it? Pride? Possession? Whatever it was, I liked seeing her wear my glasses.

This was about to get complicated, wasn't it?

Beyond my talk with Mom on Sunday morning, I hadn't spoken to my parents about Vera. My siblings hadn't asked about us either, not even Eloise when I'd gone to the hotel. Even Vance was giving me time to sort it through, but I was on the clock. This reprieve wouldn't last. They'd want to know how I was going to handle this.

Fly. Today, I was going to take Vera flying.

My parents, brothers and sisters had all noticed when my flying days had dwindled. I came to the airfield less and less often. They'd noticed, but it hadn't bothered them that I'd stopped. Maybe because I hadn't let on that it bothered me.

Not Vera. It upset her that I wasn't flying.

Today was a good excuse to get up in the air. And spend time with Vera.

Either she and I would find our way past this awkward

bump, navigate our way to a friendship again. Or everything would change.

Maybe I already knew the answer. Maybe I suspected I knew exactly where this was going. But I wasn't ready to admit it yet, not even to myself.

There'd be time to evaluate. After this flight.

Vera's shoulders crept closer and closer to her ears as we passed the sign to the airport.

"Nervous?"

She worried her bottom lip between her teeth and gave me a slight nod.

"I came out yesterday to do a few takeoffs and landings. Knock the rust off. I promise we won't crash."

"That's not..." Vera sighed. "Why am I here, Mateo? You don't need to pander to me. We can just forget about Willie's, okay?"

"What if I don't want to forget about it?"

Her gaze whipped to mine.

Finally. I had her attention.

She sure as fuck held mine.

"Let's just fly today." It was too soon to talk about anything else. "Think you can do that?"

"Yeah." She dropped her gaze to her lap. And slightly, just slightly, she inched away from the door.

I slowed and took the turnout for the airfield. The truck bounced along the patchy asphalt road. The hangars, with their white tin walls and silver metal roofs, reflected the bright morning sun. Ten buildings lined the runway. Mine was the newest.

Mom and Dad had already given us kids a portion of our inheritance. They always said it was stupid to wait until they were dead to share. They wanted to be around to witness us use that money and chase our dreams.

Everyone else had turned that money into a business or

advanced education. After I'd graduated college, I'd taken my money and bought an airplane and built a hangar.

Guilt and that hangar, my plane, went hand in hand these days. Had I pissed away my parents' money? Should I have invested it in something else?

Flying was an expensive hobby, especially when the plane's wheels didn't leave the ground.

At least it had appreciated in value.

I parked outside the hangar and climbed out of the truck, waiting for Vera to join me. Then I led her to the door, keyed in the lock's combination to the touchpad and stepped inside. The motion lights flickered on, glinting off the royal blue and silver Cirrus SR22 turbo.

"Vera, meet Four Zero Six Delta Whiskey."

"Wow," she whispered.

It wasn't a big plane. Depending on weight limits, I could fit four passengers, and the inside wasn't much bigger than that of a compact car. But this plane had taken me across thousands and thousands of miles.

It was the plane I'd flown that night I'd received the call about Alaina. About Madison. And when I'd taken my daughter from that hospital in Alaska, this was the plane that had brought us home.

Buckled in her car seat and strapped in the seat beside mine, Allie had slept through each leg of that trip. She'd only woken up when I'd stopped to refuel, feed her a bottle and change her diaper.

Only once had her ears bothered her enough to make a fuss, but I'd kept as low an altitude as possible to save her any pain. In hindsight, she'd been an excellent traveler. Better than most adults.

But that flight had been the most harrowing, exhausting flight of my life. It had taken me months to venture out to the airfield after that trip. And not once had I wanted to take

Allie flying again. I hadn't even brought her to the hangar.

"This is nice," Vera said.

"Feel free to grab a water from the fridge." I pointed to the small kitchenette.

Beside it was a lounge area with two leather couches and a coffee table. My office sat in the far corner. Beside it, a bathroom. Along with shelves for storage, there was a utility room and a cleaning supply closet.

It was the nicest hangar around, and for the past two years, it had mostly been neglected. When I'd come yesterday to fly, I'd spent three hours cleaning the months of accumulated dust. Guilt had kept me company the whole damn time.

"I'm going to do a quick preflight inspection," I told Vera, nodding to the couches. "Give me fifteen, and we'll get ready to go."

"Okay." She pushed those sunglasses into her hair and tore her gaze from the plane to meet mine. Pink infused her cheeks, the same rosy shade as her mouth.

Vera always had pink cheeks. I'd assumed it was just a natural blush. But maybe, all this time, it had been for me.

Damn.

It was gorgeous. *She* was gorgeous.

My blood stirred and rushed straight to my groin. Huh. That was new. And not entirely unwelcome.

I was in trouble, wasn't I? A fucking heap.

Focus, Mateo. We were flying today. There was no time to think about Vera's pink lips or cheeks or the way her jeans molded to her toned legs.

She walked to a couch, taking a seat on the plush leather. And I turned for my plane, waiting until I was on the opposite side before adjusting my dick.

I stepped up onto the wing and popped the door open. From my seat, I turned on the batteries, letting the screens power up, then went through my initial preflight checklist, inspecting everything from the wings to the elevator to the fuel and oil to the propeller. When I deemed everything ready to go, I walked to the button for the folding overhead door, letting it open so the air and sunshine could flood inside.

Vera stood from the couch, tucking and untucking a lock of hair behind an ear, as I used the tug to roll the plane onto the taxiway outside. With it in position, I waved her over.

"Ready?"

She nodded, joining me on her side of the plane.

"Climb up." I pointed to the footstep, then patted the wing, reaching past her to pull the door's handle.

"Okay." Her voice was shaking as she moved past me.

The smell of her hair wafted to my nose. It was sweet but subtle, like flowers and crisp apples. I leaned in closer, drawing it in.

I'd forgotten just how much I liked her perfume. While we'd danced at Vance and Lyla's wedding, I'd taken these deep inhales of that scent, wondering how I'd spent so much time with Vera but hadn't noticed just how good she smelled.

What if Vance hadn't cut in that night? What if I had had more time to get lost in the flecks of gold and cinnamon in her chocolate eyes?

What if I had snuck her away for a kiss?

Vance would have kicked my ass. Lyla would have probably been next in line.

Mom might have been understanding this weekend, but back then, she would have given me the tongue lashing of the decade.

Back then, Vera hadn't lived in the loft for long. She'd only spent months on the ranch and less than a year in Quincy. She'd been quieter then. She'd still been finding her footing.

If I had kissed Vera, chances were, my family would have gone nuclear.

Maybe the reason I hadn't noticed Vera's crush was

because I *couldn't* have noticed Vera's crush. Not back then.

"What?" she asked, that blush deepening.

"Nothing. Whenever you're ready."

She hoisted herself up on the wing, carefully stepping into the plane. Once she was in her seat, pulling on the harness, I rounded the tail and got in on my own side to buckle up.

Vera's knuckles were nearly white as she clutched her hands in her lap.

"Don't be nervous."

"Says the pilot," she muttered. "Were you nervous on your first flight?"

"Yes."

She slid the sunglasses onto her face. "Then I get to be nervous too."

"Fair point." I chuckled, then reached for her door to confirm the latch was down tight. My arm brushed against hers and tingles spread like dancing flames across my skin.

Her breath hitched.

"Just checking," I murmured, my gaze dropping to her mouth.

"Oh," she breathed, her lips a perfect *O*.

I'd never kissed anyone in this plane. Not even Madison.

Yeah, I was in trouble. So much trouble.

I tore my gaze away and plugged in Vera's headset, handing it to her so she could situate it over her ears and adjust the mic to her mouth. I did the same with my own headset, then I gave her a quick nod.

When she nodded back, I leaned my head outside, shouting, "Clear," then latched my door shut. Holding the key in the ignition, I started the engine. Its hum and vibration filled the cabin as the propeller kicked up speed.

Using the brakes to steer, I taxied to the runway, doing a quick runup of the engine as I monitored the gauges, stealing glances at Vera as I punched buttons and turned knobs.

Her eyes were squeezed shut behind her sunglasses.

"We don't have to do this."

This was the most I'd looked forward to a flight in well... years. I hadn't been this excited to fly since before my trip home from Alaska with Alaina. My heart was set on doing this today, but if Vera wanted to turn back, I'd abort this right now.

She'd love it. If I could just get us off the ground, she'd love it. I'd gamble every penny to my name that she'd love to fly.

"I want to go," she said. "I'm just... my stomach is in a knot. And I really don't want to puke in your plane."

I grinned. "I'd rather you not puke either. But if you get sick, there's a bag in the back."

"Okay."

"This plane has a parachute." I pointed to the red handle above our heads. "See that?"

Vera cracked her eyes and glanced up. "Yeah."

"If something happens to me, use both hands and pull that knob. It will shoot a rocket from a compartment in the back and deploy an airframe parachute. Float us right back to the ground."

"Are you making that up?"

"Nope. In college, when I told Mom I wanted to become a pilot, she went into Google mode. Told me to do her a favor and fly in a Cirrus so she could sleep at night."

Vera's frame relaxed. "I'm still nervous."

"Be nervous. Close your eyes. I'll tell you when to open them."

"Thanks," she whispered.

I ran through the rest of the briefing, Vera nodding along as I detailed the takeoff plan. And when we were ready, I rolled us to the runway and made the initial radio call.

"Here we go." I pushed the throttle to full power. *One. Two. Three.* We sped down the runway, and once we were fast enough to rotate, I lifted us off with a tilt of the yoke.

We soared, rising higher and higher. A grin stretched across my mouth. It never got old. That first lift, when the plane just… flew. When it did what it was meant to do.

What I was meant to do.

After calling our departure, I climbed to a cruise altitude and leveled off. When the mountains and meadows sprawled beneath us, I let the autopilot fly us on a straight course so I could focus on Vera.

Her eyes were finally open, her mouth agape in wonder.

"Well?" I asked.

"Worth it."

Thank fuck. "Where should we go? Pick a spot."

Vera glanced around, peering out her window, then pointed to a snow-capped peak in the distance.

"Sable Peak?" I asked.

"That's your favorite, right?"

"It is." I turned to the new heading, aiming us toward the peak.

"Why is it your favorite?"

"The view. It's not easy to hike up there, as you know. But you can't beat that view from the top." I loved to be in the air, but that view was arguably better than even this.

"There's a lake tucked away about half a mile past the actual trail," I continued. "Discovered it in college. I came home one weekend, went buzzing around and spotted it. The next day, I went hiking to find it. It's been my favorite spot ever since. It's remote. I like to think I'm the only person in the world who's ever touched its water."

Vera hummed, her eyes focused outside.

I flew us around the peak a couple times, giving us enough distance that we didn't need to climb higher. After a few circles, I followed the curve of the mountain ridgeline.

"Want to try?" I asked, disconnecting the autopilot.

"Try what?"

"Flying."

"Um… yes?"

"Atta girl." I'd put Vera in the left seat today. As an instructor, I could fly from either seat, but the left side was where students started.

Vera gulped and gripped the yoke. "Now what?"

I held up both hands. "You've got the flight controls. Don't crash us into the mountains."

"That's not funny, Mateo." Her lips flattened into a thin line.

"Sort of funny." I grinned. "I'll back you up. Just go for it."

"Do I just…" She tipped the yoke, the wing on her side lifting as mine dipped. And a startled, happy laugh escaped her pretty mouth. "Oh my God, I'm flying an airplane."

"You're flying an airplane, Peach."

Peach? Where the hell had that come from? It had just… slipped out. Like I should have been calling her Peach for years. Like the way I'd started calling Alaina Sprout. One day she didn't have a nickname. The next, she did. And Peach was Vera's.

She was too caught up in the flying to notice. Her forehead was furrowed in concentration. Her gaze was locked ahead.

The light that streamed through the windows loved her face. It caressed her cheeks and kissed her lips. It teased the strands of pure gold in that copper hair.

Clear and a million.

Today, I was seeing clear and a million.

"Will you teach me to fly?" she asked.

Spend hours and hours with her, alone and above the world? "Absolutely."

CHAPTER 15

MATEO

"Na-na. Pa-pa." Alaina pointed a finger over my shoulder to Mom and Dad's house.

"We'll go visit Nana and Papa in a minute, Sprout. We have to go see Vera first."

"Oh." Her favorite new word. "Ve-wa."

Allie's syllables were all divided with a slight pause. She was learning new words and using new sounds each day. But her favorite names she'd spoken for months.

Daddy. Nana. Papa. And Vera.

Her legs kicked as we walked through the barn's small door.

My heart beat a little faster as I climbed the stairs to the loft, the anticipation of seeing Vera doubling with every step.

It had been a week since I'd taken Vera on that flight. A week of self-mandated distance. These past seven days had been a test. I'd wanted to see how often she crossed my mind—so often that I'd stopped counting.

This morning, Allie and I had driven into town to get a package from the post office, and Vera's private pilot materials had been waiting. I'd decided then and there that we'd had enough distance.

My stomach knotted as I knocked. The last time I'd been

this nervous to see a woman had been in, well... it had been a long time ago.

Footsteps sounded and then the door swung open. Vera's eyes widened, her hands instantly tucking locks of damp hair behind her ears only to untuck them just as quickly. "Um, hi."

"Hi." *Damn.* I'd missed that pretty face. Her skin was fresh and clean, her cheeks flushed and those freckles on full display.

"Ve-wa." Allie careened forward, arms wide for Vera to catch her.

"Hey, Jellybean." Vera beamed at my daughter, her eyes sparkling as she lifted Allie from my arms to kiss her cheek. "What are you doing today?"

"We just came from town. Hit the post office. Stopped by the coffee shop for some breakfast."

"Muff-in," Allie told her.

"Yummy." Vera tickled her belly and shifted sideways. "Come on in."

"Thanks." I pulled the backpack off my shoulder and set it on the kitchen counter beside a pile of textbooks, Vera's laptop and a collection of maps.

Sable Peak was circled in a yellow highlighter with a larger perimeter drawn around the area. "What's this?"

"Oh, nothing." Vera folded the paper in half, pushing it aside. "Just making note of hiking trails. Since we flew that way, I thought it would be fun to hike that area more this summer."

"Ah. Well, if you give me a heads-up, I'll go with you. I know you've done it by yourself before, but that area has been known to have bears." Plus the terrain was steep and rough, so it didn't get a lot of visitors. The cell reception was shit too, and if something happened, I didn't want her stranded out there alone.

Sure, she'd lived for years in the wilderness and had more

survival skills than anyone in the greater Quincy area, but that didn't mean I wanted her alone in the mountains.

"Okay." She nodded, then pointed to the backpack. "What's all this?"

I unzipped the bag and started hauling out books. "Got your stuff in today."

"Oh."

Oh. There was a reason it was Allie's new word. She'd picked it up from Vera.

"That's a lot of books." Vera gave Allie an exaggerated frown.

There were six in total, each one thicker than the last. "There's a lot here. Don't get overwhelmed. We'll go through it all step by step."

"Where do I even start?"

"This one." I tapped the largest book with a plane on the cover. "It's a good holistic resource of everything you'll need to know. The others drill into certain topics. Read the first chapter. Then we'll review it together."

She sighed and cast a glance toward the other books on the counter. "Okay."

"There's no rush. If you can tackle a chapter a week, great. If not, we'll stretch it out."

"All right. When do you want to meet?"

"We'll plan flying time around your schedule and the weather. But for the ground school material, how about we get together on Friday evenings?"

It was the one night a week when Lyla was guaranteed to close the coffee shop. My sister would work late, stocking up inventory so she could take the weekends off and leave the shop to be run by Vera or Crystal, her other barista.

"Fridays work for me."

"Mind if we meet at the cabin? That way Allie will have her stuff and be less of a distraction."

Vera smiled down at Allie, bending until their foreheads touched. "Are you a distraction?"

Allie giggled, a sound so pure it was a treasure.

Vera puffed out her cheeks so Allie could squish them flat.

God, they were good together. So good it gave me pause. If I fucked this up, it wouldn't just be Vera who suffered. Allie would too.

Except I couldn't stay away. I didn't want to stay away.

I walked the length of the loft to the living room windows. Dad had moved the horses to the pasture alongside the gravel drive. While the rest of them were grazing, Saturn stood tall and proud in the distance, his sleek, black coat shiny in the morning light.

"Have you ever ridden a horse?" I asked, turning from the glass.

"No."

"Want to learn?"

"Someday." Vera nodded. "Your dad offered to teach me this summer."

Fuck that. I'd be the one to teach her to ride and to fly. I wanted to teach her anything and everything. I wanted time with Vera. We just needed more time.

Maybe if I'd given her that time a year ago, we'd be in a different place. Well, I'd give it to her now. Starting with Fridays at the cabin.

"Dow." Allie squirmed, so Vera set her on her feet. My daughter raced straight for the TV remote on the coffee table.

"Are you supposed to play with remotes?"

Allie ignored me completely.

"Sprout," I warned.

Vera let out a quiet laugh as she walked to the oversized leather couch and curled in a corner. She was in a thick, maroon sweater today. The color made her eyes look like pools of melted chocolate and gold. Her hair was drying slowly, lightening into strands of amber silk.

Beautiful. So damn beautiful.

"Can I see that for a minute, Jellybean?" Vera held out her hand, palm up.

Allie walked straight over and gave up the remote. "Dizzy."

"Dizzy?" Vera looked my way.

"Disney." It was always streaming at our house.

"Ah." Vera navigated through the TV's menus until she found a show for Allie to watch. Then she turned down the volume and took the batteries out of the remote before giving it back.

"Huh. Why didn't I ever think to take the batteries out? That's brilliant."

Vera's cheeks flushed.

Goddamn, that blush. I'd missed it this week. Like I'd missed the sweet smell that infused the loft.

I stared, unabashedly, taking in the delicate details of her face. The adorable chin. The straight line of her nose. She had the prettiest eyelashes.

Vera caught me staring and gave me a sideways glance. "What?"

"Nothing." I tore my eyes away, shifting them to Allie, who was sucked into the cartoon. My attention stayed on her for about ten seconds before it swung back to Vera.

She was watching Alaina too, smiling as Allie danced to a song, until she caught me staring again. "Mateo." That pink color in her face brightened. "What?"

"Nothing."

"Not nothing. You're looking at me like you want to say something."

I did want to say something. I wanted to tell her that she was beautiful. That I liked when her face was clean so I could see all of her freckles. That I'd always thought blue eyes were my favorite, but that her shade of rich, walnut brown had taken the top spot.

But she wasn't ready to hear any of that. And I wasn't ready to tell her. Not until I was sure how to do this. Sure I wouldn't mess it up.

So instead, I just said, "Thank you."

"For what?"

"For pushing me to fly." We both knew that the only reason I'd gone was because she'd instigated it. "I missed it. More than I realized."

"I had a good time."

"Do you really want to learn to be a pilot? Or are you just trying to coerce me into flying more often?"

The corners of her mouth turned up. "Both."

I chuckled. "Sneaky."

Vera tucked a lock of damp hair behind her ear, then pulled it free.

"You do that a lot. With your hair. Tuck and untuck. I haven't figured out what it means yet." My hunch was shyness. But maybe she was just nervous around me.

She averted her gaze, staring at an invisible spot on the floor.

"You hate broccoli," I said. "Whenever Mom makes it for dinner, you always dish a few pieces on your plate to be polite, but before each bite, your lip curls or you scrunch up your nose."

To my knowledge, I was the only one who'd picked up on it too. Mom kept cooking broccoli.

"Your favorite color is green. Dark green. And you're a fast runner."

She seemed to prefer hiking for exercise, but I'd watched her go out for a run from time to time. Vera had a long, easy stride. She ran with grace, poise and speed.

"Why are you saying all of this, Mateo?" Her voice was barely a whisper.

I might not have let myself cross a line. I might not have

noticed her crush. But that didn't mean I hadn't seen her. Learned about her. Paid attention to her.

"Sometimes you'll laugh so hard you snort," I said. "Instead of getting embarrassed, you just laugh harder. And you don't drink. That night at Willie's was the first time I've seen you order anything at a bar but Coke."

Vera wrapped her arms around her middle. "We don't need to talk about Willie's. Ever."

"We can."

"I don't want to."

"All right."

She blew out a long breath. "Why are you here, Mateo?"

We both knew it wasn't just to give her those ground school materials. I could have dropped them off already and been halfway home by now.

Before I could answer her question, before I could tell her that I'd just wanted to see her, a tiny person crashed into my shins.

"Daddy." Allie raised her arms in the air. "Up."

So much for the cartoons. I bent and picked her up, setting her on my side so she could look out the windows.

"Ho-sis. Wook it." She pointed through the glass. "Ho-sis."

"Those are the horses."

Vera stood from the couch, smoothing down the front of her sweater. Then she cleared her throat and walked to the kitchen. "Thanks for bringing this stuff over. I'll dive in after I finish studying today."

I wasn't ready to leave. But she was ready for us to leave.

That shifting, the shuffling, wasn't just happening to me. It was happening for Vera too. So I'd give her a chance to find a new balance.

I crossed the loft with Allie perched on my arm, pausing by the door to give her a wink. "See you Friday."

She tucked and untucked a lock of hair. "I'll be there."

CHAPTER 16

VERA

What was I doing here? I sat frozen behind the Honda's steering wheel, staring at Mateo's cabin.

How many times had I wished to be invited to his house? How many times had I fantasized about quiet nights alone in his home? Now I was here, and I couldn't bring myself to go inside.

What was happening? Things with Mateo were... strange. This had to be pity, right? He was going above and beyond to be nice. To be my friend.

Except it didn't feel like friendship. Yes, my favorite color was dark green, that wasn't a big discovery on Mateo's part. But none of the other Edens had noticed my hatred of broccoli. None of the other Edens looked at me the way Mateo had looked at me in the loft on Wednesday.

It was nothing. My imagination was running rampant. Too many years obsessing over him had led me down this road of delusion.

So what if he'd picked up on the broccoli thing? So what if he'd heard me snort when I laughed too hard?

It didn't mean anything.

It was time for me to move on from this crush.

Granted, that would be tricky now that he was my flight

instructor. Seriously, what was I thinking? I was supposed to be avoiding Mateo, not coming to his house every Friday to study aerodynamic principles.

I'd done my assigned reading in preparation for tonight, and I didn't give a damn about a single word in any of the books he'd brought to the loft.

This wasn't really about learning to fly airplanes. This was about finding Dad.

The day Mateo and I had gone flying, I'd spotted a plume of smoke in the forest. It had been small and nearly invisible, nothing more than a white wisp floating from the trees. But that plume had sparked an idea. A new plan.

I could spend years hiking around the mountains, searching for my father. And I could be looking in all the wrong spots.

There were too many mountains. Too many trees. We could pass each other moving in opposite directions and be off by one hundred yards and not have a clue.

What I needed was a focus area. I needed to narrow down my options to places where he might make camp. Where Dad would risk a fire on cool, spring mornings.

It was too hard to do that on foot. But by air? Maybe.

So here I was, pretending to be an interested student pilot, just in it for the chance to fly. Mateo would never know that it was a ruse to find Dad.

I'd already started exploring along Sable Peak in the area where I was fairly certain I'd seen that plume of smoke while flying. I hadn't found anything yet, but I was attacking the area in segments, working section by section on the maps I'd been studying.

It was a tactic Uncle Vance had mentioned. While he'd been searching for Dad years ago, he'd taken maps of an area and broken them into pieces so his hikes were systematic and deliberate.

So far, I'd covered three of my own segments. There were ten total charted for Sable Peak. With any luck, Mateo and I could fit in another flight. Maybe I'd find another clue the next time we went up in his plane.

But before any of that happened, I needed to get out of this car. Why couldn't I get out of this car?

"Get out of the car." I steeled my spine, grabbed my backpack, which was riding shotgun, and opened the door.

That first inhale of outside air settled some of my nerves.

Pine and earth and wind.

Home.

There were nights, even in the winter, when I'd sleep with the loft's windows open just to breathe in that mountain scent.

This was the first time I'd been to Mateo's cabin. He'd texted me directions last night, saving me from having to ask Anne or Harrison.

I'd seen his parents since Willie's, and even though I was sure they'd heard about my drunken idiocy, they'd pretended to be none the wiser.

I really loved Anne and Harrison.

Maybe I was being a coward, but I hoped we never had to talk about it. The same went for Vance and Lyla, who'd avoided the you-kissed-Mateo topic spectacularly.

A breeze floated more of that incredible scent on the air, and though I'd managed to get out of the car, I still wasn't ready to go inside. So I spun in a slow circle, taking it all in.

Mateo's directions had led me on a winding path across a handful of the ranch's gravel roads. I'd passed the backside of Indigo Ridge along the way, a notorious landmark in Quincy because of a tragic murder that had happened there a few years ago. From there, I'd wound my way up the mountain foothills to a meadow bordered by groves of evergreens.

The log cabin stood proudly in the grass field. Mateo had mowed recently, the stalks short and uniform. A stack of evenly chopped firewood lined one side of the wide front porch.

I loved the ranch. I loved the view from my loft. But this was exactly where I'd choose to live, right on the forest's edge. Where my backyard was the untamed wilderness.

This was the perfect balance of seclusion and convenience. It was only a short drive into town. Mateo had the luxuries of modern-day life, like plumbing and high-speed internet. But out here, away from neighbors, he had peace. A sanctuary.

As a girl, I'd dreamed of living in a city. Maybe spending a year or two in New York or San Francisco after high school. Someday, I'd like to visit a city. But only as a vacation. The idea of being constantly surrounded by people and noise and traffic made my skin crawl.

"My uncle Briggs built this place." Mateo's voice had me whirling around to face the house. He stood in the doorway, his broad shoulders filling the threshold. How long had he been watching me?

My cheeks flamed.

The corner of his mouth turned up as he leaned a shoulder against the door's frame. "Have you ever met Briggs?"

"Yes. At Lyla and Vance's wedding."

There was no mistaking Briggs as an Eden with his dark brown hair and bright blue eyes. Though there'd been so many Edens at the wedding, aunts and uncles and cousins, I hadn't been sure exactly how Briggs had fit into the mix until Harrison had pulled me aside to make an introduction to his beloved brother.

Briggs was five years older than Harrison. Before his dementia had forced him to move, he'd lived on the ranch. In this cabin.

"Dad tries to bring him out to the ranch once a week or so," Mateo said. "They'll drive around or stop and have dinner with Mom. Some days he's normal. Others, he'll get Griffin and Dad confused. It's hard to see him like that, especially for my parents."

"I'm sorry." I unstuck my feet and walked toward the porch's stairs. But when he didn't move, I stopped, standing at the bottom stair as he gazed over my head into the distance.

"Briggs was always there for me. He never had kids, but he treated us like we were his own. He never missed a single football game. When the high school basketball coach retired and they needed a new assistant coach my senior year, he volunteered. He'd take us hunting and fishing. He taught me how to rope."

Briggs sounded like Vance.

He'd been my uncle, my champion.

Mateo glanced over his shoulder, checking something inside, probably Allie. "I relate to Briggs. He's older than Dad and could have taken over the ranch or other businesses, but he didn't want that life. He didn't like the idea of being in charge. He was content to work here because he loved it. He was content with a simple life."

"That sounds like a good life."

"My brothers and sisters all have this… ambition."

"And you don't?" After just two days of trying to sort through those pilot manuals, I had a newfound respect for Mateo, getting his license *and* being a full-time college student.

Mateo shrugged. "It's different."

"Bad different?"

"Different, different," he said. "There are times when I feel this pressure. Like everyone is waiting to see what I decide to be. That they'll be disappointed if I don't do something grand or bold. But I never thought less of Briggs because he wasn't in charge or running a business. I admired him for knowing his strengths. His weaknesses. Hell, most days, I feel more like I'm walking in Briggs's footsteps than Dad's. He did what he loved. His only expectations were his own."

Was he saying that because he believed it? Or was he saying that because he wanted to make it true? "Sounds like you've got good footsteps to follow, either direction."

"Yeah." He gave me a small smile. "Hi."

"Hello."

"Come on in." He shoved off the frame and jerked his chin for me to follow him inside.

Climbing the stairs, I stepped beneath the porch's overhang and took one last glance across the meadow.

I'd had good footsteps to follow too. They'd led me here. If I never found Dad again, I would always be grateful he'd brought me to Montana.

When I faced the house, I hovered beyond the threshold, looking for a button.

"What are you doing?" Mateo asked.

"You don't have a doorbell."

"Uh, no."

"Oh. Allie loves them."

His eyebrows came together. "Yes, she does. That's why you ring the bell at Mom and Dad's?"

"Yeah." I eased the door closed behind me just as a squeal came from the living room.

"Ve-wa!" Allie ran so fast her legs couldn't keep up with her torso. She would have face planted onto the hardwood floor if Mateo hadn't swept her up, giving her a quick toss in the air before catching her.

"Slow down, Sprout." He set her down and patted her diapered butt as she rushed for me again.

Her smile was contagious as she flew into my open arms.

"Hi, Jellybean." I tickled her ribs, earning a tickle in return, then kissed her cheek. It was sticky.

There was a skillet on the stove top, and the cabin smelled like sage and syrup.

"Did you have breakfast for dinner?"

"Pa-cake."

"Yummy."

"Did you eat?" Mateo asked.

"I grabbed a sandwich before I left the coffee shop." I put Allie down to toddle off to a pile of toys in the living room.

"How was work today?"

"Hectic." School had been out for a teacher professional development day and the shop had been swarmed with teenagers and parents. Lyla and I had both opened at four this morning, and it had felt like a dead sprint the entire day. Lunch had been skipped, and by the time I'd clocked out, I'd been starving. My ham and cheese had been scarfed on the drive to the ranch.

Lyla was still there, wrapping up for the day and baking for the weekend. If I was tired, she'd be dead on her feet by the time she made it home.

"Want some water or anything before we get started?"

"Water, please."

"Make yourself at home." He jerked his chin at the dining room table, then walked to the kitchen and opened a cupboard.

The cabin was open and airy. The kitchen blended with the dining room, which flowed to the living area. The doors along the far wall must lead to the bedrooms and bathrooms. It wasn't a large house, but it was cozy and inviting.

I slid into a wooden chair at the table, taking out my book as Mateo set a glass of water beside me. Then he went to the coffee table, snagging the remote to turn on some cartoons for Allie.

"She missed her nap today. We were outside doing yard work, and I lost track of time. When we came in, I decided it was too late to try. Hopefully she'll make it another hour, but we might have to take a break so I can put her to bed."

"No problem."

The dragon I'd gotten her was staged to face the TV. Allie

climbed on, rocking it wildly back and forth as she pointed to the screen. "Dizzy."

Her dark pigtails curled at the ends, like the way Mateo's hair curled at his nape whenever he let it grow long enough.

Mateo slid into a seat, chair legs scraping on the floor.

The seat directly beside mine. Not the chair around the corner of the table. Not the chair across the table.

The chair so close to my own that the warmth from his arm seeped into mine.

He scooted closer. Another inch and our shoulders would touch. That intoxicating Mateo smell, leather and spice and wind and earth, filled my nose.

Concentrating was already going to be tough after a long day. But with him sitting so close, smelling so good, this study session was going to be brutal.

"How did the reading go?"

"Good?"

"Is that a question or a statement?"

I flipped open my book to the first chapter. "I guess we're about to find out."

Bad. It was very, very bad. All of the time I'd spent reading had been wasted. Because fifteen minutes into the discussion about lift and drag, Mateo's knee touched mine beneath the table and my brain shut off.

"So lift is the opposing force to weight. What's the opposing force to drag?" Mateo twisted slightly to stare at my profile.

If I didn't face directly forward, if I turned in the slightest to make eye contact, his mouth would be eye level. Was this how he sat with other students? Not that he had other students. Did he? Why couldn't he have just sat on the other side of the table? Or around a corner?

Wait. What was his question? "Uh... no idea."

"Thrust."

Of course the answer was thrust. A word that sounded

like sex in his rugged, deep voice.

"Right." I gulped. "Thrust."

His hand stretched across the book to flip the page and our forearms touched. Heat radiated off his large frame, enveloping me like that scent.

A thud snapped me out of the haze.

Mateo's gaze whipped to Allie, who'd fallen off her dragon. He rose, about to rush to her rescue, but she just stood up, eyes glued to the TV, and gripped the handle of the toy to climb back on. He exhaled, sinking into his seat.

I used the interruption to shift my chair over a few inches. Maybe with some space, my brain would reengage and Mateo wouldn't think I was a complete moron. Maybe words like *thrust* wouldn't make me sweat.

Except the moment he was seated and refocused, he moved his chair too. His beefy thigh pressed against mine. That heat returned.

Desire coiled low in my belly. And my brain went blank.

I swallowed a groan.

The next hour was excruciating. After getting three questions in a row wrong, he retrieved a small model airplane from a bookshelf against the living room wall. He did his best to demonstrate a plane's movement, but wrapping my mind around ailerons and elevator control, angles of attack and wing stalls—which had nothing to do with an engine apparently—was impossible. I couldn't focus.

"I'm sorry." I rubbed my temples. "I swear I'm not entirely helpless. But it's been a long day, and this material is a lot."

"You'll get it."

I slumped in my chair, and my leg slid against Mateo's. I'd gotten used to him being pressed close. But as the denim of our jeans scraped, awareness rushed in again.

He was so, so close. Why was he so close?

I glanced up at his face, expecting his profile. But he was

facing me, his eyes locked on my mouth. He looked like he wanted to kiss me.

My heart rocketed into my throat.

Did he want to kiss me? Did I want him to kiss me?

Yes. Despite the fool I'd made of myself at Willie's, despite the promise I'd made to myself to let Mateo Eden go, down deep in my heart, I wanted him to kiss me.

There were just some things I couldn't keep locked in that box.

He leaned in closer. The blue of his eyes was darker. His tongue darted out to lick his lower lip and a throb bloomed in my core.

My pulse raced, booming in my ears.

Mateo raised a hand, his fingertips skimming the hair at my temple. His eyelids fluttered closed, his breath a whisper across my cheek.

I didn't move. I didn't breathe. If I blinked, I was certain I'd wake up alone in the loft, this entire night a dream.

"Daddy, melk," Allie whined at Mateo's side.

We broke apart in a flash.

He shot out of his chair, picking up Allie.

She rubbed fists into her tired eyes as he carried her to the kitchen.

"I should get going." The book got shoved into my backpack before I ripped the zipper closed. Then I was on my feet, ready to make a run for it.

I needed air. I needed space. I needed out of this house so I could think. God, what was happening?

He'd almost kissed me. He would have kissed me, right?

"Sorry." Mateo opened the fridge and took out a sippy cup of milk.

The second she had it in her grip, Allie tipped it to her mouth and collapsed against his shoulder as she chugged.

"I'd better get her into bed. Want to stick around? It

shouldn't take long."

"That's okay." I slung my bag over my shoulder. "I'm pretty wiped. We can pick it up again Friday."

"Want to fly this weekend?"

"I'm working."

"All right. Next week?"

God, the way he said it sounded like a date. Not that I'd been asked out on many dates. But the promise in his tone made me shiver. "Sure."

Normally, I'd kiss Allie's cheek before leaving, but I was so confused by Mateo that I couldn't risk getting close. At this point, even a friendly hug would scramble my brain. "Good night."

"Vera." He stopped me just as I'd opened the door.

The night air should have cooled my face, but Mateo's stare was so intense that sweat beaded at my temples. "Yeah?"

"I see you."

My heart tumbled. My grip on the doorknob slipped loose.

This was a dream. This had to be a dream. Everything about this night had been so... off. It had to be a dream.

"Not always," I said.

He crossed the distance between us, Allie still snuggled against that broad chest. "Always."

Mateo used his free hand to pull the door open wider. Then he tucked a lock of hair behind my ear. And untucked it a moment later.

When I lifted my gaze to his, I got lost in sapphire blue. Not a person on this earth had eyes like Mateo Eden. Not his parents. Not his siblings. Not even his daughter.

"I see you, Vera."

The emotions swelled so big in my chest I couldn't breathe. How long had I hoped for this? Dreamed of this? Years. I should have known what to say and what to do. Instead, I turned for the door.

And bolted into the black night.

CHAPTER 17

MATEO

Vera wrinkled her nose as she stepped inside the cabin. "I know." I held up a hand. "It's bad."

Every window was open, along with the door. A breeze curled through the house, but the acrid scent of dinner—completely fucking burned—clung to the air.

"What were you trying to make?" Vera set her backpack on the counter, then came to the sink, peering over my shoulder to the pan soaking in suds.

"Grilled ham and cheese."

"Oh." She pulled in her lips to hide a smile. "You burned grilled ham and cheese."

"This might be a new low." Though once, I'd turned a handful of chicken nuggets into hockey pucks because I'd microwaved them for three minutes instead of thirty seconds.

"What happened?"

"I had it perfect on one side." That was the real sting here. It was going so well, that one side crisped and golden brown. "I flipped it, but Allie pooped and needed her diaper changed. So I shut off the burner to take care of her. Figured it would cook while we were in her bedroom. Came out and I'd turned the burner on full."

Rest in peace, little sandwich.

"Oh." A giggle escaped Vera's lips. She slapped a hand over her mouth to cover it, but it was pointless. She burst into hysterics, laughing so hard she snorted.

That snort, that adorable snort, made my ruined dinner worth it.

"I'm not a great cook," I told her.

"So I've heard. Your mom said she doesn't have to worry about Eloise anymore because Jasper cooks. But she's mentioned on more than one occasion that if not for peanut butter sandwiches and cold cereal, Allie might starve."

"Thanks, Mom," I deadpanned. "That is cutthroat."

"Is she wrong though?" Vera arched an eyebrow and looked to Allie's high chair, where my daughter was spooning cereal into her mouth, milk dribbling down her chin.

"Fair point. Are you hungry? I can make you cereal too. And I dare you to find anyone who can pour a better Rice Krispie to milk ratio."

"I'm good. But thank you." Vera laughed, her eyes sparkling.

Damn, she was something. I leaned in closer, that laugh drawing me in. My gaze dropped to her perfect mouth, and though I'd told myself to back off tonight, just keep the focus on studying, I wanted a kiss.

I wanted the kiss I'd almost taken last Friday.

Vera's smile faltered and she ducked her chin, like she knew exactly what I was thinking and had thrown up a stop sign. She cleared her throat and darted around me, giving me a wide berth as she joined Allie at the dining room table.

We hadn't spoken since last week. I'd been to Mom and Dad's house a few times but Vera's car had been missing from her regular parking space beside the barn.

I'd missed her. It had only been a week, but tension seeped away from my shoulders now that she was here.

Especially considering I'd been worried she wouldn't show at all.

After a week of replaying our first study session, I could admit that maybe I'd come on a bit strong. In my defense, it was becoming nearly impossible to keep my distance from Vera. There'd been too many years of staying on my side of the boundary line.

That kiss she'd given me at Willie's hadn't just been an eye-opener. It had been permission.

There were no more lines.

Something here was worth exploring, and I wasn't wasting my chance.

"How was your week?" I asked, carrying her backpack as I joined her at the table.

"Good. I worked. I've been studying a lot for a few upcoming tests. You?"

"Busy. Spent most of it helping Griffin reconfigure the corrals at his house. Allie had a doctor's appointment with Talia. Went flying for a couple hours yesterday."

"You did?"

"I did."

"I'm glad." Pride brightened her face. She should be proud. I'd flown for myself, but I'd done it because of her.

"Ready?" I patted her backpack.

Vera stood behind the chair at the head of the table. It was one of two seats where I couldn't squeeze in next to her.

Well, that wasn't going to work for me. I liked sitting so close that our thighs touched. I wanted the strands of her silky ponytail to brush my arm from time to time. I'd much rather smell her sweet scent than my scorched dinner.

She pulled out the chair and sat down, sliding her bag over.

As she loosened the zipper, I grabbed my own chair. And plopped it right beside hers.

"What are you..." She looked to the ceiling, like she was

silently praying for strength. "Mateo."

"It's easier this way."

"Studying is easier if you're sitting on top of me?" She glanced down to where our knees were just millimeters from knocking.

"I don't like to read upside down."

"You don't need to read anything. You already know this."

"I like to follow along."

Her nostrils flared. "Have you always been this stubborn? Or did I just miss it?"

"You missed it."

"Fine." She flung open her book with an eye roll.

Wherever she'd been hiding this snark for the past couple of years, I was glad to see it flourish.

It took less than five minutes for our knees to touch. Each time they bumped, she'd shy away. Then a few minutes later, she'd relax and let her guard down. We'd touch again. And the dance went round and round.

"Ahh done." Allie finished her cereal and held up her hands.

"Good job, Sprout." I gave Vera a reprieve and lifted Alaina from her high chair, quickly wiping up her face before cleaning the mess on her tray. Then I turned on a Disney show and let her play in the living room while I returned to my chair.

The moment I was seated, Vera's spine stiffened. She looked as stiff as the wood beneath her ass.

"Vera, relax."

"I can't." She huffed. "You're crowding me. I can't think with you so close."

I moved closer.

"Mateo." She jabbed her elbow into mine, then buried her face in her hands. "You're confusing me."

"About carburetor ice?" I teased.

She dropped her hands and huffed. "Mateo."

"You're confused." I tucked and untucked a lock of her hair. "I thought I was pretty clear."

"Not to me."

I forgot sometimes that she had spent so long away from the world. That she'd missed her senior year in high school and college years—years when I'd spent just as much time learning about women as I had agricultural business or piloting. What I considered fairly obvious might need to be repeated, reinforced, a few times for it to sink in deep.

"This is a date," I declared.

"But we're studying."

"It's a study date. And soon, I'd like to take you on a dinner date. And a movie date. And a coffee date. I want to date you, Vera. I want to spend time with you."

And I wanted to kiss her.

She opened her mouth and closed it. Opened it again. Then her shoulders sagged. "I don't know how to navigate this. It's... weird. I made it weird at Willie's."

"No, you didn't."

She gave me a flat look.

"You made it clear. And if it makes you feel better, I'm not exactly sure how to navigate this either."

My one and only real relationship had been with Madison. And it had ended in a fiery crash.

"We'll find our way together," I promised, then tapped her textbook. "But first, we get to learn about carburetor ice."

"Okay." She sighed.

It went against every instinct, but for the next hour as we worked, I kept my knee away from hers.

We'd take this slow. As slow as she needed.

"Ve-wa." Allie came running over with a pink plastic hammer. "Wook it."

"Oh, I love your hammer." Vera fawned over the toy before letting Allie smack it on the table to prove it worked.

While I'd been helping Griffin at the corrals this week, Allie had tagged along one day to play with her cousins. Mom had come over to help out since Winn had been at work. She'd bought toy toolboxes for each of the kids. Allie had been hooked to this hammer ever since.

She smacked it on the table again just as a yawn stretched her mouth.

I glanced at the clock on the stove. Almost bedtime. This study date was over too soon.

We could stretch bedtime a bit, but Allie was a better kid if we stuck to a routine. "I'd better get her in the tub. Would you wait?"

Vera touched a lock of Allie's hair that had escaped a pigtail. "Sure."

"Come on, Sprout. Bath time."

"No baf!" The hammer was dropped as Allie tore off for the living room, trying to hide beside the couch.

"Alaina."

"No baf."

I blew out a deep breath.

These days, this was the nightly battle. About four months ago, she'd started to fight me on bath time. Why, I had no clue. She'd squirm and kick and cry. It had become such a challenge, that Mom had stopped even trying to bathe Allie on the nights we stayed at my parents' place.

The idea of a bath just pissed my daughter off. But the bath itself? Totally fine. When I finally got her in the water, she loved it. She'd splash and play like it was her favorite activity in the world.

Two-year-olds. They made no fucking sense.

"She's going to scream," I warned Vera, then headed for the bathroom, getting the water going. I added extra bubbles in the hopes that it would lessen the fit we were about to endure.

I returned to the living room, shoulders squared for the showdown, and froze.

Vera was kneeling on the floor beside Allie, helping her out of her clothes. No screaming. No squirming. "Should we take your hammer into the bath?"

"Yeah!" Dressed only in her diaper, she ran for the toy she'd abandoned, then raced for the bathroom with it.

Who was that child? Because she wasn't my daughter.

"You have to come over for bath time every night," I told Vera.

She giggled, collecting Allie's clothes and standing from the floor.

"Daddy!" Allie called. "Bubbies."

"Be back." I winked at Vera, then went to get Allie into the bubbles. Before I disappeared into the bathroom, I glanced over my shoulder.

And caught Vera staring at my ass.

Man, did I like that. I liked the flirting and teasing. I liked the subtle touches and stolen looks. I liked the tension building between us.

It was so different than my experience with any other woman. Sex had always been the goal. An easy fuck to release some stress. Jumping straight into bed meant I'd never taken the time to appreciate these understated moments.

Just being in the same room with Vera had become a lesson in foreplay.

For the first time in my life, I wanted to stretch this out. Savor it.

Allie was ripping off her diaper when I made it to the bathroom. I snagged it from her, then plopped her in the water, moving as quickly as possible to clean her up and wash her hair.

"Time to get out."

"No!" she cried when I opened the drain. "Mo bubbies."

"All done."

"No." She kicked as I hefted her out of the tub, her skin slippery, but I kept a firm hold on her torso, plopping her on the mat and wrapping her in a hooded unicorn towel.

The pout on her face was adorable. Someday, she'd wield that against me, wouldn't she? It was already getting harder and harder to tell her no.

"Go find Vera."

The pout morphed into a toothy smile. Allie raced out of the room, bare feet slapping on the hardwood floors. "Ve-wa!"

"Jellybean."

I dried the floor and slipped into Allie's room to get her pajamas from the dresser. With a clean diaper and purple onesie in hand, I found Allie on Vera's lap, both cuddled together on the couch.

"Let's get dressed, Sprout."

Allie curled deeper into Vera's shoulder.

"Want me to help you?" Vera asked, reaching for the pajamas.

Alaina didn't fight Vera. No, the person she loved to argue with most was me.

While they worked on the diaper and clothes, I got Allie's sippy cup of milk from the fridge.

Normally, I'd take Allie to the rocking chair in her room and snuggle with her until she was asleep. Then I'd put her in her bed and sneak out. But she and Vera looked too perfect together to break up, so I turned off the main lights, leaving one on in the kitchen, and joined them on the couch.

"What should we watch?" I snagged the remote from the coffee table.

"Dizzy?" Vera asked, the corner of her mouth turning up.

"Not Dizzy."

Allie let out a whimper when I changed the channel from her cartoon, but she was getting tired and as Vera toyed with her damp hair, her eyelids began to droop.

I chose a random movie from Netflix that I'd seen before and knew wasn't violent, then turned down the volume. My arm draped across the back of the couch, my fingers reaching for the ends of Vera's ponytail.

She let me twist a lock around a finger. Another win.

Allie crawled onto my lap ten minutes into the movie and rested her cheek on my shoulder as she yawned.

My girl loved to argue and push my buttons, but I could count on my fingers how many times she'd fallen asleep somewhere other than on my chest.

"Night, Sprout." I kissed her hair as she gasped another yawn.

Minutes were all it took for her to crash.

"I should go," Vera whispered.

Except I wasn't ready for her to go, not yet. So I took more of that ponytail in my fingers, tugging just enough that she didn't move to stand. "Have you seen this movie before?"

"No. But—"

"Study date. Movie date." This time, I pulled her hair my direction until she took the hint and shifted closer.

She sighed as she sank into my side. "Just promise me the dinner date will be to a restaurant."

I chuckled. "We'll go to Knuckles."

There was a smile on her mouth when I glanced down. A smile so pretty I wanted to kiss it.

"Vera." I spoke low. Smooth. Drawing her attention away from the screen.

"What?"

"I want to kiss you."

That chocolate gaze blew wide, those pink lips parting.

"Tell me yes. Tell me you want my mouth as much as I want yours."

"I—" Her breath hitched. "Yes."

Thank fuck. I bent, ready to take the kiss I'd been dreaming about for a week.

Allie shifted, her knee colliding with my groin.

"Ooof." I winced, shifting her away. Son of a bitch. Brutal little knees.

Not only was my dick throbbing—not the good throb—but the moment was broken.

"You should put her to bed." She stood and collected her backpack from the table.

Damn. So close.

With Allie in my arms, I moved around the house, closing windows now that the burnt smell had faded. Then I met Vera at the door.

"Next week?" I lifted my hand to her cheek, my thumb skimming across freckles.

She nodded and turned for the door. But she whirled back in a flash, and before I knew it was happening, she rose up on her toes and pressed a kiss to the corner of my mouth.

Then she ran.

She was always running.

But at least this time, she'd kissed me first.

CHAPTER 18

Vera

Rain drizzled through the gaps in the trees. Mist cloaked the mountains and water dripped from the brim of my hat. My coat and clothes were soaked.

I'd been hiking around Sable Peak for hours, searching for any sign of my father. But there was nothing to find. No animal snares. No charred remains of a campfire. No footprints in the mud.

No Dad.

But I kept going, kept pushing. He had to be out here somewhere.

The steady rain drowned out any sound. If he was nearby, he'd find shelter. A place to stay dry. That had always been one of his most important rules. Stay dry. Stay warm. Stay hydrated. A person could go on an empty stomach for a day or two. But as long as we were dry, warm and had water, we'd survive.

He'd survive.

He was alive.

This far up into the mountains, there had to be a cave or something. I doubted Dad would have built a shelter. The hut he'd built years ago had been more for me than himself, so I wouldn't have to sleep on the dirt each night.

I pulled up the sleeve of my coat, checking my watch. "Damn it."

If I was going to make it to my car with enough time to get to Mateo's for our Friday study date, I had to start back now.

"Gah." A surge of anger welled. I bent and picked up a pinecone, throwing it against a nearby tree.

He was out here. I knew it down deep in my bones. He was out here. Why couldn't I find him? Why couldn't he find me?

He had to know I was searching. That I'd want to see him again.

Every hike, I left traces behind. There was no reason for me to mask my presence, so I didn't bother. Footprints. A circle of rocks. My name spelled out in sticks with the date. Every hike, for two years, I'd left a marker.

Yes, the mountains were vast. Our chances were so, so small. But if I was searching for him, and he was searching for me, it had to happen. Eventually, it had to happen, right?

Dad would be watching trailheads. It was the logical place for me to start. So for our paths to clash, it was just a matter of timing. And persistence.

I'd spent countless hours poring over maps of the area. I was working section by section, tackling the landscape in pieces. I'd been up and down each local trail at least three times.

If I just kept going, if I kept pushing, I'd find him.

I had to find him.

Unless…

What if he'd found me already? What if he'd watched me leave those messages? What if he'd kept his distance intentionally?

My breath caught.

Was he hiding from me?

No. I refused to believe it. He wouldn't ignore me. Would he?

"Dad!" My voice bounced off the trees before it was swallowed up by the steady drizzle of rain.

I shouted for him on every hike. I yelled and yelled, willing my voice to carry. Maybe if I screamed loud enough, he'd come running.

"Cormac Gallagher!"

A crow cawed in the distance, but otherwise, there was no sound. No one yelled back.

"If you can see me, you'd better come out here." I fought the urge to stomp my foot like a child. "Dad!"

Nothing but the sound of my sinking heart.

I turned, chin tucked to watch my steps, and hiked the miles to my car. My arms and legs were shaking as I slid behind the wheel, exhaustion weighing heavy in every muscle. I stripped out of my coat, tossing it in the backseat along with my hat. My hair was soaking wet. So were my jeans. My toes were almost numb as they squished in my socks and boots.

Was this search pointless? Was I wearing myself thin for nothing?

I'd been doing this with the assumption that Dad wanted to be found. What if I'd been wrong? What if he'd never intended to see me again?

My nose stung with the threat of tears as I turned on the car, cranking the heat. The windshield wipers flew across the glass, scattering and smearing drops.

I hated storms, but at least this was just rain.

It was already five thirty, and there wasn't time to go home for a hot shower before I'd agreed to be at Mateo's, so when I pulled out of the parking area, I drove straight for the cabin. The backpack with my ground school books was in the trunk.

Other than a few texts to confirm we were meeting tonight, I hadn't spoken to Mateo this week. We leapt from Friday to Friday.

The days in between gave me time to think. After all this

time, after all the waiting and crushing, it was surprisingly hard to believe he was interested.

Why had I kissed him last week? I should have waited. I should have let him kiss me. But I'd acted on impulse because...

I wasn't sure why. Maybe it wasn't all that complicated. I'd just wanted to kiss him, so I'd kissed him. Then sprinted out of his house.

Without a doubt, I was doing everything wrong. How did normal women pursue men? What would it even feel like to be normal?

Normal felt as impossible to find as my dad.

The drive to the cabin was on muddy roads. Even with the heater on full blast, my clothes were too soaked to dry.

The last thing I wanted was to study, yet the temptation of Mateo was too much to resist. So I parked my car beside his truck, retrieved my backpack and made my way to the door.

It opened before I could knock.

Mateo looked as gorgeous as ever in a long-sleeved black T-shirt. He'd pushed the sleeves up his sinewed forearms. His jeans were faded and frayed, the denim soft from years of washes and wear. And his feet were bare. That was becoming my favorite part about these visits. Last week, he'd had bare feet too, and it added an intimacy to these visits. I was coming into his home, where he walked around barefoot.

"Hey." Mateo's gaze narrowed as he looked me up and down, taking in my clothes.

"I was hiking." I shrugged. "It's wet outside."

"You don't say." He studied my face for a moment too long. "What's the weather like?"

"Uh, raining?"

"In here." He reached out and tapped my temple. "What's the weather like in here? You look upset."

"Oh." I'd hoped he wouldn't notice. What were my options

again? Overcast. Broken. Scattered. Clear and a million. Definitely not the latter. "I guess... a little overcast."

He hummed. "What's going on?"

"Nothing." Everything. I couldn't even articulate it right now.

"You can talk to me."

Not about this. "It was just a long day. I lost track of time."

"Where did you hike?"

Oh, he wasn't going to like this. "Sable Peak."

"Alone? You were supposed to call me."

"I'm fine. Soaked but in one piece. There's nothing to worry about."

His expression hardened, but instead of delivering a lecture like Uncle Vance would have, he jerked his chin for me to come inside.

It smelled like wood polish and glass cleaner.

"Get those boots off." Mateo closed the door. "Then come with me."

I bent to untie my soggy laces. "Where's Allie?"

Her toys were stowed in baskets and tubs instead of strewn across the floor.

"Sprout," Mateo called. "Vera's here."

"Ve-wa!" That squeal was music to my ears. She came racing out of her bedroom wearing a pink superhero cape. Allie didn't care that I was wet. She launched herself into my arms with a giggle.

"Hey, Jellybean." I kissed her cheek, then set her down so she wouldn't get rainwater on her clothes. "What are you doing?"

"Doss."

"Doss?" I glanced up to Mateo for an interpretation.

"Dolls."

"Ah. Dolls are fun."

"Go." She took my hand, pulling me through the house

to her room.

When Mateo joined us, he brought along a pair of folded gray sweats and a white T-shirt. "You can wear these."

"I'm sure I'll dry soon."

"You're leaving puddles on the floor."

"No, I'm—" *Shit.* There was a tiny puddle beside the hem of my pants. "Sorry."

He chuckled. "Go change, Peach."

Peach. That was the second time he'd called me by that nickname. I liked it. A lot.

I took the clothes and hurried to Allie's bathroom, swapping wet for dry before pulling my hair into a messy topknot.

The pants dwarfed my legs, pooling at my ankles. I rolled the waistband twice after cinching the drawstring tight. The shirt might as well have been a tent, the sleeves draping past my elbows, but the cotton was warm, like it hadn't been out of the dryer that long. Maybe he'd done laundry today along with cleaning. The scent of fabric softener and Mateo was a balm to my aching heart.

The clouds were clearing.

When I emerged into the living room, Allie had abandoned her dolls and tipped over a toy basket, spilling blocks and balls beside the coffee table.

"Better?" Mateo asked when I joined him in the kitchen.

"Yeah. Thanks."

He stepped close, raising his hand to my face. His thumb glided across my chin. "Feel like studying?"

"Honestly? No."

"Then how about we go flying tomorrow instead?"

"I have to work at noon."

"We'll meet at nine. Hopefully this weather will pass. And tonight, we'll just have a normal Friday evening. Good?"

Normal. Yes, I really wanted normal. "Good."

"Hungry?"

"Starved. I'd even eat a burnt grilled ham and cheese."

"I bought a take-and-bake pizza. Most likely, it will survive the oven unscathed."

"I love pizza." It was the one food I'd always craved those years in the woods. I hadn't missed cheeseburgers or tacos or spaghetti and meatballs. But pizza. I'd spent four years missing pizza.

"Pepperoni with olives. That's your favorite, right?"

"How..." How did he know that?

"Whenever we have pizza at Mom and Dad's, you take a slice of the works and pick off every topping but the pepperoni and olives." Mateo opened the fridge and pulled out a pepperoni pizza. Then he took a can of sliced olives from the cupboard.

The urge to cry or scream was so overwhelming I had to look away. It was too much. Today had been too much. I was angry at my father. I was frustrated with myself. I was stupidly happy that Mateo knew my favorite pizza toppings.

It was all too much. I wouldn't talk to anyone about Dad. I wasn't sure what to think about Mateo. The only girlfriends to confide in happened to be his sisters. The emotions were a storm of their own, raining down in heavy sheets, and with no way to let them out, they manifested as tears.

Don't cry. Not in front of Mateo. Not here. But my chin quivered. That sting in my nose was burning like fire. I squeezed my eyes shut before a tear could escape.

Don't cry, Vera.

A pair of large hands clamped around my hips. Then my feet were off the floor, and I was flying.

"Wh—" I gasped, my eyes popping open.

Mateo deposited me on the kitchen counter with a thud. "Take a breath, Vera."

I tried to fill my lungs, but the air got lodged in my throat.

Mateo took my chin in his hand, holding my gaze. "Breathe."

My inhale burned. But I breathed.

"You don't have to right now," he said. "But when you're ready, you can talk to me."

No, I couldn't. If I cracked the lid on that box, if I let even a little bit of the pain free, it would break me into a thousand pieces. Besides, he couldn't know the secrets about Dad.

"Pizza," he said. "Yeah?"

I managed a nod.

He cupped my cheek, giving me a soft smile, then hoisted me off the counter. "Go relax."

I shuffled to the living room, holding up the legs of the sweats as I walked, and curled into a corner to watch Allie.

She hefted a pink tub of Lego blocks from her toy stash and brought it over, dropping it in my lap. "He go, Ve-wa."

"What should we build?"

Allie tapped her chin. It was something she'd picked up from Papa Harrison and was about the cutest thing I'd ever seen.

"A house?" I suggested. "Or a train?"

"Tain."

"Good choice." I opened the lid and took out the pieces to string together an alphabet train.

Mateo set the table and poured us each glasses of ice water. The scents of pepperoni and marinara and baking dough filled the air as the pizza cooked. And when it was done, we sat together, the three of us, eating a normal dinner, having a normal conversation about the work he'd done on the ranch today. We watched a normal, precious little girl make a mess with pizza and the olives she tried to poke with her finger.

I helped get her ready for a bath and stood at the door to the bathroom while he washed her hair. Allie would give him orders. He'd let her boss him around.

Mateo had always been mesmerizing. The two of them together? It was magic.

When she was dressed in lavender pajamas and ready for bed, he fixed me with a stare. "Don't go."

It wasn't a request.

He disappeared to Allie's room to rock her to sleep while I retreated to the living room.

I tried sitting on the couch, but the flutters in my belly made it impossible to stay still, so I cleaned up the toys.

Mateo emerged as I was kneeling beside the coffee table to dismantle the Lego train.

"Is she asleep?" My voice was breathy, my heart racing. Would he kiss me tonight? What else was he planning?

It dawned on me for the first time just how close we were to his bedroom.

He crooked his finger as he walked toward me.

He crooked his freaking finger.

It was so unexpected, so incredibly hot, my jaw dropped. A shiver raced down my spine.

"Stand up."

I couldn't stand. I could barely breathe.

Mateo held out a hand. As soon as my palm was in his, tingles went zinging to my elbow. He hauled me to my feet, taking me by the shoulders as he closed the gap between us.

My chest brushed against his. My nipples pebbled beneath my bra.

"You kissed me last week."

I gulped. "Sorry?"

"You should be sorry." His hands threaded into the hair at my temples. "You kissed me before I could kiss you back."

"Oh." My. God.

"Oh." A grin stretched across his mouth as he bent closer. "My turn."

Mateo sealed his mouth over mine, swallowing my gasp.

He hummed, a sound so intoxicating and sinful, my body liquified. If not for the grip he had on my face, I would have crashed to my knees.

I melted against him, whimpering as he slid his tongue across my lower lip. He coaxed my mouth open, and when I parted, his tongue did a lazy swirl against mine. He tasted spicy and male and incredible.

My hands came to his chest, fisting his shirt.

His arms banded around me, holding me close, as his body, hard and strong, bent around mine.

I lifted up on my toes and snaked my arms around his neck, locking my body to his. Our tongues tangled and dueled. He nipped and sucked until I whimpered.

This kiss was better than I ever could have imagined. All those nights I'd wondered what it would be like to kiss Mateo? The dream couldn't compete with reality.

I wanted to crawl inside him and never leave. The world beyond us vanished. It got fuzzy at first, the colors blurring and swirling, then it faded to nothing.

There were no fears. No pain.

It felt so good not to worry. Not to hurt. Not to think. It was like being numb to anything except Mateo. The relief was as addicting as his lips.

He slanted his mouth over mine, delving deep to explore every corner of my mouth. He growled against my lips, the vibration of his chest making me shiver.

Fire licked my veins. The pulse between my legs was almost unbearable. More. I needed more. I loosened my hold around his shoulders to reach between us, taking the hem of his shirt in my grip. I dragged it up his ribs, then slipped my fingers beneath the cotton and flattened my palms on his stomach. My fingertips traced the hard ridges and valleys of his washboard abs. God, I wanted this shirt off. I wanted to see him, all of him.

My hand slid higher, lifting the shirt as I splayed my fingers across his ribs. But before I could reach his chest, he shifted away.

"Fuck, Vera." His breathing was as ragged as mine. His throat bobbed as his eyes locked with mine. Then he took a step away.

My heart plummeted as he righted his shirt.

That was it? We were stopping? Everything that had vanished during the kiss came rushing forward. The numbness faded.

"I promised you slow," he said.

"I never asked for slow."

"I don't... I'm not..." He dragged a hand through his hair. "I want to do this right. For your first time."

My first time? Oh. He thought I was a virgin. Considering my history, that made sense. "It wouldn't be my first time."

I'd had a boyfriend in high school and lost my virginity to him when I was sixteen. Seth Hendricks.

What was Seth doing now? Was he working or going to school? He'd been sweet and gentle. Dull. When Seth had kissed me, the world hadn't faded away.

Tonight, I needed the world to fade away. I needed Mateo to kiss me again.

"Noted." Mateo's jaw ticked. What did that mean? Was he jealous? Disappointed? "I still think we should take it slow."

Slow sounded a lot like rejection. Slow sounded a lot like pity.

I brushed past him for the bathroom, locking myself inside.

With fumbling fingers, I traded his sweats for the clothes I'd hung to dry. Except my jeans were still wet and hard to drag up my legs. My sweater was cold and smelled like rain and dirt. I didn't bother with my socks.

With them shoved in a pocket, I came out of the bathroom and found Mateo waiting.

His hands were braced on his hips. "Might as well turn around and put those dry clothes back on. You're not running out of here like this. Not again."

He'd have to barricade the door to stop me. The look on his face said he might just do it.

We stared at each other in a silent standoff. Could I beat him for the door? I was fast. But probably not fast enough.

"Daddy!" came a tiny voice from behind Allie's closed door. That sweet girl had come to my rescue.

"Shit." His nostrils flared and he held up a finger. "Do not leave."

I stayed put until he crossed Allie's threshold. Then I bolted, rushing for the door to yank on my boots. With my toes squelching in the wet insoles, I slipped out the door.

And drove home alone. Where I could suffer in peace.

Alone.

CHAPTER 19

MATEO

It was an effort not to rip the door at Eden Coffee off its hinges. The bell that jingled overhead was too fucking cheerful. So was my sister's waiting smile. Not even the smell of cinnamon and sugar could sweeten my mood.

One look at my sour expression and Lyla straightened behind the counter. "Hi," she drawled. "Bad day?"

I pointed toward the hall that led to the kitchen. "Is Vera back there?"

"No." Her eyebrows came together. "She called in sick today."

"Fuck." I rubbed a hand over my jaw. Not a chance she was actually sick.

"What's going on?" Lyla asked.

"She was supposed to meet me at the airfield this morning. Never showed." I'd waited around for an hour, texting and calling to make sure she was okay. Then I'd realized she'd stood me up.

I'd spent three hours cleaning the hangar and killing time, hoping it would burn off my frustration before I tracked Vera down at the coffee shop. The hangar was spotless. And I was still fucking pissed. I had been since the moment Vera had left the house last night.

I'd hit the brakes after that kiss and now I was the bad guy? No. Fuck no. She didn't get to keep running away from me. Avoiding me. Standing me up.

Especially after that kiss.

It was the game changer. Everything was different now.

There wasn't just something between us. There was something life-changing. And the chemistry? It was unlike anything I'd felt before. From the moment my tongue had touched Vera's, from the second I'd tasted her sweet lips, I'd been hooked. Not a chance I'd let her go now.

Did she have a clue how hard it had been for me to stop that kiss? Every cell in my being had vibrated with the need to claim her. Keep her. But I'd fought back the desire to carry her into my bedroom and worship her until dawn.

For once in my goddamn life, I wasn't going to screw up a relationship with sex.

Apparently, that made me an asshole.

"Earth to Matty." Lyla snapped her fingers in front of my face. "What is going on?"

"Nothing. I just need to talk to Vera."

"Doesn't seem like nothing." She sighed. "I'm trying really hard not to interfere and ask about that night at Willie's."

Meaning either I spilled, or she was going to ask. By some streak of luck, I'd managed to avoid discussing that night with anyone other than Mom and Vance's warning at the hotel. Given the look on Lyla's face, that streak was about to suffer a quick, efficient death. Might as well get it over with.

"Go ahead. Interfere."

Lyla gave me a sad smile. "None of us realized she felt that way about you. I guess I owe you an apology. I would have warned you."

"Don't apologize." I waved it off. "We've been spending time together. I'm teaching her how to fly."

"Oh." Surprise flickered in my sister's blue eyes. "She

didn't mention that."

"It's new."

"Do you think this is smart? Teaching her? I don't want her to get her hopes up."

Lyla assumed I'd turned Vera down. Or maybe Lyla and Vance had hoped that would be the case. Did they not think I was good enough? "I'm not teaching her to fly out of guilt, Lyla," I snapped. "She asked. I agreed."

"All right." Lyla held up a hand. "I'll stop and mind my own business. I didn't mean to insinuate that you wouldn't be anything but kind to her. I just... love her. And the trauma she's endured. It's unthinkable."

"Yes, it is." I nodded. "But she doesn't want your pity. And she's not getting mine. That's not what this is about."

"Then what is it about?"

"I like her," I admitted.

"You do?" Lyla's smile was too big. "Really?"

"Yeah. Really. She's... Vera." I wanted Vera.

And I wanted us both to walk away unscathed.

"I don't know what's going to happen," I told Lyla. "Just give me time to figure it out."

Vera and I were not on the same wavelength at the moment, and adding my family into the mix would only make it worse.

"I can do that," she said.

"Thanks."

Another customer came through the door, so I shifted out of the way.

"I'll let you get back to work."

"You could stay. We could talk. Catch up."

"I need to get Alaina," I lied. Mom was babysitting and she'd told me not to rush home, wanting the time with her granddaughter.

With a wave, I left the coffee shop and retreated to my truck.

Downtown Quincy was soaked from all the rain these past few days. The red brick buildings seemed brighter, their gutters running on full. The trees were flourishing with the water, their leaves glistening and green. My tires sloshed across the pavement as I headed down Main, and I cracked the window.

Fresh rain was a favorite smell, but like the cleaning at the hangar, it did nothing to improve my mood. When I pulled off the highway and passed beneath the ranch's archway, my hands were still strangling the wheel.

My frustration spiked when I pulled up to my parents' house. The parking space beside the barn—Vera's space—was empty.

"Sick, huh?" I scoffed, gritting my teeth as I killed the engine. Then I slammed my door too hard before stomping up the porch to Mom and Dad's.

I was one foot inside before I remembered what Vera had told me about the doorbell. So I retreated to the porch and hit the button.

Tiny feet pounded on the floor inside. Allie came running around the corner with Mom following close behind.

"Daddy!" Allie's smile was a rainbow through the clouds, and for the first time in hours, I smiled.

"Hey, Sprout." I swept her into my arms. "How was your morning?"

"Good," Mom answered for her. "How was flying?"

"I didn't go. Vera, um… canceled."

"Really? She took off this morning. I figured she was going to meet you."

"Nope," I muttered.

Mom was the only one who knew I'd been spending time with Vera. I'd asked her to keep it quiet. There weren't many secrets between my family members, but Mom was the vault. When you asked her to keep something quiet, her lips stayed sealed.

"Thanks for watching Allie."

"Of course. Are you set on taking her home? Eloise just called. I guess they're doing a story time reading at the library and she was going to take Ophelia. Asked if Allie wanted to go too."

"I don't have it in me for a story time reading, Mom."

"Oh, not you. Me. I needed to buzz into town anyway and hit the grocery store. Allie can come along."

"Are you sure?"

She nodded. "Your dad has gone to Griffin's for the afternoon. We'll get out of here. Seems like you might need an afternoon to yourself. Go for a ride or something. Your dad brought Saturn, Neptune and Mars into the small pasture the other day because he was thinking about going for a ride if the weather cleared up. Maybe the rain will stop."

Even if it didn't, a hard ride sounded like a damn good idea. "Deal."

I helped get Allie loaded in my truck, letting Mom take it instead of swapping the car seat to her Escalade, and as they drove down the lane, I headed for the stables.

Saturn wasn't at all happy when I caught him with a lead rope and hauled him into a stall. He didn't like to be away from his friends. But when I swung into my saddle and rode him out of the arena, he perked up.

My horse loved his friends. But he really loved to run.

I gave him his head, and with no particular destination in mind, I set out on a long ride through meadows and past towering trees. By the time we made it back to the stables, the tops of my jeans and coat were soaked. The rain had slowed to a sprinkle but hadn't entirely stopped.

My body was drained, from the ride and a sleepless night, and I was ready for a hot shower and a warm meal. My mood was better. Not great, but better.

"Thanks, bud." I ran a hand down Saturn's nose before

letting him free to roam the pasture and join the others. Then I put my tack away and shut off the stable's lights.

The crunch of tires on gravel sounded as I reached the door.

Vera's Honda eased into the parking space beside the barn. If my truck had been outside Mom and Dad's, would she have even come home?

I marched straight for the barn, the frustration from earlier returning with a vengeance. Guess that ride hadn't really helped.

"Vera," I snapped the moment she stepped out of her car.

Her face whipped my way.

One look at her red-rimmed eyes and my stomach dropped. "What's wrong?"

Had something happened today? Was she really sick?

I closed the distance between us, taking her in from head to toe.

She looked a lot like me—rain slogged and exhausted. The scent of pine and earth clung to her clothes and hair. Okay, so she hadn't spent the day at the hospital. She'd gone hiking again, hadn't she?

Had something happened on a trail? A too-close encounter with an animal or something?

"What happened?"

"Nothing." She looked on the verge of tears as she closed her car's door and walked for the barn.

"Vera." I followed. Not a chance she was running away from me again. "What the hell is going on?"

"Sorry, I wasn't feeling like flying today." She trudged to the loft.

I stayed close, worried that she'd falter and fall.

There was a weariness to her movements, a sluggish weight, that I'd never seen before. Like she was using every bit of strength to keep her chin up. To keep herself moving forward.

When she reached the door, her shoulders sagged. She stared at the handle like she didn't have the energy to turn it.

"I'll get it." I slid up behind her, one hand on the small of her back as I opened the door and followed her inside. "Vera, talk to me."

"It's okay." She shrugged. "Just an overcast day."

"Why?"

"I went hiking."

"Did something happen?"

"No."

I locked eyes with hers. "Don't lie to me."

She dropped her chin.

"Hey." I came closer, tugging the zipper on her coat free. With it gone, I stripped mine off, tossing both with a thud to the floor. Then I hooked a finger under her chin.

The despair in her eyes was like a knife to my heart.

Did she have any idea how hard I'd work to never see that look again?

"Is this about last night?"

She shrugged.

"So yes and no?"

"Yes and no."

"What can I do?"

Another shrug.

"Peach. Throw me a bone." I slid my hand across her cheek, my fingertips diving into her hair. She must have worn a hat on her hike today, because only the ends were damp.

"Why do you call me Peach?"

So she had noticed. She hadn't reacted when I'd said it last night. I'd assumed either she hadn't heard it or she didn't like it.

I threaded my fingers through her hair. "Because your hair reminds me of a sun-ripened peach on a hot summer day. Because you're sweet. And because it's my favorite fruit."

"No, it's not. You like strawberries best."

"Not anymore," I murmured, bending to take her lips.

She sank into the kiss, like every muscle in her body instantly relaxed. Like the world beyond us just disappeared.

I hummed and dragged my tongue across her bottom lip, testing and tasting. Then I delved deep, her soft lips and sweet taste like heaven.

Like last night, it took a conscious effort to tear myself away. But I kept her face in my hands and dropped my forehead to hers. When I cracked my eyes open, hers were waiting. "Why'd you leave last night?"

"You pushed me away."

I blinked. Pushed her away? "I stopped us before we went too far."

"Too far?" Her eyes narrowed, then she broke free of my hold. "I've spent the past two years chasing normal, Mateo. I want people to treat me like they treated me before. I want to be the person who I was before, and that just feels impossible. If not for all the fucked-up shit in my life, would you really have stopped? I want to forget. I want... you. But not if you're going to tiptoe around me. Not if you're going to treat me like I'm fragile."

The hurt in those beautiful eyes was a slap in the face. She thought I'd stopped because I pitied her.

Fuck that. I closed the distance between us, taking her face in my hands. Then I kissed her. Hard. I plundered her mouth and pressed my body against hers so she could feel exactly how much I wanted her.

She whimpered as my arousal dug into her hip. When I ripped my mouth away, we were both breathless.

"I want you. So much I can't see straight. But I don't want to fuck this up. I don't want sex to be all we have. I don't want to wake up in bed one morning and have you tell me it's been fun and all, but a relationship isn't really what you're after.

That the months we've been together meant nothing. And I don't want to walk away and find out nine months later I have a daughter no one was ever going to fucking tell me about. *That* is why I stopped kissing you last night."

The color drained from her face as the words poured from my mouth. "Oh."

"Yeah," I muttered. "Oh."

CHAPTER 20

VERA

Today had taken a toll.

Numbness had spread throughout my body. Skin, muscle, bone. It ran surface to core. Not even a hot shower had chased it away. It had started hours ago, the moment Mateo had left. It was like he'd collected all the feeling in my nerves and stuffed it in his pocket, stealing it away when he'd walked out of the loft. With every passing minute, it had crept further. Sunk deeper.

Until finally, nothing.

I'd been sitting on the couch, knees hugged to my chest, for a while now. I didn't turn to look at a clock. I just sat here wishing that the numbness would disappear.

What a stupid wish.

Without this numbness, I'd only hurt.

I ought to wish for something else, like a magic crystal that would glow red and warn me about days like today.

Days that scarred.

I'd found my father today. Sort of.

And the one person I wanted to tell, the person who might help me make sense of what had happened on my hike, was Mateo. The one person who could never know.

Maybe I'd brought this bad day upon myself for standing

him up at the airfield this morning. Karma had given me a swift kick in the ass.

My hike had been a disaster from the start. I'd left the ranch after calling in sick to work—I'd never called in sick before and the lie had festered immediately, coiling my stomach into a knot. But after Mateo's rejection—or what I'd thought was a rejection—I'd needed air. I'd needed space.

I'd needed my dad.

Or at least, the hope that I might see him again.

So I'd set out into the mountains to continue my search.

I hadn't expected to find him. Maybe that was why today had been different. I'd gone out thinking I'd leave my name carved into the trunk of a tree with today's date and that would be the end of it.

I'd hiked until hunger had clawed and I'd stopped for lunch, scarfing two protein bars. Then I'd found the best tree in sight, one with no hanging limbs that might obscure my carving. I'd just taken out my pocket knife and flipped open the blade when I'd accidentally sliced my finger.

I'd yelped and cursed. As I'd popped the cut into my mouth to suck off the blood, I'd caught movement out of the corner of my eye. For a second, I'd thought it was a bear and I was truly fucked.

But the color was wrong. Instead of a grizzly's cinnamon fur, I'd caught a flicker of orange-red popping out from behind a thick tree trunk. The red hadn't been on a head, but a face. A beard, thick and scraggly.

Dad would never stay clean shaven again, not without a razor and shaving cream. But he'd never let his beard grow unruly.

Until now.

In my mind, Dad looked the same as the day I'd left him two years ago. Stubbled. Strong. Sad.

The man I'd seen for a split second today looked like he'd

been living hard for two years. There'd been dark circles beneath his eyes. A hollowness to his cheeks. And that nasty, frizzled beard.

He must have heard my yelp of pain when I'd sliced my finger. He'd reacted on instinct, a father rushing for his injured child.

Except he hadn't come for me. He'd darted out of sight. And when I'd sprinted after him, he'd vanished by the time I'd made it to the tree.

He'd been out there, watching me. He'd stayed hidden. He had to have heard me shout his name.

And he'd left me all the same.

He'd left me.

Why?

My chin quivered, but there were no more tears to cry. I'd left them all on the forest floor as I'd hiked back to my car.

Maybe I was wrong. Maybe I was delusional and the only person hiking in the rainy mountains today had been me.

But it was so… real.

As real as a kiss from Mateo.

God, I was such a jerk. I'd been in an awful mood when I'd finally made it home. He'd surprised me and thrown me off-balance. And instead of behaving like an adult, I'd thrown a tantrum about him pushing me away.

Not once had it crossed my mind that he might have his own reasons for taking this slow. Not once had I considered his feelings.

Whatever Alaina's mother had done to him, she'd sliced deep. That wound wasn't fully healed. And rather than respect his boundaries, I'd let my own bullshit come between us.

Damn it, what was wrong with me? I buried my face in my hands, the numbness giving way to mortification and regret.

He'd left the loft right after our fight—if that even counted as a fight. Anne had returned with Allie and he'd gone to take her home. He'd left and I hadn't even apologized.

Tomorrow, I'd make this right. Tomorrow, I'd—

No. Not tomorrow.

Tonight.

He didn't seem mad, but the air between us wasn't clear. I needed it clear. I needed to know we were okay.

Springing from the couch, I hurried to my bedroom. My muscles were stiff and sore, not just from the hike but from sitting in one spot for too long. I grabbed a dark green hoodie and pulled it over the T-shirt and sweats I'd dressed in after my shower. Then, not bothering with socks, I slipped into a pair of tennis shoes, swiped my keys from the counter and flew out the door.

It was a black night, the clouds blocking out any moon or starlight. My headlights turned raindrops into specks of white and my windshield wipers worked furiously to keep the glass clear as I bounced along the muddy gravel roads to Mateo's cabin.

The porch light was on when I arrived. Alaina's bedroom was dark and only a faint glow came from the main room's windows.

I threw the hood over my hair before climbing out into the rain and running for the porch.

Like always, I didn't have to knock. By the time my foot landed on the top stair, the door opened and Mateo stood in its threshold.

"Hi," I said, breathless.

He shifted sideways, waving me inside.

I pushed away my hood but didn't bother taking off my shoes. I wasn't here to stay.

"I'm sorry," I blurted. "I know it's late. I just wanted to say that I'm sorry. I was so caught up in my own head, I didn't think about what you might be feeling."

"It's all right." He sighed, staring at me for a long moment.

Then, faster than I could blink, he caught my elbow and hauled me into his chest.

I sagged against him, wrapping my arms around his waist. "I'm sorry."

"I'm trying, Vera. I'm trying so hard to do us right."

"Us?"

He buried his nose in my hair. "Us."

My heart swelled so big it felt like it was going to come out of my throat. The clouds thinned. Gray skies made way for blue.

We stood there for a few long moments, just breathing each other in. Then Mateo's arms relaxed and I eased away.

"You were crying today."

I shrugged. "A little."

"Because of me?"

"No."

He hummed. "Want to talk about why?"

"No. Do you want to talk about her? Alaina's mom?"

He shook his head. "Not tonight."

"Are we okay?" My voice sounded too small. Too vulnerable.

He tucked and untucked a lock of my hair. "Yeah, Peach. We're okay."

Relief coursed through my veins. The numbness was gone, and with it, the knot in my gut. Maybe tonight, I'd actually be able to sleep. And tomorrow, I'd think long and hard about what to do about my father.

"Good night." I rose up on my toes, placing a kiss on his cheek. Then I flipped up my hood and opened the door to the stormy night.

"Wait." He snagged my hand before I could duck outside. "Don't go. I meant what I said earlier. I don't want to fuck this up. Part of me knows the responsible thing to do is get an umbrella and walk you to your car. But the other part wants to say fuck it. To pick you up and carry you to my bed and pray like hell I don't ruin us."

I didn't want him to get an umbrella. I didn't want to go out in that rain. "You won't ruin us."

"I might."

I laid my hand on his heart. His good heart. A heart intent on protecting mine. "I don't want to go."

He held perfectly still, waging an internal war. There was a blue umbrella propped up beside the coat hooks. For a moment, I was sure he'd pick it up.

Then he blinked, the war over, and crushed his mouth to mine.

Yes. I threw my arms around his shoulders, holding tight, as he hauled me off my feet. The kiss wasn't sweet or gentle. The moment my lips parted, Mateo's tongue swept inside to devour.

He licked and sucked, consuming me whole. The world beyond us disappeared.

I wrapped my legs around his waist, wanting to burrow deeper into his strong body.

He groaned, slanting his mouth the opposite way before pulling my bottom lip between his teeth. Then he flicked the hood off my hair, kicked the door shut and carried me through the house, straight to the open bedroom door.

We were a mess of wet lips and wandering hands. God, he had big hands. I hadn't noticed just how large until tonight. They splayed across my ribs and hips as he laid me on his soft bed. He dragged a wide palm down my thigh before cupping my ass to pull me closer as his weight settled on mine. His hard body covered mine, his hardness rubbing against my core.

I gasped, arching into his touch. It wasn't enough. I wanted more. If I didn't get out of these clothes soon, I'd combust. "Mateo."

"Fuck, I want to taste every inch of you." He dragged his lips down the column of my throat, his tongue across my skin.

I pulled at his T-shirt, fumbling, bunching it up and reaching for the hem. But he was so tight against me, all the cotton did was stretch. "Off. Take it off."

Mateo reached behind his neck and yanked it off his body.

The heat from his naked chest was like an inferno beneath my hands. It was my turn to roam, to touch every inch. My fingers dipped into the muscled grooves of his back, tracing from his spine to the dimples just above the waistband of his jeans.

I slipped my hands into his pockets, molding my grip to the curve of his behind. His ass was perfect, hard and round and... I squeezed. How many years had I wanted to slide my hands into Mateo's jeans pockets? A giddy smile broke across my face. It was better than the dream.

"Fuck, Vera." He tore his lips away from my throat and leaned back, his breath as ragged as my own.

My hands slid to his front, trailing up those washboard abs to the dusting of black, coarse hair on his chest.

The cabin's outside lights were on. They were losing the battle with the night, but they cast enough of a silvery shadow into the room to reveal the heat in Mateo's eyes. And the worry.

"You're shaking."

I was? I felt it then, the trembling in my legs and arms. It was only nerves. The good kind of nerves.

"We can stop." He swallowed hard.

Oh, hell no. We weren't stopping. I shifted to sit up, forcing him to ease away. And when I had enough space, I ripped the hoodie over my head and tossed it to the floor. "Don't stop."

The corner of his sinful mouth turned up. Then he was on me in a flash, his hands taking me beneath the arms to hoist me higher into the bed. Somehow, at the same time, he managed to strip off my T-shirt.

My bra came next. The trembling stopped, the nerves erased by lust the moment his lips captured a nipple and sucked it into his mouth.

"Oh, God." My skin, my bones, melted beneath his hot mouth.

He cupped my breast, kneading my flesh as he tortured that swollen peak with his tongue and teeth. Then he moved to the other nipple, giving it the same treatment.

He trailed his lips down my sternum, shifting lower to dip his tongue into my navel. Then he pulled at the waistband of my pants, easing them down my legs. My panties came next, dragged over my thighs in slow, torturous inches.

Goose bumps broke out across my skin as a smile toyed with my mouth. Mateo Eden, my Mateo, was stripping me bare.

"You're so damn beautiful, Vera." His voice was hoarse. "Look at me."

I opened my eyes and found his waiting.

"I see you."

My heart stopped. A full stop. He saw me. If there were any lingering doubts, they were gone by the time my heart started beating again.

I put my hand to his cheek, his stubble rough against my palm.

He twisted, kissing the inside of my wrist, then moved lower, taking my knees and pushing them apart.

His warm breath tickled my skin before he kissed my thigh. "Has anyone ever done this to you?"

"No," I confessed. High school boyfriend Seth and I had only been together twice. Both times had been nervous and awkward and we'd focused more on the deed than foreplay.

Mateo dragged his tongue through my slit.

I gasped, nearly coming off the bed.

His hands kept me pinned and he hummed a word I couldn't quite make out, but it sounded a lot like *mine.*

Every fleeting thought left my mind as Mateo fluttered his tongue on my clit. There was nothing in the world but his mouth and this pleasure. God, I loved his mouth. I hadn't spent enough time appreciating his mouth.

I panted and writhed as he lapped at my center. My whole body trembled, my toes curling into the bedding. The peak came so fast that my orgasm surprised me. One minute I was on Mateo's bed, the next I was in the stars.

He licked me relentlessly as I pulsed. He drew out the release for what felt like hours, until finally, the white spots in my vision cleared and I came back to earth.

"Delicious." He wore a smirk as he stood from the bed, like he'd just won a prize. Then he stripped out of his jeans, setting himself free.

I propped up on an elbow and my mouth watered at the sight of his cock, long and thick.

"You're…" Holy God. Definitely different than High School Seth.

Mateo went to the nightstand to retrieve a condom, rolling it on his length. Then he climbed on top of me, settling into the cradle of my hips.

He kissed my neck, whispering those lips against my pulse until I was trembling again. There was an ache in my core, a need to be filled, the desire so strong it was like that first orgasm hadn't even happened.

"Vera." He pushed the hair away from my face, then lined up at my entrance. "Close your eyes."

I shook my head. I'd spent years memorizing Mateo's expressions. This one had never been mine. Now that it was, I wasn't missing out. So I kept my gaze locked on his, taking in the midnight blue of his eyes, as he brought us together.

I moaned, stretching around his length.

"Fuck, you feel so good." His Adam's apple bobbed as he swallowed.

That sexy throat. I leaned up and dragged my tongue across that bump.

Mateo groaned and eased out only to thrust in again, this time rooting deep.

I whimpered, moving beneath him as he brought us together, over and over. His strokes were measured. Controlled. His eyes fluttered closed, his jaw flexing like he was holding back.

Next time, I wanted him to lose control. I wanted him to be real and raw and unrestrained. But tonight, he fucked me slow.

Thrust after thrust, he rocked me to the edge.

I came on a gasp, my heart thundering as I exploded. Pulse after pulse, this orgasm put the first to shame. It was like shattering into a million pieces and when those pieces came together again, I was someone new.

Mateo's. I was Mateo's.

"Fuck, Vera." He gritted his teeth, holding back for a moment. Then he came on a roar into his pillow.

We were both entirely spent and boneless when he collapsed on top of me. I savored his weight, breathing in his scent, until he rolled to his back, taking me with him as he positioned me on his chest.

Below my cheek, his heart was hammering.

He brushed an errant lock of hair away from my cheek before finally shifting us apart.

While he went to the bathroom to deal with the condom, I hugged a pillow, fighting sleep.

When Mateo returned, he curled his body around mine, holding me close. And just as I was drifting into dreamland, his lips brushed the shell of my ear as he whispered, "Mine."

CHAPTER 21

MATEO

Birds chirped beyond my bedroom windows, drawing me from sleep. I stretched my arms wide, and buried my face in a pillow, smelling Vera's sweet scent on the sheets.

I reached for her but the other side of the bed was empty. As I pushed up on an elbow, a sunbeam hit me right in the eyes. Damn, that was a bright sun. Last night's storm must have passed.

What time was it? I twisted to look at the clock on my nightstand. Eight o'clock. I'd slept two hours longer than normal. Allie rarely let me sleep past six.

Allie. "Shit."

I ripped the sheets from my legs and flew out of bed. My boxer briefs were on the floor, stuck in my jeans from where I'd shoved them off last night. I dragged both on, not bothering with my zipper, and bolted for the door.

The moment I turned the knob, I heard Allie's soft giggle. The smell of coffee and bacon hit my nose, and when I searched the house, I found my girls together in the kitchen.

Vera had Alaina on her hip. The two of them were staring out the window over the sink.

"Tee." Allie pointed.

"Yes, that's a tree. What color is it?"

"Geen." Someday, Allie would be able to say her *r*s. I hated that day already.

"And what color is the sky?"

"Boo."

"Good job, Jellybean." Vera kissed Allie's cheek. "Do you know what sound a dog makes?"

"Woof woof."

"That's right."

They smiled at each other, and my hand came to my heart.

After last night, there was no going back with Vera. She wasn't just under my skin, she'd burrowed down to my bones, infusing the marrow each passing day. The way she was with Allie was... a gift.

For the first time in her life, Allie had someone like a mother. I patted my pocket for my phone to take a picture, but it was empty. It must have fallen on the floor at some point last night. So I stared, committing the moment to memory, wishing I could bottle it up for Allie to revisit when she was older.

I watched them run through barnyard animal noises. A cat. A chicken. A sheep. A cow. Every sound was followed by a quiet laugh.

No matter what else happened today, it would be a good day.

"What sound does a pig make?" Vera asked.

Allie snorted. Not an oink. A snort.

A snort that sounded a lot like the one Vera made when she laughed too hard.

I hadn't taught Allie to snort. Vera must have. Was it possible to love someone this early in a relationship?

Though I guess we weren't exactly new, not in a lot of ways. Vera had been a part of my life for years. A part of Allie's too.

We were just starting down a different path.

And there was no looking back.

"Daddy!" Allie spotted me first. She squirmed so Vera would set her down, then her feet pounded across the floor as she raced over and into my arms.

"Morning, Sprout." I kissed her temple and pushed her hair off her face as I carried her to the kitchen. "How are my girls?"

Allie let out a string of words, something about Vera and eggs and juice.

And Vera blushed, trying to hide her rosy cheeks with her coffee mug.

God, I hoped that blush didn't fade. I hoped that twenty years from now, she blushed just as often and kept giving me that sweet, shy smile.

"Hi." I took her chin, tilting her face up. Then I brushed a kiss to her lips, my tongue darting out for a quick taste.

"Hi."

"Sorry I slept in. I haven't done that in, well… two years."

"Daddy, dow." Allie kicked her legs to be set free.

She raced off like a rocket for the toys I'd cleaned up last night. The toys I'd have to clean up again tonight.

"I hope you don't mind, but I cooked breakfast." Vera nodded to the stove, where a frying pan was out with scrambled eggs and bacon. "Allie was hungry."

"Not at all." I hauled her into my arms, her hair tickling my naked chest. "What are you doing today?"

"I have to work at ten."

"For how long?"

"Until closing."

Damn. So much for spending a day together. "All right."

"I should actually get going so I can make it home to shower and change, then get to town."

"Drive safe. The gravel roads get slick when they're wet." The warning was pointless. Vera drove exactly like my father: five miles under the speed limit and with hands placed firmly on ten and two.

I kissed her perfect mouth, then stole her coffee mug, taking a sip as she walked to the door.

She pulled on her shoes. "Bye, Allie."

"Ve-wa, you go?" Outrage contorted her little face.

The feeling was mutual.

"Sorry. I have to work."

"Oh." Allie's pout was short-lived. It disappeared a second later when she picked up a doll to brush its hair.

Damn, I regretted sleeping in. She opened the door and stepped outside before I was ready to say goodbye. "See you later."

"Bye." She smiled and jogged down the porch stairs.

I leaned against the doorway, the air cold against my naked chest, and watched as Vera got in her car. Then, with the brake lights glowing red because, like Dad, she'd ride those brakes so hard they'd need to be replaced every year, she retreated down the mountain.

With a sigh, I turned inside and went about my day, starting with a breakfast that wasn't cereal for a change. Then Allie and I got dressed in muck boots and old jeans to go outside and work on the sunken firepit I was building out back.

Allie jumped in puddles while I arranged blocks for the retaining wall. And when we were both soaked, her with water and me with sweat, I went inside to make peanut butter and jelly sandwiches for lunch.

As the afternoon passed, I checked the clock too. I picked up the house, let Allie mess it up, then picked it up again. Restless energy made it impossible for me to sit and read or watch TV.

Would it be too clingy to visit Vera at Eden Coffee? Probably. Yes. *Damn it.*

Another rainstorm brewed during Allie's nap, thwarting any plans to go outside and keep working, so I took a shower and put on clean clothes. And by the time five o'clock rolled around, two hours until Vera would be off work, I'd had enough of my own damn house.

So I loaded Allie into my truck and we set off for town to have an early dinner at Knox's restaurant.

Knuckles was on the first floor of The Eloise Inn. Two family businesses, one owned by my brother, the other my sister, that were the heart of downtown Quincy. And across the street, the other piece of my hometown's heart, Eden Coffee.

I wasn't going to visit that little green building. Yet. We'd probably go after dinner.

The restaurant was busy for a Sunday night. Though these days, it was always busy. Knox's food had a chokehold on tourists and locals alike.

Once the busy summer season started, there'd be no popping in for a quick bite unless I wanted to sit in the kitchen. Every table would be full from open to close. But even then, I didn't go often without Knox's cooking. My family took pity on my pathetic culinary skills, and Knox would swing out *extra* from Knuckles to the cabin.

There was never extra. But I think he worried Allie would come to prefer the blue box macaroni and cheese over his homemade version.

The hostess seated us at a booth in the back corner of the restaurant, a place where Allie could bounce around and not disturb other patrons. After leaving a coloring menu and crayons for my daughter, she went to get our drinks and let Knox know we were here.

My brother came out with flour dusting the sleeve of his black T-shirt. A dish rag hung from his back jeans pocket.

"Hey." Knox clapped me on the shoulder, then bent and snagged Allie from the booth for a hug. "How's my Allie girl?"

She giggled as he blew a raspberry on her neck. Then she pointed to the crayons, prattling off their colors.

He set her down, sitting in the space beside her while she went wild coloring. Her tongue stuck out of the side of her mouth as she fisted a crayon, scribbling over the kids' menu.

Those were Memphis's contribution to the restaurant. Since she'd come into my brother's life, they'd not only added coloring pages for kids at Knuckles, but the number of options on the kids' menu had doubled.

"Didn't think you'd be working tonight," I told him.

"I'm trying to put in as many hours as I can before the baby is born. And Memphis wanted a special hot dog and movie night with the boys."

Their daughter was due any day now. They were naming her Annie, after Mom. I liked that we'd have an Annie and an Allie. I hoped their similarities wouldn't end with their names and that they'd become friends, not just cousins. We all wanted our kids to be close.

"Let me know what I can do to help," I told him. "Whatever you guys need."

Knox and Memphis had come to my rescue more than a few times when Allie was a newborn. They'd done more than just show up with meals too. Not long after I'd brought Allie home from Alaska, Knox had hung out at the cabin one afternoon just so I could take a nap. And whenever I was in a bind for a babysitter, Memphis was right behind Mom in line to volunteer.

"So how are things going?" he asked. "Lyla mentioned you're teaching Vera how to fly."

News didn't take long to travel through our family, did it? "Yeah."

"How's it going with you two?"

It would be easy to blow him off. But both Griffin and Knox had always been more than just my brothers. Because they were so much older, I'd always looked up to them. Tried to be like them.

They were good men. They were good husbands and fathers.

And if I wanted to be like them, maybe all I needed to do was ask for a bit of help.

"I don't want to fuck it up with Vera." For myself. And for Allie. I didn't want to mess up the chance for her to have someone like that in her life.

"Then don't fuck it up," Knox said.

I laughed. "That easy?"

"Yeah, brother. It's that easy. Just love her. The rest takes care of itself."

Just love her.

Simple. It sounded too simple.

"If you can't do that," Knox said, "let her go."

No. Not an option. Not after last night.

Just love her.

Could I do that?

I cared about Vera. But love? It was too soon. Too early. But the potential was there, like a flower waiting to bloom. Waiting for when the time was right.

"Thanks," I told Knox.

"Anytime." He kissed Allie again, then tapped the menu. "I'm making myself a cheeseburger quesadilla for dinner. Want one?"

"Hell yes." It was my favorite concoction of his and something he refused to put on the Knuckles menu. It was for special guests only.

"Allie, do you want chicken strips and french fries?"

"Yep."

He ruffled her hair, then slid from the booth, disappearing to the kitchen as the waitress brought over our drinks.

Allie nibbled on her food. She was a good eater, albeit slow, and by the time we made it out of Knuckles, the lights were off at Eden Coffee and Vera's car was already gone from the alley.

So I headed to the ranch, bypassing Mom and Dad's house to park behind the Honda. Then I carried Allie to the loft and knocked on Vera's door.

She answered with wild hair and a massive, wet stain on the front of her Eden Coffee shirt. "Hi."

"Hey." I nodded to the stain. "You okay?"

"I was locking up and spilled my coffee." She gave herself an eye roll and opened the door so we could come inside. "Not my most graceful moment."

"Ah. Want to take a shower? Or just change your shirt before we leave?"

Vera blinked. "Uh, where are we going?"

"Home."

"Oh. Um, I didn't... I have to study tonight."

"Okay."

She didn't move. Why wasn't she moving?

"Vera, get your stuff."

"But you just said okay."

"Okay, as in you can study at home. Allie sleeps best in her bed. And I want you in mine."

Her cheeks pinkened.

It never got old.

CHAPTER 22

MATEO

Thunder shook the house, waking me from a dead sleep. I lifted my head, holding my breath as I listened for Allie's cry. But other than the clatter of rain on the roof and the grumble of lingering thunder, the cabin was quiet.

So I sagged into my pillow, stretching for Vera on the other side of the bed.

The empty bed.

This time when I sat up, it was all the way. "Vera."

My room was empty.

I tugged the covers away to slide out of bed, swiping my sweats off the floor from where she'd stripped them off me earlier. With the waistband hanging low on my hips, I searched for her in the living room and kitchen.

"Vera," I murmured.

Nothing.

What the fuck? Had she left?

After I'd picked her up from the loft, we'd driven to the cabin. She'd wanted to bring her car—I'd driven at turtle speed so she wouldn't feel rushed.

Then she'd studied while I'd gone through Allie's bedtime routine. When my daughter had been tucked into her bed, sound asleep, I'd waited for Vera to finish with her schoolwork.

The minute she'd closed her textbook, I'd picked her up from the chair and carried her to my bed. While the rain poured outside, I'd worshiped her body.

It was the best damn sex of my life. She came alive under my hands. She was shy but playful. She let me take control, let me teach her what I liked. It was easy to learn what sent her over the edge. The noises she made... just thinking about her moans made my cock twitch.

So where the hell was she? I walked to the door, peering outside. Her car was still parked beside my truck, its paint glossy from the rain. I turned, dragging a hand through my hair.

Allie's bedroom door was cracked.

I padded across the house, peering inside my daughter's room. And there was Vera, wearing my T-shirt and standing at the window, staring into the night. One arm was wrapped around her middle. The other clutched the wooden rail of Allie's toddler bed.

She gasped when I came to stand behind her, arms wrapping around her shoulders.

"Sorry," I whispered. "Thought you heard me. You okay?"

She kept her eyes trained forward, her pale face reflected in the glass. "I don't like thunderstorms."

Like the heavens had heard her whisper, lightning flashed and then a crack of thunder boomed, threatening to cleave the sky.

Vera's entire body jerked. The hold she had on Allie's bed tightened into a death grip.

She was in here, standing guard, wasn't she? She was protecting my daughter from the storm.

My heart split down the middle. One half, so fucking full that she loved Alaina enough to act as her guardian. The other half, devastated for the terrified woman in my arms.

I didn't know the whole story about the day her life had

changed, the day her father had murdered her family. I wasn't even sure if Vance and Lyla knew that whole story. But I'd bet every penny to my name that it had stormed that night.

"Come on, Peach." I peeled her fingers off Allie's bed and forced her away from the window. Then I swept her into my arms, cradling her against my chest as I carried her back to bed.

Beneath the covers, I curled my body around hers, my chest to her back. With our legs twined, I held her so tight that when the next thunderclap rattled the house, I absorbed her flinch.

"Breathe," I whispered into her hair.

"I hate this."

It was agony, hearing the pain in her voice. How had she handled storms before now? Alone? The image of her huddled in a corner, shaking, popped into my mind. Even in my arms, she trembled.

"What can I do?" I asked.

"My dad used to talk me through them. He'd make up a story or sing a stupid song. Anything to keep my mind off the thunder and lightning."

He'd comforted her through thunderstorms, even though the reason for her terror was a nightmare of his making?

Unless the trauma from her past wasn't tied to a thunderstorm and her fear was rooted in some other horrific event. Unless I'd gotten it wrong. Maybe these storms had been awful when she'd lived with him in the woods.

The only way to know was if Vera opened up. It wasn't happening tonight, not when she was locked up tight.

There was a chance she'd never share the details of her past.

But maybe it was time to share mine.

"How much did Lyla or my parents tell you about Alaina's mother?"

This time when Vera jerked, it had nothing to do with the weather. She twisted in my hold, easing away just enough that she could see my face. "Not much."

"You never asked?"

She shook her head. "No."

"Why not?"

"I wanted to hear it from you. If you wanted to tell me."

Spoken like someone with secrets she didn't want to share. Secrets she'd been pressured to share. But secrets she'd keep until she was ready to reveal them on her terms.

"Do you want the short or the long story?"

"Long."

"Long it is." I hadn't given my parents and siblings the choice. They'd received the condensed version. But I wanted Vera to have it all, start to finish. To be the one person on earth who didn't get the shortcut because it was hard to discuss.

Vera snuggled closer as a flash came outside. But when the thunder rumbled, this time she only tensed.

"I was living in Alaska when I met Allie's mom. I was working out of Fairbanks, flying supplies to remote areas of the state."

Most of the friends I'd made were other pilots who worked for tourist companies. They'd fly people around to see bears or glaciers. Drop groups off at a remote cabin to fish for a week, then go back to pick them up.

My buddies had flown people while I'd transported cargo. My employers were an older couple who'd owned their company and small fleet for over twenty years. They reminded me a lot of my parents. Completely in love, even after having been married for decades. Hardworking. Honest. Kind.

When I'd put out feelers for jobs in Alaska, I hadn't known what to expect. It was lucky that they'd called me first, that we'd hit it off so well on our initial phone call. And when they'd offered me a job to fly one of their cargo planes, I'd accepted and moved my life to Fairbanks.

"I liked the town," I told Vera. "It was similar to Quincy. A little bigger."

Tourism was a driving force in the local economy, and for the most part, the people were friendly and welcoming.

"My friends and I would go hiking in the summer on an off day. We'd meet up for drinks at our favorite bar. That's where I met Madison."

"That was her name?" Vera asked. "Allie's mother?"

I nodded. "She had blond hair and hazel eyes. Her nose turned up at the tip. Allie looks nothing like her."

Because she was mine. Even if Madison's family hadn't insisted on a paternity test, there wasn't a doubt in my mind. One look at Alaina and those Eden genes shined bright.

Vera curled closer as the thunder continued, seeking comfort and offering it too as she listened.

"Our relationship was casual. We'd cross paths and hook up for a night. That went on for a few months. Then the occasional night together became not so occasional. Every weekend turned into three or four times a week. Then we were seeing each other every night. And I just… fell for her."

It was the first time I'd fallen for a woman. I'd never seen the end coming. No matter how many times I replayed our relationship, I still couldn't spot the warning signs. There'd been no hints that she was growing tired of my company. She'd appeared just as committed. Just as addicted.

"One night, I showed up at her house, thinking it would be like any other night. We'd have dinner. Hang out for a while. Go to bed. She answered the door and stared at me like I was a stranger. Wouldn't even let me inside. Told me it was fun but she didn't want anything beyond sex."

The way she'd stared at me, like I'd meant nothing. I'd never felt used before that moment.

"It was..." I blew out a long breath. "Shocking. I cared for her."

"Did you love her?"

"I don't know," I murmured. "Maybe. Too much has happened since. Too much that's tainted what might have been love. Does that make sense?"

"Perfect sense."

Did Vera feel that way about someone? Her father, maybe?

I buried my nose in her hair, breathing in that floral and apple scent. It made telling this story easier. It made me realize how much Madison and I had been missing. How we never would have worked, despite my best efforts.

Because I was meant to be here in this bed. With Vera.

"I came home the week after Madison ended it. Quit my job. Gave up my apartment. I hadn't planned to leave Alaska, but I realized just how alone I was up there. My friends were fine, but they weren't my family. I got homesick for Montana. Alaska is beautiful. But it's not home."

So I'd returned to the ranch and picked up exactly where I'd left off.

Maybe I still wasn't sure what exactly I'd been searching for in Alaska. But when I'd come home, my expectations had changed. I'd realized that working for my parents and siblings was better than being alone.

"I helped Griffin on the ranch. Pitched in at Mom and Dad's. Did whatever Eloise needed at the hotel." Especially after the shooting that had happened in the lobby. She'd had a hard time coming back to work after a disgruntled ex-employee had tried to kill her. Would have killed her, had Jasper not jumped in front of the bullet.

"That first year back, I was busy. Besides work, there was a lot to be done on the cabin. I put on a new roof and expanded the clearing. If I got a whim, I'd go fly. And then Lyla got attacked." Vera's father had nearly strangled my sister. He'd let her go, but not without leaving bruises all over her throat. "We all searched for him. Did you know that?"

Vera stiffened. "Mateo, I—"

"Later." We'd talk about that incident and her father later. She nodded.

That had all happened before Vera had escaped and shown up in Idaho on Vance's doorstep.

She'd been in Montana then, hadn't she? She'd lived in the mountains where she still loved to hike. Did she ever revisit their old campsites? Had she found him already? Was she meeting him on her hikes?

Curious as I was, this wasn't the time. Not as the loudest blast of thunder shook the walls and the rain pelted the tin roof.

Vera jerked, nuzzling closer. I listened for Allie again. If this storm kept up, it would wake her too. But there wasn't a sound.

"A buddy of mine, another pilot, was getting married that June, so I flew back for a quick weekend trip to go to the wedding. After the reception, I went to my favorite old bar for a drink. Madison was there. We hooked up." Try as I might, I'd still cared for her. Still wanted her. "I knew the score."

And she'd made sure to remind me the minute I'd climbed out of her bed to deal with the condom.

A condom that had broken.

"I came home after the wedding. Put her out of my mind for good. Until months later, when I was about to come to a family dinner, and got a call from one of Madison's friends. We'd met before. She'd go with Madison to the bar from time to time. I'm not even sure how she got my number, but I'm glad she had it."

When she'd told me her name, I hadn't even remembered who it was.

"Mateo?"

"Yes."

"This is Leesa."

"Who?"

"Leesa. Madison's friend."

"When I left Alaska after that wedding, I hadn't expected to hear from Madison again. We were done. She was done. I'd already moved." I'd given her up.

Maybe that had been my mistake. Maybe I should have stuck around. So much would be different if I'd stayed.

Madison might still be alive.

"Leesa told me to get to Alaska. Right away. That Madison was... gone. I didn't understand it at first. I thought she was asking me to get there to help find her, like a search and rescue."

But when Leesa had started crying, when she'd said that Madison was dead, I'd dropped to my knees on the cabin's kitchen floor.

"Madison started hemorrhaging after Allie was born. The doctors couldn't stop it. She died in the delivery room."

"Oh, God," Vera gasped. "Mateo. I'm so sorry."

My throat was thick, the words hard to choke out. "She didn't tell me. Nine months and she never told me she was pregnant."

I took a minute, breathing through the tightness in my chest. Madison's death had been a tragedy. But everything else had been a betrayal. It was harder to talk about than the rest and was the part that didn't make the story short.

"Allie was two days old when Leesa called me."

"Wait. What?" Vera pushed back, eyes wide.

I nodded. "Madison's family was going to take Allie. Only a few people knew I was her father, and they decided after Madison died, they weren't going to tell me. Because Madison was never going to tell me. Leesa thought it was wrong. So she went behind their backs and made that phone call."

Thank fuck. I wouldn't have known my daughter otherwise. I'd have missed out on her entire life.

"When I showed up in Alaska and marched into the hospital, well… it was a mess. Madison's family refused to acknowledge me. They said I wasn't Allie's father. I had to fight to get a paternity test."

"Seriously?" Vera's eyes bugged out. "How could they do that?"

"They wanted her." I shrugged. "I'm just glad I was able to make it there so fast. Before they let anyone take Allie home."

If not for my own plane, I wouldn't have made it. That had been another harrowing flight, riddled with nerves and shock and adrenaline. Exactly the mental headspace they teach pilots to avoid.

"When the dust settled, after the paternity test results came in, the hospital released Allie to me. Madison's parents were furious. Threatened to go to court for custody. I knew I needed to get the hell out of Alaska. But even then, I promised they could have a relationship with her. That they were welcome in Quincy at any time."

"Have they ever visited?"

"Not once." No visits. No birthday cards. No Christmas presents. No phone calls. They were as dead to Allie as her mother. "I haven't spoken to them since the hospital."

"Idiots," Vera scoffed. "They don't even know what they're missing."

"Yeah." I breathed her in, a smile ghosting my lips. God, I loved that she was mad. That she knew how special Allie was. That she'd fight to stay in my daughter's life.

This woman. She was spinning everything around, like I'd been wearing a shirt backward for years and she'd finally made me turn it right.

"Do you think Madison would have ever told you?" Vera asked. "About Allie?"

"I don't know," I murmured. "I spent a lot of time with Leesa at the hospital. She was the one who'd brought Madison to the hospital when she'd gone into labor. She'd stuck around after Madison died. When I asked her the same question, she just stayed quiet. I think she wanted to give her friend the benefit of the doubt."

Vera gave me a sad smile. "Understandable."

"Someday, Allie will ask about her mom. I hope by then, I'll know what to say."

"You will." She lifted her hand to my cheek. "Thanks for telling me."

Thunder boomed again, but Vera didn't so much as blink. She kept her eyes locked on mine, and when I bent to take her mouth, she sank into the kiss.

My sweats were stripped to the floor once again. The T-shirt she was wearing was dragged over her head. And when I slid inside her tight body, the world faded away. The storm. The past. All that mattered was Vera.

When we broke apart hours later, limbs tangled and skin sweat-slicked, the thunder's roar had faded to a rumble. The wind had stopped whipping against the walls. The rain was slow and steady, white noise that followed us both into sleep.

The next morning, when I woke to find Vera in the kitchen with Allie again, the sky was blue. The sun was shining.

The weather today, inside and out, was clear and a million.

CHAPTER 23

VERA

Lyla nudged my elbow with hers as we stood behind the counter at Eden Coffee. "So... flying lessons?"

I laughed. "How long have you been wanting to talk about this?"

"Since Mateo came in here on Saturday."

"Ah." I nodded. "I'm proud of you for waiting four whole days."

"It took every ounce of my willpower."

Part of me wanted to keep it all inside. Whatever was happening with Mateo was... unbelievable. Incredible. If I talked about it, would I jinx it? But at some point, everyone in his family was going to know that I'd spent the last four nights in his bed—if they didn't already.

I had enough secrets to keep. Mateo didn't need to be another one.

"I sort of stood him up on Saturday," I said. "He wasn't very happy about it."

"So that's why he was in such a bad mood. Well, he was overdue for an ego check," she teased. "He hasn't been stood up enough in his life."

"It wasn't my finest moment. I felt bad and apologized. We talked it out and I guess... we're together? I don't know. I've had a crush on him for so long that it still feels surreal. And it's moving so fast I haven't had time to really figure it out."

Mateo's plan to take it slow had been entirely discarded. If I wasn't working, I was at the cabin. Last night when I'd suggested I sleep in my own bed at the loft for a change, Mateo had hidden my keys so I couldn't leave.

I'd found them in the freezer this morning.

"Tell him to slow down," Lyla said.

"I don't want to."

She giggled. "Okay, then buckle up and enjoy the ride."

God, what a ride it had been. Was it possible to become a sex addict in just four nights? Because I was hooked on Mateo. I realized now why he'd been worried that sex would become the focus. It was quickly becoming an obsession.

He worshiped my body and made me feel cherished. Craved. He never made me feel naive. He loved discovering and claiming any firsts. My pleasure was his priority, his reward, and he did not disappoint.

But while I loved having him inside my body, our nights together were more than just trading orgasms. There was intimacy in every touch. In every moment of sleep.

Whenever I rolled to the other side of the bed, he'd drag me back to his. I slept pressed against his side, wrapped in his strong arms, with his heat surrounding me and his nose buried in my hair.

He touched me constantly. A brush of his knuckles against mine when we crossed paths in the living room. A tuck and untuck of my hair behind an ear when we were at the dinner table. Little caresses that were playful and sweet but promised there'd be more as soon as Allie was tucked in her bed.

"You're happy?" Lyla asked. I loved her for the concern etched on her beautiful face.

"I'm happy."

She didn't need to worry about my heart. Down deep, I

knew Mateo wouldn't break it.

He wouldn't have chased me otherwise. If he wasn't in this to stay, he wouldn't have started an us in the first place. Not just for my sake. But Allie's. He wouldn't let a woman into her life who might disappear.

"When you get a chance, maybe give Vance a call," Lyla said. "He's been worried since Willie's."

"He's always worried."

She gave me a sad smile. "Can you blame him?"

"No." After everything, if I were Vance, I'd be worried too. "I'll call him later. See if he wants to meet for lunch."

"He'd like that." She pulled me in for a quick sideways hug, then sighed as she surveyed the display case and its empty spaces. "Looks like I need to get busy. What should I make? Muffins? Scones?"

"Carrot cake muffins?"

"With cream cheese frosting. Absolutely." But before she could head for the kitchen to bake, the door opened, the shop's bell a cheerful chime.

A man wearing a pair of pressed slacks, a crisp white shirt and a black blazer strode across the room. His blond hair was parted in a severe line above his left eyebrow. His gait was unhurried, but something about him made the hair on the back of my neck rise.

A gust of cold air and sharp energy accompanied him as he approached the counter.

I stiffened as he smiled. That was a wolf's smile.

Lyla must have noticed it too. She didn't move as he stopped in front of us. "What can we get for you?"

"Coffee. Cream and sugar."

"Of course." She gave him a fake smile, then nodded for me to get his coffee. Like she didn't want me anywhere near this counter. "Anything else?"

His gaze shifted to me. He stared for too long, unblinking

as he took in my hair and face. "Vera Gallagher?"

My stomach dropped.

He was a cop, wasn't he? Given the suit, probably a federal agent.

I hadn't looked closely enough at his torso when he'd walked inside, but I'd bet my paycheck there was a holster and sidearm beneath that blazer.

What was he doing here? What did he want? My heart was beating too fast. My palms felt clammy, but I held my chin high and gave him a saccharine smile. "Yes? I'm Vera Gallagher. Can I help you?"

He held out a hand, not to shake mine, but to hand over the crisp, white business card I hadn't noticed him pull from his pocket. "Agent Ian Swenson."

An FBI agent. *Fuck.* My nerves spiked, but I kept my smile fixed, my shoulders relaxed, and tucked his card in the pocket of my apron. "What can I do for you, Agent Swenson?"

"I'd love a moment to talk."

"About?"

"Your father."

My stomach plummeted to my tennis shoes. "Oh. Um, well, obviously I'm working."

"I'll wait." That wolf's smile widened.

I hated him already.

"Let me get your coffee," I said, holding up a finger. Then I moved to the coffee cups, plucking a clean ceramic mug from the tray and filling it with black coffee. His eyes bored into me the entire time.

When I set his mug on the counter in front of him, I pointed to the station against the wall where he could find cream and sugar. "Two dollars."

His eyes narrowing, he took a money clip from his pocket and slapped a five-dollar bill on the counter. "Keep the change. I'll just find a table to wait."

As in, don't keep me waiting. *Asshole.*

I glared at his back as he carried his mug away.

Lyla leaned in close to whisper in my ear. "Have you met him before?"

"No." That was not the agent assigned to my dad's case. That guy had been older and shorter. I'd met him in Idaho two years ago. Even after Vance and I had moved away from Coeur d'Alene to Quincy, I'd wondered if he'd follow me here. If he'd check in on me from time to time.

But I hadn't heard so much as a whisper from the FBI in two years.

Either this Agent Swenson was here to ask questions about the past. Or he was here to break some horrific news.

Maybe they'd found Dad. Maybe he'd mentally cracked, hurt someone again and finally been caught. Maybe he hadn't been in the woods on Saturday and my imagination was just playing tricks on me. Maybe Dad was alive but locked in a jail cell.

"I'm calling Vance." Lyla fished her phone from her apron, but before she could make the call, I put my hand on her wrist.

I shook my head, gaze locked on Agent Swenson's shoulders as he walked to a table. "Let me find out what he wants first."

If Vance rushed down to the cafe, he'd take over this discussion. Maybe Swenson would see it as Vance simply trying to protect me. Or maybe he'd think we both had something to hide.

Lyla's eyebrows came together but she nodded. "Talk loud. I'll eavesdrop."

Swenson took the table closest to the counter, probably because he wanted to eavesdrop too.

I rounded the counter and took a chair opposite his.

He relaxed into his seat and kicked a leg up over his knee, like he was here to talk about sports or the weather.

He swirled a straw in his coffee, trying to appear unhurried and carefree. But his muddy hazel eyes betrayed him. They were locked on mine with an intensity that almost made me squirm.

Almost, but not quite.

"You want to talk about my father." I leaned my forearms on the table. "What about him?"

"Have you heard from him?"

"You mean like a phone call or weekend visit? No. I haven't seen my father in over two years."

"He hasn't made contact with you?"

"Why would he?"

"You're his only surviving daughter." He could have just said daughter. But he had to add those other words. *Only surviving.* It was a knife, opening the wound of my sisters' deaths.

This bastard could rot.

"Is there a point to this visit, Agent Swenson?"

"I'm new on this case. The previous agent retired."

Shit. I'd liked the previous agent. He'd been conveniently scarce. Why did I have the feeling that Swenson was about to make my life miserable?

"According to his notes, it had been a while since he checked in with you. Last you spoke was in Idaho, correct?"

"Yes." Back when Vance was managing the authorities and the press. Maybe I should have let Lyla call him down.

"He didn't realize you'd moved to Montana," Swenson said.

"Was I supposed to run that by him first?"

"No."

Silence stretched between us as he sipped his coffee, eyes never leaving mine.

Intimidation was his go-to tactic, wasn't it? He was an arrogant cop who thought he could frighten a woman. Asshole.

I wasn't obligated to talk. To anyone. So I sat perfectly still, hands clasped in my lap, and let Swenson stare.

Was there more to this visit? Or was it really just an introduction? An assessment? Why, after all this time, was the FBI in Montana? Why now?

If they'd arrested Dad, I would have heard about it, right? Or Swenson would have mentioned it already. Vance or Winn would have probably heard too.

The longer we sat and stared, the longer this visit felt tactical. Swenson wasn't here to deliver news. He was here for information. His gaze was too assessing. Too suspicious. Too curious.

Exactly what I didn't need in my life.

The door's jingle sounded, drawing my attention, and a sweet voice echoed through the room.

"Ve-wa!" Allie raced across the cafe, her feet unable to keep up with her body. She crashed on her hands and knees, but shoved herself back up and kept on running.

"Hey, Jellybean." I stood from my chair in time to scoop her up and kiss her cheek, then turned as Mateo walked over.

He had his attention locked on Agent Swenson. When he finally met my gaze, a thousand questions lingered behind those blue eyes.

"Hey, Peach." Mateo pulled me in for a kiss on the cheek. "Hi."

"What's going on?"

"Nothing." I waved off Swenson, dismissing him like the pest he was. "What are you guys doing?"

"Thought we'd come visit."

The scrape of chair legs from the table had us both turning as Swenson stood, his coffee mug now empty. He wore an arrogant smirk as he rounded the table. "You've got my card, Vera."

"I sure do." I patted my apron's pocket.

Swenson whistled as he walked to the door, stepping outside and onto the sidewalk. Then he disappeared from view, looking like a man out for an afternoon stroll, not a snake in the grass.

I turned, finding Lyla's eyes waiting. When I gave her a single nod, she left the counter for the kitchen. To call Vance.

"Who was that?" Mateo asked.

Allie played with the ends of my ponytail, oblivious to the edge in his voice and the nervous breath I finally let loose.

"An FBI agent."

Mateo's jaw flexed. "What did he want?"

"To know if I've had any contact with my father."

"You left your father almost two years ago. And the FBI is just now getting around to a visit?" He sounded mad, like the system had failed me.

"He's new on the case," I told Mateo. And hopefully, like his predecessor, Swenson would give up as soon as he realized that, short of a miracle, he'd never find Cormac Gallagher. "I'm sure this visit was just protocol."

"Or maybe the FBI has finally decided it's time for justice. It's not right, Vera. That your dad is out there living without consequences after what he's done."

What Mateo thought Dad had done.

Yes, Dad was guilty of hurting Lyla. I'd always be angry at him for that. But for everything else?

If the FBI found Dad, there wouldn't be justice.

Dad had seen to that already.

God, what a mess. Was it too much to ask that I'd just be forgotten? That he'd be forgotten? Apparently so.

"Maybe you should call him," Mateo said. "The agent. Tell him everything you know. If he's new, he might have better luck at finding your father. Put him away for good."

The anger in his voice made my insides churn.

Mateo didn't know the whole truth. It didn't surprise me he was furious about what Dad had done to Lyla. I was upset about it too.

Dad wasn't innocent. But he wasn't guilty either.

Lyla cleared her throat, coming to stand at my side. She

smiled at her brother, let him kiss her cheek, then turned to me. And between us passed a silent exchange.

If I was in this with Mateo, if I was going to keep him in my life, my secrets couldn't stay hidden forever.

Whether I wanted to or not, one day soon, I'd have to tell him the truth.

I'd have to open that box.

CHAPTER 24

VERA

Guilt settled like a one-ton boulder in my gut as I tiptoed from Mateo's bedroom. He was sound asleep, his hair a disheveled mess like it was every morning. I eased the door closed and froze, breath held and ears straining for any noise.

I was quiet in the mornings when I woke up first, but I wasn't silent. Mateo never stirred as I made coffee or breakfast if Allie was hungry. It would be just my luck that today he'd wake up early too.

The house was still, not a sound came from beyond the door, so I eased backward and padded to Allie's room, peeking in to make sure she was sound asleep too.

Her hair, like her father's, was a wild mess of silky brown waves. Her lips were pursed, her eyelashes perfect crescents above her smooth cheeks.

I'd miss her this morning. I'd miss having alone time with her before Mateo woke up. But what I needed to do today couldn't wait.

On hushed footsteps, I snuck to the cabin's door and left as it clicked shut. With my keys in hand, I hurried across the porch, careful not to make a sound on the boards that creaked. And when I reached the last stair, I bounded to the dirt, jogging to my car in bare feet.

Robins tweeted in the morning light, greeting the dawn. A chill snaked down my spine as I climbed into my car and turned on the engine, eyes glued to the house, hoping like hell the door didn't whip open as I reversed away.

I didn't breathe until I was half a mile away. The pit in my stomach deepened with every minute. God, Mateo was going to be so pissed. My groan filled the car.

We hadn't talked about Agent Swenson last night. When I'd made it to the cabin after work, Allie had been throwing a fit about her bath so I'd helped Mateo get her ready for bed. And once she was asleep, our mouths had been used for anything but talking.

But I was only delaying the inevitable.

Mateo would need to know the truth about Dad. Just... not yet.

Even Vance had agreed we needed to be thoughtful about what and how we shared now that the FBI was in Quincy. He'd come to the coffee shop yesterday about five minutes after Mateo had left. Luckily, it had been a slow afternoon, so we'd been able to sit down and replay Swenson's visit.

Vance's theory was that Swenson was a young, cocky agent trying to prove himself. What better way to impress his superiors than to solve a cold case that would make a media splash?

I'd been in enough headlines to last a lifetime. In Quincy, I was just Vera. I wasn't *that* girl who'd survived *that* night.

Swenson would have to find a new case to crack because I refused to be in the news again. He'd find nothing in Montana. I'd make sure of it.

The sun's first rays crept over the mountain horizon as I drove off the ranch. By the time I made it to town, the sky was a kaleidoscope of blues and golds. This was Dad's favorite time of day. He always preferred the sunrise to sunset. He said there was nothing more hopeful than the light of dawn, a fresh start on a new day to move past yesterday's mistakes.

There was no such thing as moving on, especially for Dad. He'd forever be tied to his sins. Trapped by old horrors.

Maybe the same was true for me. Maybe it would never go away.

Maybe that was what we both deserved.

As the highway turned into Main Street, I slowed to a crawl, creeping toward The Eloise Inn. The hotel stood proudly as the focal point and tallest building in downtown Quincy. Most of the lights were off, guests still tucked into warm, plush beds.

But a few rooms had a golden glow from behind their drawn curtains, including the corner room on the third floor.

Agent Swenson's room.

Lyla had gone to the hotel yesterday to visit Eloise. While she was there, she'd found out which room was Swenson's.

An early riser. The clock on my dash showed it wasn't quite five.

I looped around the back of the hotel to the parking lot. Swenson's car, a simple black SUV with Washington plates, was in the second row. Its windshield was coated with dew. Lyla had gotten the make, model and plate number from Eloise too.

Good. He was still in the hotel.

So far, my morning was going to plan.

While Mateo had dozed soundly last night, I'd stared at the dark ceiling, unable to shut my mind off. I'd spent too many years living under a cloud of paranoia. Dad's. My own. My irrational fears had reached their peak around two.

I'd convinced myself that Swenson had been outside, staking out the cabin, waiting for me to lead him to Dad. So I'd decided that before I left for the mountains today, first, I'd make sure I wasn't being followed.

Vance said there was a slight risk that Swenson had

gotten a warrant for my cell phone history. That he could have surveillance on my location and know about my hikes. Maybe he'd even bugged my car. But Vance had also said there wouldn't be much probable cause for such extreme measures.

Yes, Dad was a fugitive. But the FBI had bigger cases than my father.

So as long as Swenson wasn't physically following me, there wasn't much likelihood he'd have a clue where I was going.

Relief came in a long breath and I aimed my car back to Main, putting Quincy in my rearview. I took the familiar roads through the countryside toward Sable Peak. Then, parking in the same place where I'd been leaving my car for weeks, I retrieved my pack from the trunk, secured it on my shoulders and started my climb.

The ground was slick with frost. The trees would keep the forest's floor shaded for another few hours. My breath fogged in white clouds that billowed behind me, and even though it was chilly, my muscles warmed. Sweat beaded at my temples.

I stayed on the trail for a mile before I veered off in the direction I'd taken on Saturday. The day I thought I'd spotted Dad.

Was he here? Was that why Swenson had come to Montana? Was it possible that Dad had been seen by a hiker? Maybe he'd gone into town for something critical, like first aid supplies, and someone had recognized his red hair and face.

It wasn't exactly easy for Dad to blend in with a six-inch scar running from eye to chin.

He'd earned it from a car accident of sorts. He'd been in his twenties, out for a run, and came across a kid playing basketball in his driveway. The ball had rolled into the street just as an oncoming car was passing by. Dad had watched as the kid chased his ball, oblivious to the danger. And so Dad had sprinted to the rescue, pushing the kid out of the way and taking the brunt of the hit.

I was proud of that scar. Even if the world thought he was evil, even if that scar only added to the illusion, my dad was a hero. To that boy he'd saved. And to me.

Off the trail, the hike was harder. I had to pick my way over rocks and branches, around bushes and trees. Dad had taught me how to hide footprints. When we'd been together, I'd jump over muddy patches. I'd walk on pine needles rather than dirt.

But today wasn't about hiding my tracks. Today was about speed, so I took the easiest path through the underbrush.

Another hour and my legs were straining, my lungs burned. But I kept pushing hard until I reached the spot I'd been Saturday.

I took a moment to regain my breath, fishing my water bottle from my pack for a drink. Then I cupped my hands around my mouth and let out a piercing whistle.

Like always, silence was my only reply.

My shoulders sagged. *Damn.*

Of course he wasn't out here. It was early. He was probably still wherever he'd made camp. And if he really was hiding from me, then he wouldn't stick around this area. Still, I had to try. This was as good of a place to start as any.

I took the pocket knife from my backpack, opening it more carefully this time. And I found a nearby tree, ready to make the carving I hadn't on Saturday. My initials with the date. Except just as I cut away a piece of loose bark, I hesitated.

What if Swenson came out here? He certainly didn't seem like the hiking type, not with his starched clothes and polished shoes, but he might surprise me. Finding my footprints was one thing. That would be easy enough to chalk up to a simple hike.

But a deliberate marking? I didn't need him stumbling upon a carving and deciding to stick around Montana for the foreseeable future.

So I closed my knife and tucked it away and, for good measure, whistled one more time.

"Are you out here?"

My mind knew the answer, even though my heart refused to believe it.

This was a foolish search by a foolish girl. Why couldn't I let this go? Why couldn't I just stop? Part of me wanted to keep going, keep looking. The day was young and I could cover a few more miles before I needed to turn back.

But the other part was so tired. So sick of these mountains. I could stay here alone. Or I could go back to the cabin and spend the day with Mateo and Allie.

I whistled.

Nothing.

I just wanted to go home.

On a sigh, I turned around, ready to hike back to the trail. But as I took my first step, I heard something different. Something not born from the woods.

A nearly inaudible whistle. The sound was so faint, it could have been a trick of the wind.

But my heart stopped, my entire body going still, as I listened.

More nothing.

It was probably just the wind. Maybe a strange bird. But just to be sure, I cupped my hands around my mouth for one last whistle, this one as loud as I could muster.

My pulse boomed so loudly in my ears that I barely heard the reply. But it was there, in the distance, a whistle just like mine.

"Oh my God. Dad!" I almost tripped on my next step but caught my balance. Then I ran, not uphill or deeper into the mountains, but in the direction from which I'd come, toward the trail. Maybe he'd come across my footprints in the frost. Maybe he'd followed me this way and was rushing to catch up.

I whistled again, my backpack bouncing on my shoulders as I hurried, a pace between a jog and a walk.

The replying whistle got louder. Clearer. Both of us moving in the right direction toward each other.

He was here. He had to be here. He was alive and coming for me.

"Dad!" I rounded a tree, jumped over an exposed root, then slowed to listen, my chest heaving.

The whistle. It was close.

I scanned the trees, searching past brush and branches. When the sound came again, I followed it to my right. My boots thudded on dirt and needles, sweat dripped down my spine, but I pushed harder. Faster. Until the whistle was so loud he had to be close.

I skirted a patch of thick underbrush, and there, standing in a gap between two thick evergreens, was the man who'd heard my call.

My heart stopped.

Mateo, blue eyes blazing with fury, stood with his arms crossed over his chest.

"What the fuck is going on, Vera?"

CHAPTER 25

MATEO

"Mateo, I—"

"Not yet, Vera." I stalked down the trail, careful not to go too fast so she could keep up.

We'd been walking for a while, probably a mile, maybe more, and though she was ready to talk, I was not. The fury coursing through my veins was a vicious beast, and I needed more time to put it on its leash.

What was she thinking? What the hell was going on?

I'd give her credit for a stealthy escape this morning. She'd been quiet. But not quiet enough.

I hadn't woken when she'd slipped out of bed or left the house. But that old Honda's engine didn't exactly purr. It had been enough to rouse me from sleep, and when I'd realized what was happening, I'd shot out of bed, making it to the front door just in time to see her taillights disappear.

By the time I'd gotten dressed, then woken up Alaina to change her diaper before loading her into the car, I hadn't known exactly where Vera might have gone, but I'd had a hunch. So I'd dropped Allie at Mom and Dad's place, grateful they were able to babysit, then hustled to Sable Peak, hoping like hell I'd find Vera on her hike.

Locating the Honda had been easy enough. But Vera?

I'd followed the trail, hoping I'd be able to outpace her and catch up. But damn it, she was fast. And then she'd abandoned the trail.

If not for all the mud, I would have missed the spot where she'd veered off the path. Luck had been on my side, and I'd spotted a footprint. They'd been few and far between, but I'd managed to head in the same direction.

She'd whistled. If not for that, I wouldn't have found her. I'd lost her trail and had been going in a different direction entirely when I'd heard the shrill noise in the distance. Then she'd yelled.

She'd yelled for her fucking father.

Deep down, I'd suspected this. That these hikes were tied to Cormac. But I didn't want to believe it. Was she searching for him? Or had she found him already? Maybe, if I'd waited a bit longer, I would have caught them together.

Fuck. Was she hiding him? Helping him? After all he'd done, how could she?

It was no coincidence that she'd come out here today, the morning after that FBI agent had arrived in Quincy. And instead of telling me about it, she'd just run away. Would she ever drop her guard and *talk* to me? Or would she always keep me in the dark?

My hands fisted and unfisted, and by the time we made it back to our vehicles, I was still really fucking pissed.

I dug my truck's keys from a pocket and unlocked the doors, opening the passenger side first. "Get in."

"But my car—"

"Can rust out here for all I care."

She frowned. "Mateo."

"Get. In."

"Don't be mad at me."

"Mad?" I scoffed. "You fucking scared me, Vera."

Her face blanched. "I'm sorry."

"Don't ever do that to me again. Don't ever leave without telling me where you're going. If something is wrong, talk. To. Me." I jabbed a finger into my chest with each word.

That was the real problem here. Not that she'd gone hiking alone, though I didn't like it. Not that she'd snuck out of bed and my house. If she kept holding these secrets, if she kept setting me apart, we'd never survive it.

"I'm sorry, Mateo."

The regret on her face eased some of my anger. "You're searching for him."

She nodded.

"Why?" There was venom in my question.

Vera swallowed hard. "He's my dad."

Yes, he was her dad. She loved him still, didn't she? After everything he'd done, she loved him. Had he brainwashed her or something? I didn't know how to deal with that. I didn't know how to deal with this. Hell, this was fucked up. Absolutely, incredibly fucked up.

How did I fix this? I dragged a hand through my hair. "Have you been seeing him?"

She shook her head. "No."

"But you've been looking for him. For how long?"

"Two years. Since we came back to Montana."

Two years? Well, I'd give Vera one thing. She was stubborn as hell.

Was that why she'd moved to Quincy with Vance? I'd assumed it was to stay close to Vance and Lyla. But she was really here to find her father, wasn't she?

"How do you know he's in Montana?"

"I don't but…" She dropped her gaze, eyes closing. "This is where we were living."

That, I knew. But it was only a fraction of the story, wasn't it? How exactly had she ended up in Idaho with Vance? What did my sister know that she wasn't telling us?

Whatever story Vera, Lyla and Vance had been spinning was probably bullshit. My sister had been lying to me, to all of us, for years.

It hurt. Our family was better than that. But I'd give Lyla the benefit of the doubt. I'd give her the courtesy she hadn't extended to me. If she'd lied, it had to have been for a good reason.

Probably for the sake of the woman at my side.

"Time for the truth, Peach. The whole truth."

Vera's shoulders sagged, like the weight of that truth was a heavy burden. When was she going to realize that she didn't need to carry it alone?

She walked to her car, climbing up on the Honda's hood. With her backpack stripped and resting behind her, she pulled her knees into her chest.

That familiar defensive position.

Someday, she'd learn she didn't need it. Not with me.

I sat on the hood beside her, the heels of my boots braced on the bumper. Then I gave her the minutes she needed to tear down the walls guarding the truth.

"Dad grew up in Alaska. He became a cop and when he moved to Idaho, he worked for a backcountry unit because he loved being outside. He always said that he was born out of time. That he would have loved to have been on the Lewis and Clark Expedition. He was into survivalist stuff, always researching how to make different snares or traps. He could look at any berry and tell you if it was poisonous or not. And he said that someday, he wanted to apply for that show *Alone*."

If Cormac had been a survivalist, no wonder they'd lived off the grid. There was no way an average person could stay alive. But if he had the skills? Yeah, he could live off the grid for a long damn time.

"I don't want to talk about that night." More walls. Walls that were not coming down, not today.

"All right."

"He didn't kill them."

My gaze whipped to her profile. What? Cormac was innocent? How was that possible?

Vera sat perfectly still, barely breathing, as she stared into nothingness. "My sisters. He didn't kill them."

Then who?

"But he did kill her." Vera's voice was ice.

Her.

Her mother. Norah Gallagher.

Cormac had killed her mother. Why?

Was it because Norah had killed Vera's twin sisters? Oh, fuck.

This wasn't a little secret. This was *the* secret.

Her mother had murdered her sisters. And for years, the world had believed Vera had drowned with them.

My brain struggled to rewrite everything I'd thought I'd known. Everything.

If Cormac had murdered her mother, he was far from harmless. But if her mother had killed her sisters, well... maybe he'd had a reason. What the fuck? What the hell had happened that night?

"Dad took me away," she said. "He loaded up everything he could in a hurry. His gear and guns. Clothes. Boots. Medicine. Not a lot of my stuff, not so much that people would notice my things missing, but enough. We stopped at an ATM for cash. I stayed out of sight. And then we left Idaho. We drove all night and made it to the Olympic National Forest before dawn. We ditched the truck at a gas station, then started walking. I lost track of time, so I'm not sure how long we went before he finally let us stop. That first year is kind of blurry."

Blurry? He'd taken her the night her mother had drowned her sisters. Yeah, that time would have been *blurry* for me too.

So Cormac had kept Vera with him. Why? He had to have

known how hard that lifestyle would be. Why hadn't he let her go and walked away?

Stupid question. A team of wild horses couldn't drag me away from Allie. And if he had murdered Norah, his choices were to run or go to prison. The former meant staying with Vera. Maybe he'd thought the best place for her was at his side. I couldn't exactly fault him for it.

Well, she wasn't brainwashed. That was something. She'd stayed with her dad because... he was her dad. Maybe not quite the villain I'd thought minutes ago.

But he shouldn't have taken her. He should have left her behind. Vance would have helped her. He could have gotten her into grief counseling and therapy.

Cormac had taken a traumatized teenager and isolated her from the world. He'd done it to keep her close. Because he hadn't wanted to lose her.

I wouldn't have wanted to part with Allie either. That I could understand. But everything else? Despite Vera's love for her father, Cormac was far from blameless. It was going to take some time for this to sink in. To make sense of it all.

"We moved around a lot," she said. "Stayed hidden. Stayed in the mountains."

There was no shortage of remote locations in the Pacific Northwest. Hell, if Cormac knew what he was doing, he could have just bounced from national forest to national forest. From Idaho to Washington to Oregon to Montana. There were thousands upon thousands of acres of untamed wilderness, most of which had never seen a human being.

"It wasn't horrible." Vera shrugged. "Dad did his best to make it comfortable. We kept moving, kept biding time."

"Time for what?"

"Time to be forgotten. Dad's goal was always to get to Canada. He thought maybe if we traveled far enough north, we could set up in a small town where no one would recognize him. But he was worried that crossing the border would be a risk. Even though it's relatively unguarded, he worried there might be surveillance equipment, like drones, or thermal imaging cameras. Maybe the roads had embedded sensors. He just didn't want to chance it too soon, so we waited. Kept moving. Kept hiding. And eventually, we came to Montana."

To Quincy.

"I got sick about four years ago. We'd had a few weeks where there wasn't a ton to eat. My body was worn down, and I think I was dehydrated. It wasn't anything serious but Dad didn't want to risk pushing too hard. We'd just made it to Montana. He found a place tucked far away and let me rest for about a month. He built us a shelter. Hunted a lot. Once I started feeling better, I didn't want to leave. I was tired of always being on the move. So we stayed."

If they'd arrived in Montana four years ago, that meant they'd been living out here for two years. Two goddamn years. I loved camping. Give me two weeks, even two months, and I'd be happy. But two years? Damn.

"Is that the longest you stayed anywhere?"

She nodded. "I liked it here."

"Where?"

Vera pointed north. "About ten miles from here. I'll take you there someday. It's not exactly easy to get to, but it was close enough to town that I could go in for supplies."

I blinked. "You came in to Quincy?"

"About once a month."

Had we crossed paths? Huh.

Vera probably knew the mountains around Quincy better than me or my brothers or even Dad. It made me feel better about all the hiking she did. Not great, but it eased a few fears. No wonder Vance never objected to her hikes.

"This is where Vance found you, isn't it?" I guessed. "You didn't just show up on his doorstep in Idaho."

"Yeah. They were partners. Did you know that? He never gave up on finding Dad. Not because of their friendship. Vance thought, like everyone else, that Dad had killed us all."

Vance had come to Montana for justice. After Lyla was attacked, the police had put out a bulletin describing Cormac. His build. His red hair. The scar across his face. Vance had seen the APB and come here.

"I'd come to town for supplies. Vance saw me. Chased me down. I took him to Dad."

"Then what?"

"Dad told him the truth. Lyla was there too."

I blinked. "What? Vance let that motherfucker around her after he tried to kill her?"

Vera flinched and guilt flooded her gaze. "I didn't know what he did to her. Not until after Vance found us. I'm sorry. He shouldn't have done it. He promised he wouldn't have let it go too far, he was just trying to scare her enough to buy himself time and get away. He was worried that someone would find me. I'm not making excuses for him. I'm just... I'm sorry. I wish it had never happened."

"And what does Lyla think about all this?"

Vera gave me a sad smile. "She has Vance."

If Cormac hadn't attacked her, Vance never would have come to Quincy.

And he never would have found Vera.

Son of a bitch. I'd still hate Cormac for what he'd put Lyla through. But damn if it hadn't changed everything.

"You know the rest," Vera said. "I left with Vance. We knew it would be impossible to convince people he didn't murder my sisters, so we didn't bother trying. We decided to tell everyone I'd left him in Idaho. Let them keep thinking he's a monster. Better that than have the FBI in Montana."

Well, they were here now. "You came out today to try and find him and warn him away."

"Yes. He should leave."

"How do you know he's here?"

"I don't." She hugged her knees tighter. "I just... hoped. I didn't think he'd really leave me."

If Cormac had kept Vera hidden all these years, if he'd been determined to keep her close, my guess was he hadn't gone far.

"He's all I have left, Mateo. I know he's not perfect. I know he's done some horrible things. But he's my family. I need to find him." A tear rolled down her cheek. "He's my dad."

"Hey." I cupped her cheek in my hand, forcing her to face me. "He's not all you have. Not anymore."

She sniffled, her chin quivering. "I'm sorry. I know I should have told you a long time ago but... how? It wasn't like I could show up at a family dinner and say, 'Oh, remember that time my dad almost killed Lyla? Yeah, it's cool now.' "

How the hell could she make me want to laugh right now? This woman. I wrapped her up, hauling her into my chest to kiss the top of her hair. "From now on, we go out here together."

"W-what? You want to help?"

"Yeah. And I don't want you out here alone. Not anymore."

Her eyes softened. "Thank you. But I have to come out here alone. If he sees you, he won't show himself."

"Oh, I think he will." I was banking on Cormac's protective instincts to come roaring to life. If he saw me with Vera, his curiosity might get the better of him. He'd want to meet the man sleeping with his daughter. "Am I a part of your life?"

"Yes."

"Then he's got to meet me at some point."

"But—"

"Just say yes, Peach."

She sighed. "Yes."

"No more hiking alone. Promise?"

"Promise."

I bent and dropped a kiss to her mouth, then slid off the hood of the car and held out my hand. "Let's go get Allie and head home."

She set her hand in mine, but not to climb off the hood. Her grip tightened. "Mateo?"

"Yeah, darlin'."

Her chin quivered. "Thank you."

With a tug, I pulled until she was on her feet and in my arms. Then I held on to her. There wasn't much else to say, not until I could puzzle it all out in my head, so I just held on to her.

Tight enough that maybe the next time she thought about going it alone, she'd remember there was no need.

CHAPTER 26

VERA

My fingertips kneaded my temples in slow, measured circles. Maybe if I pressed hard enough, I could force the information to stay locked in my brain for my upcoming exams.

Since Mateo and I had started this relationship, I'd neglected my online classes. I just couldn't muster the motivation to spend hours with my nose in a textbook when I'd rather spend my time with him. But too many nights learning sexual positions rather than psychology and I was far, far behind.

Yesterday, after Mateo had found me on Sable Peak and we'd brought Allie home, I should have knocked out a few hours with my textbooks. But I'd been too raw after that confession about Dad, so I'd opted to relax with Mateo and play with Allie. After we'd put her to bed, instead of studying for even thirty minutes, I'd let him carry me to bed, where we'd fucked for hours.

Those orgasms might cost me my final grades.

I had two tests next week I was ill prepared to take, and as much as I would have loved to relax at the cabin after working at the coffee shop this morning, I'd come to the loft and forced myself to study.

I'd never understood the concept of cramming until now. My head was so full of facts and information that even the idea of what to eat for dinner made my skull ache.

A thud echoed. Was someone coming up the stairs? Or was it just my brain throbbing?

"Vera." Mateo knocked on the door.

"Come in."

"Hi—" His eyebrows came together when he saw me. "What's wrong?"

"Nothing but impending failure." I swung a hand out at the sea of papers and books spread across the coffee table. "Ask me how studying is going."

He crossed the room and sank down beside me on the couch. "Have you been studying all day?"

"Since I got home from work." I sagged into his side. "My head hurts. And it's Friday. We're supposed to study ground school stuff. But, Mateo, I can't. I might die if I have to read another word. And I don't even really want to be a pilot. The flying part is fun and cool, but I don't care about weather systems or magnetic variation or runway diagrams."

The words came out in a rush. I hadn't even realized how I was feeling until this moment.

"Don't be mad."

Mateo shifted, taking my face in his hands. "I don't care if you want to be a pilot or not. You can just come fly with me."

"Okay." I exhaled. "You're sure you're not disappointed?"

"Not a bit. People change their minds all the time once they get into it. Becoming a pilot is hard."

"After that first flight, I just thought maybe it would make finding Dad easier. That's why I asked you to teach me. And if you had to teach me, it would give you a reason to fly."

"Peach." His eyes softened.

"You love it, Mateo. I saw it when we were up there. If you could do anything in the world, from Quincy, what would you do?"

"Fly. But I don't know how to turn it into a career. Not here."

My heart sank. "You were born to fly. Promise me you'll go more often. Please?"

He studied me for a long moment, then nodded. "Promise."

"Good."

Mateo tugged on the end of my ponytail. "And what about you? What do you love?"

You. "Naps."

The corner of his mouth turned up. "No naps. I came over to get you for an impromptu family dinner. Everyone is at Mom and Dad's."

"Oh."

"That's your tired *oh*."

I blinked. "Huh?"

"You have different *oh*s. That's the tired one. You have another when you're surprised. One when you're entertaining Allie, pretending to be enamored with whatever she's showing you. And the *oh* you make when I go like this." He bent, his lips finding my pulse.

The moment his tongue skated across my skin, I shivered. "Oh."

His chuckle was deep and sexy. "Are you hungry?"

My fingers threaded through his hair as I hummed.

"I'm taking that as a no." He laid me down, pressing me into the couch as his weight settled on mine. His mouth worked lower, tracing the line of my collarbone to the hollow beneath my throat.

I smiled for the first time in hours, letting him erase the stress and exhaustion from the day as he trailed kisses across my jaw and up to my ear.

He broke away to lift me up, rip the tee off my body and unclasp my bra. Light streamed through the windows, highlighting the flex of his jaw as he worked my jeans off my hips and legs.

The blue of his eyes darkened as he stripped my panties away next. When every article of clothing I'd donned this morning was puddled on the floor, he stood from the couch and stared at my naked body.

The perusal was slow and deliberate, moving from head to toe. With every passing moment, my heart beat faster. Heat bloomed across my skin as my core throbbed.

I reached for him but he didn't move. So I spread my legs wider, cupping my breasts with my hands. Every time we were together, I found myself growing more confident. My cheeks flushed, both with desire and a rush of nerves. Without the cover of darkness, this was as bold as I'd ever been.

I liked it. Did he?

His gaze locked on my pussy, and when that Adam's apple bobbed, I held back a smile. He liked it. "You're fucking perfect, Peach."

With one hand, Mateo yanked off his plain black T-shirt, dropping it to the floor. My mouth watered at the sight of his broad chest and those washboard abs. Though I did love dragging my tongue over his throat, that V at his hips was my favorite place to lick.

The oval medallion of his belt buckle clinked as he worked it loose, the noise carrying through the loft. He let it hang loose as he flipped the button on his jeans open. His fingers were poised, about to drag down the zipper, when I threw a leg over the back of the couch.

"Hell, woman." He rocked back on his heels. "You're drenched."

I was blushing. But it felt like a reward these days, not something to hide. So I let my gaze wander over his body. The roped arms. The chest so solid it was like carved stone, yet the perfect pillow to sleep on each night. The thick, bulky thighs that strained the denim of his jeans.

Mateo toed off his boots and shed the jeans. His cock sprang free the moment they were gone.

No underwear. My core clenched. God, that was hot. Why was that hot?

He fisted his shaft, stroking it a few times as we stared at each other. Then he dropped a knee to the couch and covered me with that muscled body, his skin hot against mine.

His hands dove into my hair, his eyes locked on mine.

I leaned up, ready for a kiss, but he backed away. "What?"

"I—" He shook his head. "You're beautiful."

Before I could respond, his mouth crushed mine, his tongue sweeping inside. He rocked against me, his arousal pressed against my slit and the root of his cock rubbing against my clit.

"More," I panted into his mouth. "I need you inside."

He growled, nipping at my jaw. Then he fitted himself at my entrance and thrust home, filling me completely.

I cried out as I stretched around him, my body fluttering around his length. Every night I tried to draw it out, to hold back that first orgasm, but no matter how hard I fought, it was pointless. My body was at Mateo's mercy, and as he kissed me deeper, his hands fisting my hair with a tug, my inner walls clenched.

He eased out and slammed inside again. The sound of our bodies colliding mingled with ragged breaths. "You feel so damn good."

"Yes." My fingers clawed into his shoulders as he pounded us together.

"I'm going to fuck you hard and fast, darlin'. Then tonight, we'll go slow and play." He slid a hand to my ass, squeezing the cheek. A promise of the play to come later.

My pussy clenched. "Yes."

His hips never slowed, his thrusts hitting a spot inside that made my limbs tremble. He delivered on his promise, fucking me hard and fast until I writhed beneath him.

"Come, Vera. Come with me." He reached between us and flicked my clit.

"Oh, God." I detonated, my back arching off the couch as I cried his name. That coarse dusting of hair on his chest tickled my nipples as I came apart. The world blurred to nothing but the clenching of my body, rocking me top to bottom.

Mateo let out a string of curses as I squeezed around him. His nostrils flared, his jaw clenching, then he tilted his head to the loft's ceiling and let out a roar as his own release took over.

His come leaked hot between us. A sheen of sweat glistened on my skin. My chest heaved as I tried to regain my breath. When I finally managed to crack my eyes open, Mateo was locked above me, arms braced on the couch as the final waves of his own orgasm faded.

Last night had been the first time we'd had sex without a condom. I was on birth control and neither of us had been with anyone in a while.

Now there was nothing between us. That made it even better.

"Fuck, Peach. It's always so good." He kissed my chest, right over my heart, then eased away. But he didn't leave the couch. He reached between us, finding my sensitive flesh. Then with a smirk, he pushed his come inside me with a finger.

I gasped, my mouth parting. "Oh."

"That's a new *oh*. I like it." He licked his lower lip. Then he licked mine.

He kept me pinned to the couch as he played with me for a few moments, his fingers slick and warm. But he didn't make me come, not again. *Tease.*

Another preview of what would come later when we were in bed.

When he took his hand away, I whimpered.

He bent to suck a nipple into his mouth, releasing it with a pop, then he stood and hauled me off the couch. "Get dressed."

"Do I have time for a shower?"

"Nope." He smacked my ass. "I want you to be sticky with me all night."

"Mateo." I rolled my eyes. "That is so…" My brain was too fried from the studying and sex to think of the right word.

"Sexy." He bent to hand me my tee from where it had landed on my psychology textbook. "It's fucking sexy knowing that I'm all over your skin. And tonight, after we get dirty again, I'll wash it all off in the shower together. Now get dressed."

I pulled my lips in to hide a smile, then reached for my discarded clothes. After smoothing out my hair and attempting to cool my too-pink cheeks by fanning my face—I didn't need to go to family dinner looking freshly fucked—I took Mateo's hand and let him lead me to Anne and Harrison's house.

The noise enveloped us as we walked through the door. Like always, we found everyone crowded in the kitchen.

"There she is," Harrison announced with a smile. That grin spread as his gaze shifted to where Mateo still had my fingers firmly threaded in his.

Everyone stared.

Uncle Vance stared.

So much for meeting him for lunch to explain.

The bubble that had been surrounding Mateo and me burst so loudly my ears popped.

I tried to wiggle my hand free, heat spreading across my cheeks, but Mateo's grip only tightened. I was so focused on my hand, I didn't notice until it was too late that he took hold of my chin, pinching it between his index finger and thumb, to tilt my face up to his.

He kissed me, hard and firm, then let me go with a smug grin.

My eyes bugged out, darting past him to an entire kitchen of Edens. Still staring.

This time when I wiggled my fingers, he let them go. But only so he could use that arm to haul me into his side.

"Peach, it's not like they all don't know why it took me thirty minutes to collect you for dinner."

"Oh my God." I turned crimson from head to toe. "I can't believe you just said that."

Griffin barked a laugh, attempting to hide it in his tumbler of whiskey.

"I think I need another beer for this dinner." Vance stood from his stool and went straight for the fridge.

Mateo chuckled, holding me closer.

My hand shot out like a whip, smacking him in the gut. "It's not funny."

"Hey, don't get mad at me for kissing you in front of everyone. You started it."

"I did no—" *Shit.* Yes, I'd been the one to kiss him first. That night at Willie's. God, it seemed like eons ago.

That smirk of his stretched to a dazzling, dreamy smile.

I couldn't help it. When he smiled like that, it was automatic for me to smile back.

Vance came over, fresh beer in hand. He took a long gulp, staring at me as he swallowed. The worry line was creased deep between his eyebrows. "Hey, kiddo."

"Hi, Uncle Vance."

He motioned between the two of us. "It's official. You're together?"

"Yeah," Mateo answered before I could reply.

I looked up at Mateo, finding his blue eyes waiting. "We're together."

He winked, then kissed my forehead.

Vance clapped Mateo on the shoulder. It looked friendly enough, but Mateo winced so hard that I felt it too.

The first warning. It probably wouldn't be Vance's last. They might be brothers-in-law, but he was on my side first and foremost.

"I'm getting a beer. What do you want?" Mateo asked me. "Water."

He'd just left my side to get our drinks when the kids streamed out of the playroom and into the kitchen.

Allie came rushing over, arms raised in the air. Her cheeks were rosy, like she'd been running full-out to keep up with her older cousins. "Ve-wa. Up."

"There's my Jellybean." I settled her on my hip, then brushed an errant strand of hair off her forehead.

"Fiss." *Fish.* She smooshed my cheeks together.

It was our newest game. I made a fish face and kissed her with my fish lips, earning a giggle.

"Gen." *Again.*

I did it again and again, until Anne announced dinner was almost ready and everyone shuffled to the dining room table to find a seat.

The table wasn't made for this many people. There was hardly an inch between chairs but somehow, we made it all work. And for the first time in the two years I'd been eating dinners with the Eden family, I sat beside Mateo.

When he dished his garden salad, he moved the tomatoes from his plate to mine.

CHAPTER 27

MATEO

The check on my kitchen counter was annoying me. It snared my attention for what felt like the billionth time since I'd left it by the coffee pot earlier. It was pale blue and printed with black ink. Simple. Standard. But for as many times as I'd looked at it today, it might as well have been neon yellow with three-dimensional letters and a flashing strobe light.

Griffin had given it to me today when I'd gone to his place to finish up the rework of his corrals. When the last panel had been put into place, he'd asked me to come inside. Then he'd handed over that check.

My paycheck.

It certainly wasn't the first. He'd been paying me when he paid the other ranch hands. But today's check was the first I didn't want.

I hadn't filled out Eloise's direct deposit form either.

Working on the ranch was my job. A job I'd always enjoyed. Not loved. Enjoyed. It, along with the work I did at the hotel, paid the bills.

I wasn't a man who needed wealth to feel successful. I counted blessings, not pennies. My good fortune came from those I loved, especially the little girl asleep for her afternoon nap and the woman who had captured my heart in a matter of weeks.

But I still needed money. Allie would need to go to college one day. I'd love to take Vera on a trip somewhere. Maybe we'd fly to the desert this winter and escape the snow.

It should be enough. Working for my family's ranch, living to make Allie and Vera smile and build a future together should be enough.

It wasn't enough.

Vera's words from last week kept haunting me. Every time I looked at that paycheck, I heard her voice.

You were born to fly.

That woman knew me arguably better than I knew myself. She was right. It was time to finally make a move. But what? Crop-dusting was… crop-dusting. There wasn't a lot of need for it in this area of Montana because the land was rugged. More trees than prairie. More cattle than wheat.

There was flying during forest fire season, but that would keep me away from home for months in a bad fire year. I couldn't be apart from Allie or Vera for that long.

Maybe I could start a flight school in Quincy. I'd probably have one student a year, at most.

Or… we moved.

I loved flying. No question. And if I had no attachments, I'd go back to Alaska and fly every day. But that wasn't where I wanted to raise Allie. And I wouldn't move Vera. Not only because she was so intent on finding her father, but because she needed Montana. She needed Quincy. She needed the Edens.

And if we did find Cormac Gallagher, then I really wasn't sure what we'd do.

We hadn't talked about Cormac since that day on Sable Peak. We hadn't gone hiking again. Vera had been busy studying, taking her two exams and working. When she came to the cabin every evening, the last thing I wanted was to weigh her down with anything heavy, so I hadn't asked about her father. We hadn't discussed the FBI agent either.

Swenson had left two days after talking to Vera at Eden Coffee. I'd asked Eloise to tell me when he'd checked out of the hotel. For now, I could put him out of my mind. But not Cormac.

Maybe the reason I hadn't brought it up to Vera was because I still wasn't sure what to make of it. What to think of Cormac. Of Vera's mother.

Norah. Her name was Norah. As far as I could remember, I'd never heard Vera say that name. In two years, I couldn't recall a single time when she'd spoken her sisters' names either.

And up until last week, she hadn't talked about Cormac.

That bastard had tried to strangle my sister. I wasn't sure I'd ever be able to let that go. He could have killed her, whether he'd intended to or not. Whether he'd done it to protect Vera or not. He'd choked my sister.

How was I supposed to be okay with this? How was Lyla? Or Vance?

The crunch of wheels on gravel tore me from my thoughts, and I walked out of the kitchen to the front door, opening it as Vance's truck parked beside mine.

He was dressed for work in a button-down Quincy Police Department shirt, his badge and gun holstered on the belt of his jeans. He carried a vase of pink roses as he walked to the porch and climbed the stairs. "Hey."

"Nice flowers."

"They're for Vera. Figured she'd probably enjoy them more if they were here than at the loft."

"Come on in." I jerked my chin for him to follow me inside, then closed the door behind us. "I was just thinking about you."

"That sounds dangerous." He set the vase down, then leaned against the counter, like it was the only thing keeping him upright.

"I was, uh, thinking about Cormac."

"Ah." Vance nodded. "How much did Vera tell you?"

"Enough. Not everything. But enough."

"Sorry." His shoulders drooped. "We probably should have come clean with the truth a while ago, but..."

"You're protecting him too." What was it about Cormac Gallagher that inspired so much loyalty?

"We're protecting Vera. We're just trying to do what's best for her. If Cormac goes to prison, she'll be devastated."

Yeah, it would break her heart. And knowing her, if Cormac was arrested, she'd go visit him every week. That was not the life I wanted for her.

"And Lyla?" I asked. "How does she feel about it?"

"Conflicted," Vance said. "We both are. I'll never forgive him for what he did to her. But... it's complicated."

Complicated. As much as I hated that word, I understood. My feelings toward Madison would always be complicated. And that was it. They were just complicated.

There was no making sense of it. No matter how hard I tried, not everything was cut and dry, black and white. Sometimes, it was a goddamn muddy mess.

"What are the flowers for?" I asked.

Vance didn't answer. He stared off into space, a sheen of tears in his eyes.

Fuck.

"It's today," I guessed. The anniversary of the night that had changed Vera's life. Her sisters' deaths.

Vance nodded.

I dragged a hand over my face. "She didn't say anything."

Vera had left for work this morning like she had all of the other mornings this week. She'd played with Allie over a cup of coffee, then kissed me goodbye before heading into town. Last night, while we'd watched TV on the couch, she hadn't mentioned a thing about today. She hadn't hinted that it was significant.

"No, I doubt she would." Vance sighed. "Last year, she pretended like it was just another day. Wouldn't talk to me about anything. Would hardly look at me. Year before that, she avoided me completely. She went hiking and didn't come back until after dark."

"Looking for Cormac?"

"Probably."

Damn it. Was she at work today? She'd promised not to go searching for Cormac alone, but what if she'd done it anyway? I'd understand. Today of all days, I'd understand.

"She's at work," Vance said, reading my thoughts. "Drove by on my way out. Saw her through the windows."

"You didn't want to deliver those flowers in person?"

He shook his head. "I think she wants to pretend it never happened. That's what she did all those years with Cormac. When I found them, he told me she refused to talk about it. And when he explained it all, she wasn't there. She'd left so she wouldn't have to hear it."

My heart twisted. The pain Vera must keep locked inside. The secrets. How could she bear it?

"I'd better get back to work." Vance shoved off the counter and walked toward the door.

But before he slipped out, I put a hand on his shoulder, giving it a squeeze. "I'm sorry."

"Me too." He gave me a sad smile, then headed for his truck, waving as he backed out and drove away.

Vera wasn't the only person who mourned those girls today. Did Cormac know what day it was?

If something happened to Allie, I—

No. I couldn't even think about that. The grief Cormac

must have felt. The grief he'd always carry.

Instead of dragging Vera into the wilderness, he should have left her behind where she could have gotten help. But he'd lost two daughters. Could I really blame him for not wanting to lose another?

Damn. Yeah, it was complicated.

I stood on the porch, staring into the distance until long after the dust had settled from his tires.

How did I help Vera if I didn't know what had actually happened? What did I say?

"Daddy." Allie's voice pulled me back inside as she came out of her room, fists rubbing sleepy eyes.

"Hi, Sprout." I went and picked her up. "Did you have a good nap?"

She snuggled into my shoulder, eyelids still heavy. So we cuddled on the couch until she woke up enough to go with me outside to do some more work on the firepit.

It was dark by the time Vera's headlights flashed outside. Hours past closing time at Eden Coffee. But she'd had to do an assignment for one of her classes and said she might just stay at the cafe after closing to knock it out before the weekend.

Had she stayed at the coffee shop? Or had she done something alone tonight, something to honor her sisters?

"Hey." She came inside, as beautiful as ever. Tired, but no more than any other night following a long day at the coffee shop. If not for Vance, I never would have known about today.

"Hi, darlin'." I shut off the TV and stood from the couch. When she walked through the door to this house, she got a kiss. And even though I still wasn't sure what to say, even after thinking about it for hours, she was getting that kiss.

So I crossed the room, framed her face in my palms and kissed that perfect mouth.

She smiled as she toed off her shoes, gripping my forearm

to keep her balance. That smile wavered when she glanced past my shoulder and saw the roses on the counter.

"Those are from Vance."

"Oh." It was her sad *oh*. The sound of realization that she couldn't keep everything hidden, not from me. Vera's eyes closed, her shoulders slumped. "He told you. What today is."

"Why didn't you?"

She let me go and walked to the counter, reaching out to touch a bloom. But she yanked her finger away before it could skim a petal.

"The thorns are on the stems, Peach."

She stared at the flowers, and if I wasn't standing here, I had a hunch she'd toss them in the trash.

"Want to talk?"

"No."

I sighed and walked up behind her, wrapping an arm around her shoulders. Then I kissed her hair. "Vera—"

"Where's Allie?"

"Asleep."

She tore herself out of my hold. "I'm going to go kiss her good night."

Her silky hair, tied up in a ponytail, swished across her shoulders as she left for Allie's room.

I scrubbed both hands over my face. If only I knew what to say to get her to open up. To just let it out. But she wasn't just kissing my daughter good night. She was fortifying walls, adding another layer of bricks and chains.

When she emerged, easing Allie's door closed, her shoulders were pinned, chin lifted. Her hands might have well been raised into fists, ready to defend those walls.

"Vera." I put a hand to my heart, then held it out, palm open. "I'm here."

"I... can't." Her voice cracked. "I can't talk about it. Please, Mateo. Don't ask."

"It kills me to know you're hurting and trying so hard to hide it. You don't have to. Not from me."

She dropped her chin.

"What can I do?"

"Help me keep it locked away."

"Keep what locked away?"

"All of it," she whispered, lifting her gaze. In those pretty brown eyes, a plea. *Don't push.*

Then I wouldn't push.

"I don't want to be a hired hand or a maintenance man," I blurted. It felt cathartic to let it out. To voice the thought that felt like a betrayal to my family and a balm to my soul.

I didn't want to be a hired hand or a maintenance man. Or I didn't want to *only* be those things.

"What if I started a flight school?" This wasn't at all what I wanted to talk about tonight, but for tonight, it would do. I'd leave those walls alone.

She blinked. "A flight school?"

"Yeah. There isn't one in Quincy. It would be small. There aren't many pilots in town, but right now, anyone wanting to learn has to travel to Missoula. I doubt I'll make much money. If any. Hell, I doubt I'll have many students."

I walked over to take her hand, then I pulled her around the house as I shut off the lights.

"I'll still have to keep working on the ranch for Griffin and at the hotel for Eloise. But if I can drum up a student or two, it'd mean I'd get to fly."

Quincy was growing. People were leaving the larger cities in the Pacific Northwest to raise families in small towns that ran at a slower pace. The elementary school was at capacity and this year's graduating class was the largest in a decade.

Maybe a newcomer would want to learn how to fly. Maybe a millionaire or two would move to town and need a private pilot to help them commute to Denver or Salt Lake on occasion. Maybe every couple of years, a high school student would dream of getting his or her wings.

"What do you think?" I asked when the last light was off and we were standing outside the bedroom door.

Vera lifted our clasped hands until my knuckles were resting over her heart. "I love this idea."

"Me too." There was plenty to think through, but it wasn't the first time I'd tossed around the idea. But it was the first time I could see myself making it happen.

It was her doing. Her encouragement.

With my free hand, I tucked a lock of hair behind her ear and untucked it. Maybe I'd changed the subject for a few minutes, but that sadness was still so deep in her gaze.

It hadn't been like that this morning. She'd hidden it well. But after a long day, there was no masking it now. That agony in her gaze was like a knife to the heart.

"I wish I could take it from you."

She swallowed hard. "I would never let you."

No, she'd keep it all herself, thinking it would save me pain. Didn't she realize it hurt to see her hurt? Frustration swelled, escaping my chest as a low, menacing growl. "Stubborn woman."

There was nothing to do about her secrets, not tonight. And if she wanted to forget, to block it all out, then I'd play that game.

I wrapped her in my arms and picked her up off her feet, lifting her high enough so we were eye to eye.

She threaded her fingers through my hair, her nails scraping against my scalp as she brought them to my nape. "Thank you."

"Say it with a kiss."

Her mouth dropped to mine, kissing the corner of my lips. She peppered gentle, soft touches from side to side, until finally, that sweet tongue darted out for a taste.

I held her, feet off the floor, her chest crushed to mine, until I was done letting her play. Then I carried her into the bedroom, closing the door behind us before stripping her out of her tee and jeans.

When she was dressed only in her pale pink bra and panties, I tugged loose the elastic band around her ponytail, spilling that coppery hair around her shoulders. Then I pointed to the bed. "On your back."

A smile tugged at her mouth before she brought her lower lip between her teeth. She obeyed, she always obeyed, and climbed onto the bed. Red and gold locks spread across the white quilt like flames.

"Close your eyes." When they were closed, I stripped out of my T-shirt and tossed it aside.

Vera's breathing turned ragged as the sound of my belt unbuckling and my jeans being shoved to the floor filled the room.

My cock sprang free, hard and aching to plunge inside her tight body. But tonight, we'd drag this out. We'd see how many orgasms I could coax from her before she passed out.

I moved to stand at the edge of the bed, taking her knees and pushing them apart. The sight of her on my bed never got old. I fisted my shaft, giving it a firm stroke. Then I dropped to my knees and started worshiping her skin with my tongue, starting at her hips and working my way across her panties, leaving them on to tease.

"Mateo." She squirmed, arching those hips toward my mouth.

I kissed the inside of her thigh, exactly where she was the most ticklish.

Her giggle was music to my ears. "Stop torturing me."

"No." I moved to the other leg while dragging a finger over the center of her panties, earning a hiss. "Soaked. Always so wet for me."

A whimper escaped as I pulled her panties aside, feasting my eyes on that glistening pink flesh.

"First, I'm going to fuck you with my fingers. Then you'll get my tongue. And after you come twice, you can have my cock."

"Yes," she breathed.

I slid a hand up her stomach to her bra, lifting a cup to expose a breast. Then I rolled her nipple and gave it a pinch.

She yelped but pushed into my touch, wanting it again.

This time as I pinched her, I slipped a finger inside her wet heat.

"Oh," she gasped, her inner walls already fluttering. Damn it, she was perfect. The way she responded to my touch, the sounds she made. Like she was made for me.

Like she was always meant to be mine.

I took my finger out and popped it into my mouth. "You taste so sweet."

"Mateo, make me come. I need to come."

"Patience." I kissed her hip, then slid two fingers in this time, working them in and out. I curled my hand to massage that spot inside that made her shake while my palm flattened on her clit.

"Baby." Her breath hitched.

Fucking hell. She wasn't the first woman to call me baby. But she'd be the last. "Say it again."

"Baby." She arched into my touch, and the moment her toes curled, I grinned, loving the hell out of orgasm number one.

Number two was twice as sweet. With her taste on my tongue, I picked her up and moved her deeper into the bed to settle in the cradle of her hips.

She panted, her skin covered in a sheen of sweat. The flush of her cheeks had spread across her chest and breasts.

"You have never looked more beautiful."

Her eyes fluttered open.

"I—" Loved her.

I loved her.

It was a fight, but I held back the words. Not today. Not with those pink roses on the kitchen counter. So instead of telling her how I felt, I showed her, loving her with every stroke that brought us together.

We tumbled over the abyss in tandem, falling farther and farther until we were nothing but tangled limbs and thundering hearts.

When we'd regained our breaths, I settled her into the crook of my shoulder.

Her leg was draped across mine, her breath whispering over the plane of my chest.

By rights, we should both be exhausted. But when I closed my eyes, sleep was impossible. Maybe because I could feel the tension in Vera's shoulders.

She was trying not to cry.

What happened that night? It was on the tip of my tongue to beg for the truth. For her. For me. I was flying in the dark here. How did I help her without a light? Especially when she wouldn't let me? *What happened?*

I swallowed that question and traded it for another. A question similar to the one that had given me a purpose on one of my darkest days. "What should we call it?"

Her fingertips drew invisible swirls over my bare chest. "Call what?"

"The flight school. What should we call it?"

She rose up, tears swimming in those pretty eyes. Hair tumbling around us.

I pushed it off her face, tracing the line of her cheek with my thumb. "Help me think up a name."

"Okay." She snuggled into my chest and returned to drawing patterns on my skin. "Let's start with the *A*s."

CHAPTER 28

VERA

I shut the lid to my laptop, took off my headphones and collapsed in my chair. For the past hour, I'd been polishing my final paper for Personality Theory and Research. It was now uploaded and turned in to my professor. That was it for my semester. For the next three months, I was free to enjoy the summer.

It was easier to breathe without the weight of school on my shoulders. The past five days had been stressful, balancing exams and studying and work and life.

The latter had suffered the most. Most nights, I'd come to Mateo's and immediately taken this very chair, confiscating the dining room table as my workspace. He'd leave me in peace and keep Allie out of my hair, and when she was asleep, he'd retreat to the bedroom to read.

Usually by the time I snuck in after midnight, he'd be asleep, book open on his chest.

Even though it had been a grueling race to the end of the term, I'd really enjoyed my classes. I wanted to keep learning.

What would have happened if instead of burying our feelings for four years, Dad and I had had someone to talk to? Someone to confide in, like a therapist or counselor?

It had been impossible, given the situation. And even if I'd wanted to talk about it with Dad, which I hadn't, he'd been equally wrecked by that night. But maybe I wouldn't be as closed off if I'd had a different outlet.

Maybe someday, I could be that outlet for others.

The sound of hammering came from outside. I stood from the table, stretching my tense shoulders, then slipped on a pair of tennis shoes to head out back.

April had come and gone in a rain-soaked blur, but the beginning of May had been a ray of sunshine. The air smelled crisp, like clean pine and fresh-cut grass.

Mateo had taken Allie outside all afternoon so I could concentrate and finish my paper.

"Daddy!" Her shout carried through the air as I jogged down the porch steps and rounded the side of the house. She had something in her hand, holding it up as she raced toward where he was working on the firepit. Though considering how big he was making the circle of stone pavers, it was turning into more of a patio.

"Sprout." He tore off his leather gloves and turned his hat backward as she came running over to where he was working.

"Is a pitty wok."

"That is a pretty rock." He took it from her, inspecting all sides. "What should we do with it?"

She took it from him, wound up an arm and threw it as far as she could. It landed about five feet away. "Ah gone."

He chuckled, shaking his head, then gave her a swat on the butt. "Go find me another one."

"Okay." Off she raced, crouching as she picked through the grass.

Mateo stared at her with a soft smile, watching her for a moment with pure, endless love. Then he went back to work, pulling on his gloves before picking up a block to take toward what would be a circular retaining wall.

The muscles of his biceps strained at the sleeves of his

T-shirt. The white cotton clung to his shoulders and back, damp from sweat. His jeans, dusty and dirty, hugged the bulk of his thighs and molded to the curve of his ass.

I leaned against the corner of the cabin and enjoyed the view.

My view.

This was mine. He was mine.

I was keeping him forever.

The anniversary of that night was never easy. Usually the pain lingered for days and days. Without him, it would have been unbearable. It never got easier. It never got lighter. The only thing that seemed to dull the pain was blocking it out. Letting that numbness take over. Pretending like it didn't exist.

I loved Mateo for trying to understand. I loved him for not pushing me to talk. I loved him for the distraction of a flight school and the name we still hadn't chosen.

I loved him.

For always.

Mateo worked to place the block, fitting it into the row he was assembling. Once it was set, he stood tall and wiped his brow with the back of his arm. "Are you going to stand there and drool or come help me?"

"Drool," I called.

He chuckled, twisting to flash me that blinding white smile. "Finish your paper?"

I raised both arms in the air. "Done!"

"That's my girl." He tore off those gloves and waved me over.

I ran for him, laughing as I launched myself into his arms and wrapped my legs around his hips.

"Proud of you, Peach. You worked your ass off this week."

"I'm proud of me too." I kissed him, letting him spin us in a circle before putting me on my feet. "This looks good."

"It's coming along." He took my hand, leading me around the space.

He'd carved out a circular area and covered it in gray stones. "The retaining wall on that side will double as seating. I'll put a smooth block on top. Then these open sections I'm going to build pergolas and hang swings."

"Love it." Leaning against his arm, I pictured us sitting together on that swing, watching Allie race around the yard.

"I'm about done for today. We need groceries," he said. "I was going to take Allie into town to distract her while you were working."

"She's happy playing." The knees of her pants were dirty and wet. The pigtails he'd put into her hair had completely fallen out and now it was sticking up at odd angles. "I'll go. You can finish up and relax."

"You sure?"

I nodded. "Yep."

"Okay, darlin'."

"Your dad calls your mom darlin'."

Mateo nodded. "He does."

"I like it."

"Good." He bent to kiss my hair, then like he had for Allie, gave me a swat on the ass to send me on my way. "Oh, hey, Vera?"

"Yeah?" I turned.

"I keep some of my tools at the hotel for maintenance stuff, but I need to sharpen the blade on the lawn mower and don't have my wrenches to take it off. Eloise was going to set them out. Would you stop by and grab them for me? Save me a trip."

"No problem." I blew him a kiss, then went to the house, scribbling out a quick grocery list before grabbing my keys and setting off for town.

Main Street was busy for a Wednesday afternoon. Now that the rain had stopped, storefronts and window displays were being refreshed for the upcoming tourist season. The kitchen goods shop had a basket of petunias beside its front door. Though it was nothing compared to the traffic we'd see this summer, the sidewalks were busier than I'd seen in months. There were buckets of tulips next to the carts inside the grocery store.

I picked up a bundle before quickly running through my list.

"Hey, Vera," the cashier said as I piled items on the conveyor belt.

"Hi, Maxine. How are you?"

"Good. Tired. I got a puppy. He kept me up all night." She'd been talking about getting a dog for months. "But he's cute so I'll forgive him. Want to see a picture?"

"Of course." I put the last of my items on the belt, then moved closer as she swiped through photos on her phone. "He's precious."

Should we get a dog? Mateo was great with Anne and Harrison's dogs. Allie would be adorable with a puppy.

Maxine set her phone aside and began ringing up my foodstuffs, chatting as she bagged.

The normalcy of it hit me like a slap in the face. A good slap, if there was such a thing. Going to the store. Chatting with Maxine. Contemplating a pet.

Normal.

This was normal.

At some point in the past two years, I'd stopped being new to Quincy. I'd stopped being a stranger. I'd stopped being that woman who'd lived as a survivalist in the woods for four years.

Normal. This was a normal day. Running errands. Doing yard work.

God, I loved normal. I wanted another ten normal days. Another hundred. A thousand. I didn't want fame or fortune. I just wanted this.

To be the woman who I might have become if not for *before*. A normal life.

With Mateo. With Allie.

And maybe, if I was lucky, with my dad.

Mateo and I hadn't had time to go on a hike since I'd been so focused on school, but we were going out tomorrow. Maybe this time, with him along, I'd get lucky.

"Thanks, Maxine." I waved as I took my groceries and headed to the car.

With them loaded, I made my way to The Eloise Inn, breathing in the scent of lemon and verbena from the candle burning on the coffee table in the sitting area. For the first time in months, there was no fire crackling in the grand room's stone hearth.

Eloise smiled from her seat behind the mahogany reception counter as I crossed the lobby. "Hey."

"Hi. I'm here to pick up Mateo's tools."

"Oh, perfect." She bent to pull out a tool set from beneath the counter.

"Thanks." I scanned the room, searching for Jasper and their daughter. "Are you here alone?"

"Yeah." She pouted. "Jasper stayed home with Ophelia today. I think she's getting a summer cold or something because she's got an awful cough."

"Oh. Sorry."

Eloise shrugged. "It's okay. I've been finagling the summer schedule, which takes forever. We're booked but it's been slow today. No needy guests. Not that I'm complaining. In a month, I won't have a minute to think."

I opened my mouth, about to ask if she'd filled the vacant housekeeper position, when a throat cleared from the direction of the elevators. My smile dropped as the man approached.

Agent Ian Swenson, walking with that cocky swagger,

headed straight for me. "Miss Gallagher."

"Agent Swenson." I forced a smile and lied through my teeth. "Nice to see you again."

He narrowed his gaze. "Is it?"

Absolutely not.

Ironic, that he was here today. Not thirty minutes had passed since I'd been mentally rejoicing my newfound normalcy.

Of course it wouldn't last. Of course something would ruin it.

I'd never be normal. No matter how much time passed, I didn't get to be the woman I would have been before.

Silly of me to think otherwise.

"I didn't realize you were still in Quincy," I said.

He'd left, right? I was sure he'd left. I hadn't seen him in weeks. He hadn't come to the coffee shop again or tracked me down at home. I hadn't seen his SUV in the parking lot.

"Just arrived," he said, gesturing for the sitting area in front of the fireplace. "A moment?"

I didn't want to give him a moment. What if I said no? "Sure."

He headed for a couch, not even bothering to let me go first. The asshole just expected me to follow.

"Everything okay?" Eloise mouthed, concern etched on her pretty face.

I nodded, steeling my spine as I joined Swenson.

He didn't sit on the leather couch or one of the plush chairs, so I didn't either.

I stood opposite him, the coffee table between us, and did my best not to fidget.

Why was he here? Again?

"Would you like to sit?" he asked.

"No, thanks."

He studied me for a long moment with those boring hazel

eyes. "I'm not the enemy, Miss Gallagher."

"Then what are you?"

"Curious."

Any other answer would have been better. "About what?"

"You."

"Me," I scoffed. "There's nothing to be curious about, Agent Swenson. I work at a coffee shop. I take online college classes. I'm a safe driver and a mediocre cook. What you might find interesting about me is in the past. I'm trying to get on with my life. You being here makes that impossible. So forgive me if I don't roll out the welcome mat. I don't want you here."

For the first time since I'd met him, his face softened. Without that harsh, intimidating edge, he looked human. Handsome, even. "That's fair."

I sighed, my shoulders relaxing away from my ears. "Okay. Can I go?"

"Not yet." The softness disappeared so fast I wondered if I'd imagined it. He stared at me without blinking, like he didn't want to miss a second of my reaction to whatever it was he'd come here to say.

My insides knotted.

"Miss Gallagher, we have reason to believe your father is dead."

My gasp echoed to the lobby's wooden rafters.

CHAPTER 29

MATEO

"So this is why you've been so quiet while I was working." I planted my hands on my hips and stared at my daughter.

Allie smiled up at me, eyes dancing, from the puddle she was sitting in. Her hands were caked in dirt as she held them up, fingers splayed. "Wook it mud."

"I'm looking at the mud, Sprout." It was on her hands, her arms, her nose, her cheeks. Those clothes were going to be a bitch to get clean, but if parenthood had taught me anything, it was how to use stain remover.

"You need a bath."

Her grin dropped and her eyes widened, then she shoved to her feet and ran away. "No baf."

Why was it she let Vera put her in the tub without protest, but I still had to endure this fight?

I gave her a head start, then I chased her through the meadow, letting her think she was outpacing me for a bit. When I caught her, I tossed her into the air, drowning in that precious giggle as she came falling down.

"No baf." She kicked and wiggled in my hold, but I tucked her under my arm like she was a football and stalked for the house. The squirming stopped and she held out her hands like she was an airplane.

I shifted my grip, holding her with a hand on her belly and the other on her knees, and flew her toward the house just as the sound of a car door slammed. We rounded the corner, all smiles, until I saw Vera standing beside the Honda.

The color was drained from her face and if not for the hand braced on the side of the car, she looked ready to collapse.

It was instant, the way my heart lurched. Her suffering was mine. After quickly setting Allie on her feet, I ran to Vera and took her shoulders in my hands. "What's wrong?"

She squeezed her eyes shut and fell into my chest, nose buried in my T-shirt to draw in a long breath. "I'm okay. I just... let's go inside and talk."

"No, tell me—"

"Ve-wa!" Allie interrupted us to proudly showcase the mess she'd made. "Mud."

Vera managed a smile as she crouched down to touch my daughter's hair. "Look at you, Jellybean. Should we go wash up?"

"No." Allie scrunched up her nose and raced the other direction. Maybe she'd be a pill for us both today.

"Talk to me." I dropped to a knee beside Vera. "I'm worried."

"Inside." She stared at Allie for a long moment, then shoved to her feet. "Let's get the groceries."

"Fuck the groceries." I shot to my feet. "What the hell is going on?"

When she looked up at me, the tears swimming in her eyes ripped my heart from my chest. "I went to the hotel. That FBI agent, Swenson, was there."

"He's back?" Why the hell hadn't Eloise told me he'd checked in? "Why's he here?"

She swallowed hard. "My dad."

Fuck. My stomach dropped. "They found him."

"No." She shook her head. "Allie, don't touch that."

My gaze whipped toward the house, where Allie was rifling through the tool box I'd left on the porch. The last thing I needed was for her to poke an eye out with a screwdriver. So I jogged over, taking it from her despite her wail of a protest, then closed the box and swept her up.

"Leave the groceries," I called over my shoulder, taking Allie up the porch. "I'll get them in a minute."

No shock, she didn't listen.

After I'd stripped a squirming and screeching Allie out of her filthy clothes and put her in the bath, Vera had unloaded everything from the car and was putting the last box of cereal in the pantry off the laundry room.

"Damn, but you are stubborn, woman." I frowned and clasped my hand over hers, hauling her to the bathroom where Allie was splashing around in the bubbles and playing with her plastic boats.

Vera sighed and sat on the tile floor, knees hugged, with her back to the sink cabinets.

I took the space beside her, keeping close so our arms touched. And even though I was about to come loose at the seams, I waited. One minute. Two minutes. Three.

Stubborn didn't even begin to cover Vera's will. It was iron. She'd talk, but only when she was ready. So I put a hand on her knee, traced circles with my thumb, and waited.

"Swenson said they believe my dad is dead."

"What?" My jaw dropped. "How?"

"There was a young hiker in Yosemite who got swept up in a river and died. When the park authorities went to recover the woman's body, they found an old pack on the riverbanks. It was Dad's. His old driver's license was inside. They think he might have, um... drowned."

The way her voice cracked on that word, *drowned*, tore through my chest. That was how her sisters had died. And Swenson had delivered that news to her today while she'd been wholly unprepared, running errands.

"Swenson is a motherfucker," I clipped.

Allie's face turned to us from the bathtub, and I cringed. Before she started preschool, I really needed to clean up my language.

"He shouldn't have talked to you today," I gritted out. "Not like that."

"Nope."

"What did you say?"

"Nothing really." Vera shrugged. "I was at the hotel, picking up those tools from Eloise. He was coming off the elevator so it was a coincidence I even saw him. But I have to think he would have tracked me down at the coffee shop or maybe come to the ranch. I don't know. He asked for a minute. I talked with him in the lobby. When he told me about the pack, I sat on the couch, sort of... numb."

And alone. She'd been alone. "I should have been there with you."

"How could you have known?"

Swenson was a smarmy bastard. First the surprise visit weeks ago at the coffee shop. Now this. "Next time you see him, you turn and walk away," I said. "Call me or Vance. But I don't want you talking to him alone again, Vera."

"Okay."

"Promise me."

"Promise."

The pressure in my chest eased. "What else did he say? Did they find anything else of your dad's?" Like his body?

I hated to even ask, to push for details, but if all they'd found was a backpack that didn't exactly mean Cormac was dead.

"No. Just the pack and wallet." Vera rested her temple against my shoulder.

Swenson had nothing. No proof. What the fuck was the

point of this visit?

"He came here to drop a bomb and get your reaction." He was fishing to see if Vera knew of Cormac's whereabouts.

"Yep."

What a motherfucker.

"Dad isn't dead." There was so much resolve in her voice, that iron will sharpening to a blade. If by sheer mental force Vera could keep Cormac alive, she'd do it.

"Why would he go to Yosemite?" She pinched the bridge of her nose. "I can't figure it out. There are too many people. We always avoided the national parks whenever possible because they're so busy. But Swenson showed me a picture of the pack and asked me to confirm it was Dad's. Green and black. There was a tear in the strap that he'd fixed with duct tape. Dad didn't go anywhere without it."

"Then he did go to Yosemite."

"Yes? I can't see him giving it to someone else. So it had to be him. But none of it makes sense. Going south was never the plan. He always wanted to get across the border to Canada. Maybe he planted it there? To make the police think he was staying in California?"

"Maybe. But there's no way for him to know about Swenson being put on his case."

"No. Except it wouldn't matter. It's true that every year we stayed away, Dad relaxed more and more. But he never dropped his guard. He always assumed that people were still searching for him."

A safe assumption, especially with Swenson in the mix. "Did Swenson say when they'd found it?"

Vera shook her head. "No."

Cormac could have taken that pack there two years ago, after Vera had left. He could have pitched it thinking no one would ever find it.

Or, he'd left it intentionally, expecting someone to find it much, much sooner than now. Maybe after Vera had gone with Vance, Cormac had wanted to give the illusion of distance. She'd been in Idaho. So he'd gone to California.

"What else did Swenson say?"

"Nothing, really. All he told me was that they think Dad might have..." *Drowned*. "And then he showed me pictures. That was about the extent of our visit."

Swenson could have made a phone call, not taken a trip to Montana. He could have sent those pictures through email. "Do you think Swenson actually believes he's dead?"

"No." She replied instantly, no hesitation. "Like you said, he came here to get my reaction. Maybe to remind me that he's not going to forget about Dad."

The arrogant bastard probably wanted to break a cold case, earn some notoriety. Whatever the hell motivated Agent Swenson, I didn't really give a fuck. I just wanted him gone and to stay gone.

Swenson probably wasn't the kind of man to look the other way, even if he knew the truth.

Weeks ago, I would have loved nothing more than to see Cormac rot in prison for the rest of his life. But after Vera had told me the truth, after I'd considered it over and over and over again, I simply wanted Cormac to be forgotten. And maybe for Vera to have some sort of closure where her father was concerned.

"I saw him," she whispered.

"Who? Swenson?"

"Dad." Vera looked up at me. "I thought I saw him. It was a while ago and I wasn't sure if I was just making it up in my head because it happened so fast. But I think I might have seen him."

"Where?"

"Sable Peak. Not far from where we were a couple weeks ago."

"But he didn't approach you?"

"No. He was there. Then gone. Faster than I could blink. I thought maybe I was imagining it. But maybe... What if it was him?"

Then Cormac had seen Vera, and he'd stayed away. Why? Why wouldn't he talk to her? Hug her? Show himself? That made no sense. Maybe these past two years in the wilderness, the bastard had started to lose his damn mind.

"He looked awful. I'm worried he's going to lose his mind out there, all alone. Or maybe he'll just give up. I don't know. But we need to find him." Vera's voice was hard with ruthless determination. I wasn't the only one in this bathroom who wanted answers from Cormac Gallagher.

"Then we keep looking," I said. "Should we bring Vance in to help?"

"No."

"He found your dad once. Could help do it again."

"Vance found *me*," she corrected. "I'll find Dad."

Then she'd have help. "Tomorrow."

We'd always planned to go out tomorrow. Swenson's visit wouldn't change that plan, but I'd be damn careful to ensure we were alone.

I kissed Vera's hair, then shifted to get one of Allie's hooded towels from the cabinet. But before I could stand, Vera grabbed my wrist.

"Thank you." Her eyes were so sad. "It's nice not to be alone in this."

My heart pinched, and *fuck*, it hurt. I hauled her into my chest, letting her bury her nose in my neck as I held her tight. "I got you, Peach."

CHAPTER 30

VERA

Mateo's low chuckle made me pause.

"What?" I threw the question over my shoulder.

"Where's the fire?"

I stopped and turned. "Huh?"

Mateo had stopped too, hands on hips, on the path behind me. "You're practically sprinting up this mountain, darlin'."

"Oh." My muscles were warm but not burning. My heart rate was elevated but my lungs weren't straining to keep up. "This is just… how I hike."

Mateo's eyes softened as he stepped closer, looking down at me from under the brim of his hat. "You're the fastest hiker I've ever known. When I followed you up here that morning you snuck out, it was everything I could do to keep up. You move like a ghost through these woods. It's incredible. But we're not exactly going for a sneak attack, Peach. We're hoping to be noticed."

"Oh."

He was right. Stealth was not the goal.

But this was how Dad had taught me to hike. To move without a sound. To blend into nature's noises so my own would go unnoticed. Light feet. Strong muscles. Silent mouths. Especially if we were anywhere near a hiking trail like the one beneath my feet.

The only time we were loud was when we were deep in the woods where the forests were thick and progress slow. Those days, we'd talk or whistle. Sometimes Dad would sing so that we were making enough noise to spook nearby predators, like bears or mountain lions, who wouldn't react well to being surprised.

"I'll slow down," I told Mateo.

"Lead on." With a wink, he swatted my ass.

I set out again, this time deliberately slowing my steps. When I lifted a foot to clear a stick, I quickly changed the movement and stomped on it instead.

The snap made me cringe. For four years I'd dodged branches and twigs. That crunch felt wrong down to my bones.

We'd veered off Sable Peak's trailhead two miles ago, following no particular path as we wandered through the wilderness. I'd shared my maps with Mateo earlier this week, and we'd agreed on this section to tackle next. To stick around Sable Peak until it was done. After that, I wasn't sure where to go next.

There were too many mountains. Too many places for Dad to hide. Maybe we'd have to enlist Vance's help after all. Vance had been trained for this sort of thing, but at the moment, I wanted that to be our last resort.

Vance was building his career as a Quincy cop. If we found Dad, it would mean new secrets. New lies. I didn't want to ask Vance to lie for me again.

"Vera."

Behind me, Mateo was lagging. I'd been going too fast again. "Shit. Sorry."

He chuckled. "Let me take the lead for a bit."

"Okay." I waited for him to catch up and pass me, then fell in step behind him. At least the view was nice.

He was wearing a pair of his faded Wranglers, the denim

clinging to the curve of his butt and legs. There was something about the back pockets of those jeans. Now that I could, I slid my hands into his pockets whenever possible.

"I can feel your eyes on my ass." He twisted and shot me a wicked grin.

I giggled. "Guilty."

"To be fair, I was staring at yours all morning." He stopped, waiting until I reached his side. Then he bent down to brush a kiss to my mouth. "You okay?"

I lifted a shoulder. "I'm glad you're here with me."

"We'll find him." The confidence in his voice was catching. We would find him.

Our morning had started early. We'd dropped Allie off at Eloise and Jasper's A-frame house to spend the day playing. Then, like I'd done the last time Swenson had been in Quincy, we'd driven by The Eloise Inn before heading to the mountains—Swenson's car was in the lot and the light to his room was on.

Still, I'd checked the mirrors countless times as we'd driven to the trailhead, but Mateo's truck was the only one in sight as we'd parked, and if Swenson was following us, he'd need to be a hell of a hiker.

Mateo might tease me about racing up the mountain, but his pace would outmatch almost anyone's.

"What do you think would have happened if Vance hadn't found you?" Mateo asked as we kept walking.

"I don't know." I'd asked myself that same question a thousand times.

Life out here had gotten both easier and harder. Easier because we'd had a routine. A home of sorts. Harder because... it was a hard life. Food wasn't guaranteed. Winters were brutal. Squatting to pee wasn't exactly glamorous. It had become more and more difficult to summon the strength to keep up with Dad. With every passing month, my energy had waned.

"Living out here always felt temporary," I told Mateo. "Those years when we were constantly on the move, it was running. Adrenaline was a big motivator in the beginning. I never expected it to last forever. I thought at some point, we'd stop. But Dad just kept going. Kept running. He didn't stop until I got sick."

Maybe that was why I'd gotten sick. The idea of moving on, of enduring endless miles, had shut my body down.

"It got easier when we came to Montana." I tilted my gaze to the treetops and the blue sky peeking past their limbs.

These mountains had been my refuge. This was where I'd finally... breathed. For the first time since that night, this was where I'd outwardly mourned.

This forest had caught my countless tears. The moments I'd had to myself while Dad was hunting or setting snares and traps, I'd let the lid of that box crack open, just a little. And I'd let myself grieve for my sisters.

Maybe I'd never talk about them again, but I'd cried rivers for Elsie and Hadley. These trees had drunk the tears. The azure-blue sky had swallowed my cries. While I'd mourned two beautiful souls, these mountains had never left my side.

"This was home. We made a home," I said. "But it wasn't home. It was temporary too. Eventually, I knew we'd run out of money. Not that we spent much, but there were just certain supplies from town I'd get each month. I'd pick up certain foods whenever Dad worried we weren't getting enough fat in our diet. It all cost money. Every trip to town was a risk. Down deep, I knew it couldn't last."

And it didn't. Vance had caught me on a trip to Quincy.

I'd run from him that day. It had been out of fear for Dad that I'd raced in the opposite direction when I'd recognized his face. But my first reaction, before the panic had set in, had been this crippling relief that it was over. That we could stop running.

That I could live again.

"I think Dad knew I was fading. It was his idea that I go back with Vance."

Mateo slowed to a stop, waiting for me to step up beside him. "Can I tell you something?"

"Always."

"Part of me is terrified that when we find your father, you'll stay with him." The air rushed from his lungs, like he'd been holding that secret in for weeks.

"No. Even if we find him, I won't stay." I missed Dad so much it hurt, but this wasn't the life for me. "Dad loves it out here. This is where he belongs now. What happened... it broke him. Broke us."

Mateo's hand took mine. "Not you."

I was broken, whether he thought so or not. Irrevocably broken, like Dad? No. But a part of me had shattered that night and no amount of time or love would ever repair what had been destroyed. All I could hope for was enough strength to move forward. To balance the broken with unbroken and find peace.

All this time, I'd been worried about normal.

But my definition of normal was wrong, wasn't it? Normal didn't mean I became the woman I would have been if not for that night.

Maybe my version of normal meant finding peace with a very not-normal past.

Maybe if I'd had a therapist or counselor years ago, it wouldn't have taken me so long to come to that realization.

"I've been thinking about school," I said.

"Yeah?"

"I've been enjoying my psychology classes. When I registered at the beginning of the semester, I was hoping maybe it would help me understand my parents. But the more I learn, the more I want to keep learning. Maybe I could become a social worker or a counselor or... I don't know. It was just a thought."

"I like that idea." Mateo used our clasped hands to tug me into his arms. "Whatever you decide, you know I'm in your corner."

"I know." I smiled against the thermal shirt that pulled tight across his broad chest. "It's a lot of school. I might not be able to take them all online."

"We'll make it work." Mateo kissed my hair and let me go. But he kept my hand in his as we continued to hike, picking our way past trees as we scanned our surroundings.

We hadn't put a limit on how long we'd stay out today, but as the sun passed directly overhead, the disappointment in another unproductive journey settled like a gray cloud. Another hour at most, and we'd need to head back to the truck.

That hour passed too quickly. The forest wasn't as thick here, and the grass swished against the hem of my jeans, the taller stalks brushing my calves. White and yellow wildflowers dotted the field of green. It was hard to appreciate its beauty today with that cloud hanging over my head.

"We should probably turn around," I said.

Mateo let go of my hand and took a step forward, like he hadn't heard me.

"Mateo."

He lifted a finger to his lips.

I clamped my mouth shut and craned my ears, listening for anything as my eyes swept from left to right. There was no one. No sound.

He jerked his chin for me to follow as he took off into the field, walking so fast I had to jog every other step to keep up.

Mateo's gaze roved from side to side, searching. The minute he spotted whatever it was he'd been looking for he changed paths, marching straight toward a row of bushes in the distance. His body blocked my view until we were just ten feet away.

I saw the gap in the bushes first. The small hole and narrow, trodden path in the grass. Dad had taught me to identify bunny trails where rabbits would leave the safety of the thicket to feed on wild carrot and sweet cicely.

So focused on the trail, it wasn't until I was standing directly beside Mateo that I spotted a fluff of white and tan, stark against the greenery.

A rabbit.

My heart climbed into my throat as Mateo bent to inspect the dead animal. A thin wire was looped around its neck.

I knew that wire.

Two years ago, before I'd left, I'd bought Dad three new rolls of that malleable, thin gauge wire for his snares. Mateo had found his snare line.

"How?"

Mateo glanced up. "I heard it scream."

Rabbits often let out a scream of terror and panic before they died. A sound that made my heart twist so violently I'd stopped going with Dad whenever he checked his snare line.

There had to be more. My gaze darted around, searching for more trails and wires.

Twenty feet from where Mateo was still kneeling, a shrub had been nibbled recently. I slowed, crouching to find a gap in the grass.

The wire was nearly invisible, but I'd built enough snares to pick it out against the foliage. Its loop was about the size of Dad's palm. He'd tied it to a nearby shrub, positioning the loop about four finger widths off the ground. A stick had been shoved into the earth below the snare's loop, something Dad liked to do to ensure the animals didn't duck under the wire but instead jumped through it. Then the wire would kink around the rabbit's neck so it couldn't get loose.

"It's him," I said as Mateo came to stand by my side.

"You're sure?"

"Yes."

I shifted the pack off my shoulders, unzipping the front pocket to retrieve the note I'd written in the kitchen this morning.

It should have been easy, leaving it on the grass for my father to find. But I stared at the words for a long moment, doubting what I'd written.

Stop hiding from me.

Everything would change when he found this note.

Because if nothing changed, if he ignored it, it would break my heart.

CHAPTER 31

MATEO

That son of a bitch Cormac Gallagher was breaking Vera's heart.

"Want me to fly another loop?" I asked Vera.

"No." She glanced out her window, peering toward the terrain below the plane. There was nothing but trees and fields and rugged Montana beauty. "Let's just go home."

"All right." I banked the plane and put us on a heading for Quincy's airfield.

There was no way to spot anyone from up here. The forest was too thick to spot a shelter. The weather had warmed enough in early June that, even though the nighttime temperatures were chilly, there was no need for Cormac to have a fire burning during the day. And other than a plume of smoke, there'd be no way to see one man through the trees. I should have warned her this would be pointless.

But when Vera had asked to fly around Sable Peak, I hadn't been able to tell her no.

It had been a month since we'd found that snare line. Since she'd left that note.

Cormac had taken it. And ignored it.

We'd gone hiking ten times since. The first trip had been three days after she'd left her message. The snares had vanished. We'd scoured the area, searching for other signs that Cormac was around. But rather than face his daughter, rather than show her he cared, he'd disappeared.

Clearly, Cormac had abandoned the spot where he'd been living, but on foot, there was only so much ground we could cover. Hence today's flight. We'd left Alaina with my parents and come to the airfield at sunrise to fly for a couple of hours.

I was giving this two more weeks. Then, regardless of how much Vera resisted, I was putting an end to the madness.

Every time we came home empty-handed, some of the spark would fade from her eyes. More than once, I'd seen her fighting tears on the drives home. She'd retreated this past month, pulling deeper and deeper into herself.

Her arms wrapped around her middle. Her shoulders curled inward into the straps of her harness.

"Sorry." I put my hand on her thigh.

"Thanks for trying." She shrugged and kept her gaze aimed outside as we flew past Sable Peak.

The highest ridge was still capped in white. The small mountain lake was a bright aqua beneath the morning sun, a circle of blue against the sea of evergreen.

When the peak and mountains were behind us, as we flew over the open plains that surrounded Quincy, Vera shifted to face forward, her hands clasped in her lap. Her disappointment was louder than the plane's engine.

A lone tear streaked down her cheek. She caught it, but not fast enough for me to miss it.

Fuck the two weeks I'd planned. This was enough. We were ending this today. Cormac didn't deserve her.

What the hell kind of man would do this to his daughter? Did he think he was saving her? Setting her free? How could he have spent so many years with her but not know her at all?

Vera's loyalty knew no bounds. She'd torture herself for his absence until the end of her days.

"Want to take the controls?" I asked, needing to do something to make this better. "Fly for a bit?"

"That's okay."

"Are you sure? You could do some steep turns or maneuvers, something fun. We could go buzz the cabin or Mom and Dad's house."

"Let's just finish up at the hangar. I kind of want to clean the loft today. You can just drop me off when you pick up Allie."

The loft didn't need to be cleaned. She was hardly there these days other than to grab clothes. At most, there was a bit of dust. But this was Vera wanting to run. To hide from me so she could deal with the emotions alone.

"Quincy traffic," I announced into the common traffic advisory frequency. "Cirrus Four Zero Six Delta Whiskey. Ten miles south. Inbound for a full stop."

She wanted to clean? Fine. Then we'd both clean. And if she didn't want my help, then I'd camp out on her sectional and pore through the piles of paperwork for the flight school.

As a certified instructor, I could train student pilots, but to actually start a flight school, there were different rules and requirements from the FAA. I'd spent the past month establishing a business and getting the necessary insurance. Then I'd spent countless hours developing training curriculum.

I'd missed teaching too. I hadn't realized how much until I'd sat with Vera for our few study sessions. The last time I'd had a student pilot under my wing had been in college. Vera might have groaned at the ground school material, but I'd missed those books. I'd missed breaking down the basics and explaining the aerodynamics.

It would take months, maybe longer, to put the flight school's plan together for approval. There was no rush to start, but I didn't want to wait. For the first time in my life, I felt like I was doing exactly what I was supposed to be doing.

That I was moving in the right direction.

That feeling was more than just the flight school. It was Allie. It was Vera. Life was good. Now if I could only take away the sadness hiding behind Vera's sunglasses.

She stayed quiet as we landed and taxied to the hangar. The drive to the ranch was equally as silent. When we stopped at Mom and Dad's, she surprised me by staying in the truck while I went in to get Allie. I'd expected to find her gone when we came out.

"Thought you wanted to clean."

"I'll do it later." She knew I wasn't going to leave her alone.

By the time we made it to the cabin, Vera had curled herself into a ball in the passenger seat. Did she even realize how far away she'd huddled toward the door? The instant I parked, she blew outside, hurrying for the house.

Allie had drifted off on the ride home, and since it was her naptime, I carefully lifted her out of her seat and carried her inside, taking her straight to bed. With the sound machine cranked to drown out any noise, I closed the door and came out to find Vera in the kitchen.

Keys in hand.

"I think I'm—"

"No." I planted my hands on my hips. "You're not going anywhere."

"Mateo, I'm in a bad mood. Let me go deal with it somewhere else before it ruins your day too."

Instead of talking to me, she was going to run.

Not today.

"Put the keys down, darlin'."

She sighed. "Please."

"Keys down." Either she dropped those keys or I'd blockade the fucking door.

It took a moment, but she tossed them onto the counter. Without them to hold, it looked like she didn't know what to do with her hands. She lifted them, dropped them. Lifted them again, her fingers splayed in the air, until they dove into her hair, pulling at the red strands. "I don't want to be here."

That stung. But it wasn't about me.

Vera didn't know how to talk through the big emotions. She'd spent too many years hiding from them, burying them.

There wasn't a lot I could do. But I could love her. I could be here.

"Why don't you want to be here?"

"Because I'm... mad." Her voice cracked. "Sad. Frustrated. Angry. You name it, Mateo. That's how I feel. It's too much, and I want to scream."

"So scream."

She huffed. "Just let me go and I'll—"

"Deal with it on your own? No. We've got things to discuss."

"What things?"

"For starters, we're done searching for your father." Cormac had blown his chance at a reunion with his daughter.

Her body stiffened. "I'm not quitting."

"You are."

"You don't get to dictate—"

"I won't let him keep hurting you. I will not."

"He's my father, Mateo."

"Then he should fucking act like it." I wasn't shouting. Yet. But I was damn close. "It's breaking your heart. What do you expect me to do? Stand by and watch it happen?"

Her chin started to quiver. "There has to be a reason for what he's doing. He must think it's for my own good or something, I don't know. But I'm afraid he's not in a good mindset. He attacked Lyla, Mateo. He *hurt* her. He's not thinking clearly. What if he's spiraled even more? I just need to find him and talk to him."

"No." I raked a hand through my hair. "Damn it. No. He found that note, and he stayed away. He doesn't want to talk."

"It might not have been him."

"Vera," I deadpanned.

Her expression shuttered, like a wall slammed down in front of her face.

"Every time we go up, it takes a piece of you." I gave her a sad smile. "I'm scared you'll give and give until there's nothing left."

Tears flooded her eyes. "He's my dad. He's my family."

"I—" My brain screeched to a halt.

She said it. She meant it. She was hell-bent on finding Cormac because she considered him her family. But if she didn't find him, if she never saw her father again, she knew she had our family, right?

She knew she wasn't alone, didn't she?

My frustration vanished. In its place, this crushing regret that maybe I hadn't done or said enough so she'd see just how much family she had under this roof.

I loved her. More than my own life. Allie loved her. We were her family. With or without her father.

"You did Allie's bath last night."

She swallowed hard and wiped at the corners of her eyes. "Yeah. So?"

"She rarely throws a fit for you. You tell her it's time for a bath, and she thinks that's the best idea in the world. Because it's you. You're her Ve-wa. Every time she says it, she might as well be calling you Mommy."

Vera's mouth parted.

"I didn't think she'd ever have that. A mother. I didn't even want to let myself dream she could. But she does. It's you. You are her family. You are hers." I crossed the room and took her face in my hands, holding those beautiful chocolate eyes. "And you're mine. *We* are your family."

A tear cascaded down her cheek.

I caught it with my thumb. "I love you, Vera. I fucking

love you. I won't leave you. And I won't let you go."

It took a moment for my words to creep past those walls, but the moment they made it, the light that transformed her face was the most beautiful sight I'd ever seen.

"I love you." The words had barely made it out of her mouth before she jumped, launching herself into my arms to crush her mouth to mine.

I swept her into my arms, slanting my mouth over hers. If all I accomplished for the rest of my life was to kiss Vera every morning and every night, I'd consider it a life well lived.

She wrapped her arms around my shoulders and her legs around my waist, clinging to me as I deepened the kiss and walked us into the bedroom.

I shut the door. She hopped down to flip the lock. Then we stripped out of our clothes, fumbling and frenzied, without fanfare, until she was in my arms again and her soft, smooth skin was warm against mine.

Our mouths collided, teeth clashing and lips frantic, as I laid her on the bed. My cock nudged against her core, aching to slide into her tight heat, but I held off, bracing my body above hers as my elbows bracketed her face.

"I love you."

Her eyes were like chocolate pools, the gold flecks dancing in the light as it streamed through the bedroom windows. "I love you too."

Thank fuck she'd kissed me that night at Willie's.

I took her mouth, savoring the kiss as her body rocked against mine. Tonight, I'd take my time. I'd draw out her pleasure for hours. But right now, there was no telling how long Allie would sleep, and I wasn't waiting. With a slow, deliberate thrust, I slid inside.

Heaven. "You feel so good."

She clawed at my shoulders, her back arching off the

bed as she stretched around my length. "Mateo. Move, baby. Please."

All my life, I'd live for the sound of my name while I was buried inside her.

I withdrew and slammed inside again, earning a hitch in her breath.

Her grip on my shoulders only tightened as my fingers dove into her hair. With it threaded in my fists, I pistoned in and out, faster and faster.

"I love you," I breathed. With every thrust of my hips, I whispered it into her ear like a prayer.

"Yes," she whimpered as her pussy clenched around me. God, that first orgasm. It always came fast. Hard. It usually came without much warning, sometimes surprising us both.

Vera's cries echoed off the walls, her body quaking beneath mine.

Pulse after pulse, she shattered. God, the sounds. The feel of her body. The pressure at the base of my spine was almost unbearable. I gritted my teeth, wanting to draw it out for just another minute, another second, but the way she clenched was too incredible.

I came on a groan, muffling it in a pillow as I poured inside her. Every muscle in my body tensed and trembled, my mind going blank as white spots stole my sight. I'd lost count of the times I'd come inside Vera's body.

But this orgasm was different. This was the release that tore me into shreds, and when the pieces came floating together, nothing would ever be the same again. From this moment on, it was us.

Her legs wrapped around my hips as we both collapsed, boneless and panting. The stars behind my eyes finally faded, and when I cracked my eyes open, lifting up to stare down at Vera, I found her gaze waiting.

The hair at her temples was damp with sweat. Her cheeks

were flushed. Her lips were rosy and damp.

Never before had she looked more beautiful.

Never would I love a woman more.

"How's the weather, Peach?"

"Better than I expected," she whispered. "It started overcast and gray."

"And now?"

She smiled. "Clear and a million."

CHAPTER 32

VERA

"This is everything?" Vance asked as he took the backpack from the trunk of my Honda.

"It's only a weekend camping trip." I'd lived for four years on about as much.

He chuckled as he carried it to his truck, opening the tailgate. Beneath the smooth black cover, there was barely room for my backpack. "Tell that to my wife."

"Hey." Lyla scolded as she came through Eden Coffee's back door to the alley. "I heard that. Babies come with stuff, Vance."

"You're right, Blue," he said. "Anything else you want to pack up?"

"No, I think—shoot. The cookies. Be right back."

As she disappeared into the cafe, Vance and I shared a look.

"What is all this?" I asked as he stowed my backpack.

"Well, my backpack is in there somewhere. But we've also got Trey's portable crib. Enough baby food for a month. Three bottles of sunscreen. Five coolers. And this morning, I had to sit on her biggest suitcase so she could zip it up."

"Then I know who to go to if I forgot anything."

He slammed the tailgate shut. "When I teased her about

it, she told me it was a fraction of what her parents were bringing."

"Yeah, Anne's been prepping for this trip all week." I moved for the backseat, but before I could climb inside, Lyla came rushing out with a plastic container of cookies and waved me away. "I'll sit back there with Trey. You can ride shotgun."

"Are you sure?"

"Yep." She smiled and popped the lid to the container, letting me and Vance each take a chocolate chip cookie before we all climbed in the truck.

Vance hit the ignition button. "Ready?"

"Let the Eden family campout begin," Lyla said.

He reversed away from the coffee shop, leaving my car behind, and headed down Main.

This weekend marked the inaugural family camping trip. Attendance was mandatory. Anne and Harrison had threatened to cease any and all future babysitting if people didn't show up for this trip.

Even without the idle threats, no one had balked at the idea of a weekend getaway.

Talia had taken the weekend off from the hospital. Eloise had ensured her staff had the hotel covered. The ranch hands could survive a weekend without Griffin. Knuckles was being run by Knox's sous chef. And Lyla had handed the reins of Eden Coffee to Crystal.

Even though it was tourist season and everyone was swamped, Anne and Harrison had insisted on just one weekend.

One break from work. One weekend as a family.

Everyone else had already left Quincy. Mateo had promised Anne and Harrison he'd help get the campsite ready, so while he and Allie had headed up early, I'd stayed in town to work and ride up with Vance and Lyla.

"So where are we going?" I asked.

"Some new spot Dad discovered," Lyla answered from beside Trey's car seat. "He said it was about an hour from here. Why we're not just camping at the ranch like we did as kids I have no idea. But he's excited and he planned it all out. Do you have the directions?"

Vance plucked a sticky note from the dash. "Got 'em."

Lyla yawned, reclining in her seat.

Five miles later, as we sped down the highway, Vance glanced into his rearview and smiled. "They're out."

When I looked to the back, Lyla was resting on Trey's car seat, both sound asleep.

"I'm glad you rode with us today," he said. "I've missed you, kiddo."

"Missed you too." I saw him at least once a week at the coffee shop, but our regular lunches had dwindled this year. He was busy with Lyla and Trey. I had Mateo and Allie. Time alone had become sporadic.

"So... I hear you've got a new address."

My cheeks flushed. "As of yesterday."

The loft was no longer my home.

It had been two weeks since Mateo had told me he loved me, and there were moments when I still didn't quite believe it was real. It would probably take that and longer for our living arrangement to sink in.

Mateo and I hadn't talked about me moving into the cabin. He'd just taken it upon himself to pack my stuff from the loft.

I'd come home from work on Monday night to find the dining room table crowded with everything I'd had in my bathroom. Lotions and curling irons and makeup and nail polishes. Everything had been strewn on the table because he'd wanted me to claim whatever space in his—our—bathroom that I wanted.

Tuesday, I came home to find my clothes on his—our—bed.

Maybe it was too soon to live together. Maybe not. I wasn't going to overthink it. I liked that we shared a home.

So on Wednesday, when I hadn't had to work, we'd gone to the loft together and finished packing. Then yesterday, I'd spent the evening deep cleaning and saying goodbye to the first home I'd built on my own.

I was going to miss that loft.

"Are you happy?" Vance asked.

"More than I ever thought possible."

He stretched a hand over, placing it on my shoulder. "I'm sorry."

"For what?"

"For treating you like you're fragile."

"Oh." It came from a good place. Vance worried. In Dad's absence, Vance had stepped in to fill that role. But yes, he treated me like I was going to break.

"Mateo doesn't. And that's part of why you love him."

I nodded. "Yes."

"Then I'm glad. For you both."

"Thanks." I smiled at him just as a yawn tugged at my mouth.

"Tired?"

"Yeah. It was an early morning and Allie had a bad night. She woke up twice and finally just crawled in bed with us."

"The nights when Trey sleeps with us are the worst." He groaned. "He always manages to dig his feet into my back."

"Allie had hers in my face." I yawned again. "I gave up trying to sleep around three."

"You're good for her."

"I love her." She was mine.

"Take a nap too," he said when I yawned for the third time.

"I'm okay."

"Vera." He shot me a flat look. "Sleep."

"We haven't gotten to talk much."

"We have all weekend."

I shifted in my seat, leaning against the door. "Thirty minutes. Wake me up before we get there."

"You bet." He plucked a sticky note from the console, rereading Harrison's directions.

While I'd spent my week packing up the loft, Anne and Harrison had worked tirelessly to load up their fifth-wheel camper. Meanwhile, everyone else would be sleeping in tents. Maybe I could convince Mateo to sleep outside one night beneath the stars.

Dad and I used to sleep beneath the stars. We'd spend hours pointing out constellations before drifting off to sleep. Did he still do that? Did he hold his hand in the air and trace them out with a fingertip?

Mateo and I hadn't gone hiking again. For my heart's sake, the break had been necessary. But down deep, it felt unfinished. I wasn't ready to stop looking for Dad, no matter how much Mateo insisted.

Part of me wanted to talk to Vance about it and get his thoughts. But I was afraid he'd agree with Mateo. So I closed my eyes and let the whir of tires on pavement lull me to sleep.

I jolted awake as we came to a stop. Gone was the highway. Instead, we were parked beside Mateo's truck against a grove of trees. "We're here already?"

"You were out," Vance said. "I didn't have the heart to wake you."

I blinked sleep from my eyes. "Sorry."

"Don't be." He hopped out, going to the back to help Lyla.

"Ready for your first camping trip?" she asked Trey as she unbuckled his harness.

The sound of laughter and talking reached my ears. When I opened my door, I was hit with the scents of pine and grass and… water.

"You made it." Harrison came to my side and hauled me

into a hug. "How you doing?"

"Good," I breathed, still foggy from the nap. "Where's Mateo?"

"Swimming in the lake with Allie."

A lake? My heart stopped. "W-what?"

"Where's your stuff? I'll take it to your tent." Harrison went to the tailgate, oblivious to the wash of panic coursing through my veins.

A lake. No one had mentioned a lake. They'd only talked about the campsite at Alder. Mateo had packed his fly-fishing rod and he'd told me to bring a swimsuit but I'd assumed it was for a river.

"Where are we?" My voice rattled.

"Alder Campground." Harrison smiled and grabbed my bag. "Is this all you brought?"

I managed a nod.

"Come on." He threw an arm around my shoulders, leading me to the campground.

The site they'd picked was an open expanse large enough for the fifth wheel and all of our vehicles. Tents had been set up throughout the space, everyone choosing a different spot beneath the shade of the surrounding trees.

The firepit was already circled by collapsible chairs and coolers. A stack of wood was piled nearby. An umbrella with towels and blankets was set up on a patch of grass for the kids to play beneath.

Talia was putting sunscreen on Jude. Memphis had baby Annie strapped to her chest and was talking with Winn and Eloise.

And beyond it all, the guys were in the water with the kids.

My heart beat so loudly in my ears I could barely hear their laughter.

A lake. It was just a lake. *Breathe.*

"Daddy!" Drake came racing past us wearing a life jacket.

His blond hair, the same shade as Memphis's, flopped as he ran straight for the water, where Knox was waiting.

The water.

A lake.

I couldn't fill my lungs. I couldn't breathe.

"Want something to drink?" Harrison asked, setting my backpack by the campfire and opening a cooler. "Water or pop? I picked up your favorite cream soda."

A lake. We were at a lake. The kids were swimming in a lake.

"Vera?" Harrison stood. "What is it?"

I took a step forward, then another.

Mateo was standing close to the shoreline wearing nothing but low-slung black swim trunks, a pair of mirrored sunglasses and that dazzling smile. The water lapped at his calves.

Allie was beside him, dressed in a frilly lavender swimsuit and splashing in the rippled waves. Her sunglasses were purple and heart shaped.

She wasn't wearing a life jacket. Why wasn't she wearing a life jacket? She could drown. She could drown in that water. She could die in that lake.

I took another step, the panic rising so fast it nearly suffocated. "Mateo."

He didn't hear me. He was talking to his brothers.

"Mateo."

His attention shifted, and when he saw me, that smile widened.

"Get her out of the water."

He shifted his sunglasses into his hair. "What?"

"Get her out of the water." She was in the water. She was in that lake. She couldn't swim.

She couldn't swim and she was in the lake without a lifejacket. I took another step forward, my knees nearly buckling. "Get her out. Get her out of that water."

"Peach."

"Get her out of that lake, Mateo!" My voice ricocheted.

Talking ceased. The laughter died, even from the kids. Everyone turned to look at me.

But I didn't move. I didn't breathe. Not until Mateo bent and snatched up Allie, ignoring her protests as he hauled her out of the water.

"Vera." Vance's hand landed on my shoulder, but I shrugged it off.

Then I ran.

CHAPTER 33

MATEO

"Daddy! No!" Allie kicked and screamed.

"Mom," I hollered.

She already had her arms outstretched to take Allie. "I've got her."

I handed off my daughter, then tore off after Vera, but in my soaked flip-flops, I'd never catch her. So I kicked off the sandals and bolted for my tent, snagging the tennis shoes I'd had on earlier. By the time I had them on, Vera was nowhere in sight. "Fuck."

But Vance was chasing after her. I'd caught sight of him before he'd disappeared past a cluster of trees. Foster, Jasper and Dad were hot on his heels. Griffin and Knox, who hadn't stopped to change their shoes, joined the chase.

I outran them all, passing them without a word as I sprinted to find her.

When I caught up to Vance, my lungs and legs burning, he just pointed ahead to where a flash of red-orange streaked in the distance.

"Vera!"

She ignored my shout and kept running, faster than I'd ever seen her move. Like if she were quick enough, she could escape the past.

She ran.

I let her run.

But she was done running alone.

I pushed my body harder, faster, and when I finally caught up, I didn't stop her. Every fiber of my being wanted to grab her and put this to an end. Except she wasn't done yet. She needed to keep going.

So I settled in behind her, keeping pace.

She ran.

And I followed.

By the time her strides slowed, I was sweating and breathless. Her run became a jog, then a walk. Then she buried her face in her hands and the wail that escaped her palms tore through my heart.

"Peach." I wrapped her up, hauling her into my chest.

"Let me go." A sob broke from her mouth as she tried to wrench her body free.

I held on tighter. "I love you."

She fought me again, squirming and jerking, trying to wiggle loose. She could fight all she wanted.

I wasn't letting her go.

"I got you."

Her shoulders began to shake and the protest leeched from her body.

"I love you." Nothing else mattered. On the hardest days of her life, I'd be here to remind her that I loved her.

"Mateo." Another sob cracked clear, then she sagged against me.

"I'm here. I'm not letting go."

"It hurts." She sobbed without stopping this time, the cries cleaving me in pieces.

"I know, darlin'." I held her tighter, a lump forming in my throat. Her pain. My pain.

"It's open."

"What's open?"

She cried harder. "The box. It's open and it hurts."

Oh, God. This was killing her. For too long, she'd kept it all locked up. "Let it out."

"I c-can't."

"Yes, you can." I buried my nose in her hair. "Give it to me."

"She killed them." Her entire body went slack, so I turned her in my arms and cradled her against my shoulder as we dropped to our knees. "She killed them. Hadley and Elsie. She killed my sisters. She tried to kill me."

Her mother.

It was what I'd assumed, but to hear it from her lips was like having a whip slice into my bare back, cutting to the bone.

Was this the first time she'd spoken the truth? She'd never told anyone that before, had she? She'd just locked it away. She'd run from the truth.

Pain, rage, lit my blood into a wildfire, but I didn't so much as move. I kept my arms locked around Vera, knowing we hadn't even started yet.

It took her a while to stop crying. The forest moved around us, oblivious to the magnitude of this moment. Birds flew and chirped. Trees swayed and pine cones clacked against branches as they fell.

And I just held Vera, feeling eyes on my back.

Dad. My brothers. They wouldn't approach. They'd keep their distance and give us this moment. But they were close, ready to help me pick her up when the time came.

"I was on the swim team," Vera whispered with a hitch. "I was a good swimmer. We lived on a lake. I loved to swim. We had a boat. Dad taught us to waterski. And he'd take us to a quiet spot so we could jump in and swim."

The lake. That was the trigger. She'd seen Allie in the lake.

A lake, like the one where she'd lived. Where her sisters had drowned.

Fuck. Why hadn't I thought of that?

"I'm sorry. I'm so fucking sorry, Vera. I shouldn't have brought you here." I should have taken one look at that lake when we'd arrived this morning and turned this camping trip around.

She nuzzled deeper, like if she crawled into my chest, that would make it all go away.

If I could take it from her, I would in a blink.

"She was acting strange when we got home from school that day."

She. Not Mom. She.

"I've never seen anyone high like that. I didn't hang out with the kids who smoked pot but I'd seen them high before. This was different. Not just from weed. And it was more than just being drunk, but I wasn't sure. I didn't drink. Ever. Not just because Dad was a cop and he taught us about being responsible, but because I didn't like getting in trouble."

A good girl. My good girl.

I hated her mother for putting her through this. I hated her father for letting this fester. Six fucking years this had lived inside her and she'd dealt with it all on her own.

"She was drinking wine." Vera shuddered as more wounds ripped open. "At four o'clock in the afternoon. I thought she was just drunk. She didn't drink like that. At least not normally. But there'd been something wrong with her. Twice I'd come home and she was drunk. Not slurring or out of it, but almost... hungover. I tried to hide it from Hadley and Elsie."

Maybe her mother had started drinking the minute her kids had left for school. And sobered up by the time they'd made it home. Or by the time Cormac, an adult who knew what drunk and high looked like, had made it home.

"I didn't tell Dad." Her voice cracked. "Why didn't I tell Dad?"

The guilt that came with that question was about as hard to stomach as her pain. "This isn't your fault."

"I should have told him. Before."

Before her mother attempted murder.

"Dad was at some coaches meeting at the school," she said. "Concussion training, I think, for the volunteers. She was acting off, so I told Hadley and Elsie to go upstairs and do their homework until he got home. There was a thunderstorm. It was loud and the rain was hard."

I was right. That was why she'd gotten scared the night of the storm weeks ago. Because there'd been a storm that night.

"She got frantic. Every time there was thunder, she'd pull at her hair and start talking to herself. It scared me. Every time I tried to talk to her, calm her down, she'd look at me like I was a stranger. She didn't have a clue that I was her daughter. I was about to call Dad and have him come home but then she screamed. She screamed so loud, Mateo. I had to cover my ears."

Fucking hell. Her mother had gone off the deep end, and she'd had to witness it all.

"She ran outside. Right into the storm. It was still early. Gray. The storm blocked out the sun but it wasn't dark yet. She ran for the dock and climbed on the boat, untying it before I could stop her. I tried to get her to stop. We all did."

Vera's body began to tremble and she burrowed deeper.

I stroked her hair, holding her so impossibly tight that my muscles locked in place. They'd be stiff when I finally let go.

"I wish I could go back to that moment." A fresh wave of tears soaked my skin. "I would do anything to keep my sisters off that boat."

"I'm sorry," I murmured.

"She took off. Drove away from the dock so fast it threw me to the floor. Elsie almost tipped over the edge but Hadley caught her. The waves were... impossible. The water just kept coming into the boat, crashing over the hull, and she was out of control, going faster and swerving in all directions. I finally managed to get to my feet and pull her away from the steering wheel. I was going to drive us home but then she said something about swimming lessons. I didn't understand."

Vera pulled away from my chest, staring up at me with so much regret in those beautiful eyes I wanted to scream.

It wasn't fair that she'd endured this. It wasn't fucking fair.

"Swimming lessons?"

She nodded, her chin quivering. "She took Hadley's arm and pushed her to the edge of the boat. A wave rocked us hard and then my sister was just... gone."

I closed my eyes. "Christ."

"I dove in after her, and it was so cold. It made it hard to breathe and took me a minute to snap out of it. But I swam for Hadley as fast as I could, trying to keep my head above the waves. They were too big. It was too cold. I turned back to look at the boat and Elsie was gone. I was going to swim back and find her too but she drove away. She... left us." Her face crumpled. "She left us."

Sitting on my lap, cradled in my arms, Vera broke to pieces.

The sobs that wracked her chest shook her entire body. They were endless. Each time I thought they'd stop, a fresh wave would hit and start the anguish anew.

Was that how it had been that night? Wave after wave slamming her toward the depths.

"I lost them," she cried, clinging to me. "I lost them, Mateo. I couldn't find Hadley. I tried to find Elsie but she was gone. I lost them."

"This is not on you, Vera."

"I should have found them. I was their big sister. I was on the swim team. I should have saved them."

"Look at me." I took her face, pulling it away from my

shoulder. "You did not lose them."

She squeezed her eyes shut. "I left them. I thought they'd swim for home, so when I couldn't see them, that's what I did. I kicked off my shoes because it's hard to swim in shoes. They probably didn't think to take off their shoes, did they?"

"I don't know, darlin'." I kissed her forehead, catching tears with my thumbs.

Fuck you, Norah Gallagher. For what she'd done to her daughter, I hoped that woman had landed in an especially hot corner of hell.

"I thought I'd find them." Vera's breath hitched. "I stayed on the dock for hours, letting it rain and waiting for them to make it. The boat was gone. I thought she might have sunk it. I wanted her to sink it."

To sink with it.

"Then Dad was there. He was soaking wet. I've never seen him so scared. But he was alone, and I knew... we were alone." She crumpled again, curling so tightly she fit like a ball in my lap. "They were so scared. They died scared. Because I didn't save them."

My heart broke. Over and over and over again.

"I'm sorry, Vera. I'm so sorry."

She cried for so long I started to worry she'd never stop. But eventually, the shaking in her shoulders stopped, and with it, the tears. Her body slumped against mine, not even having the strength to sit upright. Too much heartache and it was shutting her down.

I shifted and picked her up, cradling her against my chest as I walked to a nearby tree. Then I sat at its trunk, using it as a backrest even though the bark dug into my bare skin. It was nothing compared to what Vera had endured alone.

The strength she'd had at seventeen to swim home. To keep swimming. To not give up. *Damn.* I'd never hurt so much for another person and been so proud at the same time.

I held her, unmoving, until she eventually leaned away to meet my gaze.

"She was an addict." The life had drained from Vera's voice. It was flat and dull. "I never talked to Dad about it. He tried, in the beginning. But I shut him out. I just… couldn't."

"Understandable." I tucked a lock of hair behind her ear, then untucked it.

"When Vance and Lyla found me, Dad told them the truth. They didn't know I was listening, but I was outside our shelter, eavesdropping. I heard every word."

She inhaled a long, deep breath. It was the first time she'd filled her lungs in hours. The breath to start another story.

One more story.

Her father's.

"Dad met her at a bar in Alaska. Whenever they told us the story, he said he took one look at her and left his friends in the dust. Proposed to her the next day. Love at first sight. That's what I believed for most of my life."

"Not anymore?"

She stared at me, her eyes softening. "Not for them."

But for her. She'd loved me from first sight. For the rest of my life, I'd regret not being able to say the same.

"How did they actually meet?" I asked.

"In that bar. He went to the bathroom and found her passed out with a heroin needle stuck in her arm."

"Heroin?"

Vera nodded. "He took her to the hospital. The next day, went to check on her. He said once she was out of rehab to give him a call, and he'd buy her a cookies-and-cream milkshake."

"Did he?"

"Yeah. They started dating. She got pregnant with me, so they got married. Dad thought everything was fine, but he came home from work one day when I was nine months old and she was passed out drunk on vodka in the bathtub. She'd left me in my crib for hours with a dirty diaper and no food."

The mental image was jarring. Maybe because Allie was so young. I could still see her at that age. I could hear her crying from her crib, arms outstretched, when she'd wake up from a nap and want me to come rescue her.

"Apparently, they got her on some medication for postpartum depression. They moved to Idaho so they wouldn't have those long, dark winters in Alaska."

I'd lived through one of those winters and it was brutal. Montana might be cold six or more months out of the year, but at least the sun was usually shining.

"According to Dad, her family was toxic. I don't remember them because Dad refused to let them be around us after we moved. We never went back to Alaska, even though that's where his parents lived. They came to Idaho to visit us until they died. Dad used his inheritance to buy us that house on the lake and get the boat."

Every added detail was like another tiny cut. Another dash of salt on an open wound. Did Cormac regret every decision he'd ever made? My heart softened for her father. In his shoes, I would have blamed one person.

Myself.

"They waited awhile before having Elsie and Hadley. Dad wanted to make sure she was okay. That she'd be a good mother." Venom dripped from Vera's voice. "She *was* a good mother. She'd leave me notes in my lunch box. She'd braid my hair and talk to me about the boys I liked. She'd hug me whenever I was close. She'd kiss my temple and tell me she loved me to the moon and back. I loved her too."

Loved. Not love. Vera's love for Norah had drowned with her sisters.

"A friend of hers from Alaska came to visit. They went to lunch. Dad didn't go along. He told Vance he didn't think much about it. But that must have been the turning point for her to start using again."

Cormac hadn't noticed? I held that question inside. I had a lot of blame to put on that man. For my sister. For Vera. But a friend of mine from college had been addicted to meth. I hadn't known about it until he'd gotten arrested for breaking into his grandparents' house to steal some jewelry and pawn it for drug money.

Addicts were good at hiding their vices.

"Dad came home that night and found her alone," Vera said.

So Norah had made it home with the boat while her daughters had been drowning in the lake and Vera had been swimming for her life.

"Dad asked her what was going on, and she kept talking about swimming lessons. She thought he was a lifeguard and asked him to get her kids from the pool. He went outside, found the boat on the shore, not tied up. After he put it all together, he strangled her."

I flinched.

The way she said it, so cold and detached.

Her father had murdered her mother, and Vera spoke about it like the truth that it was. Did she ever resent him for that? No. Probably not. Not after what Norah had done.

"Dad went looking for us. Ran the boat almost out of gas. I was on the dock when he got back."

And then he'd swept her away from the world. He'd hidden her and let the world think she was dead. That he was a man who'd murdered his family.

Would I have done any different? Would I have taken Vera away from that horror? He would have gone to prison. At seventeen, she would have been left as a ward of the state. That, or sent to live with family. Possibly Norah's toxic parents from Alaska.

Did she have other family? Vance seemed to be her only

link to the past, and he wasn't a real uncle, just a friend.

Then there would have been the media attention. A tragic case like that... reporters would have been crawling all over her. They sure as hell had when she'd appeared years later, not dead. They would have suffocated her.

Maybe Cormac had done the right thing taking her away after all.

"Mateo?" Her face was splotchy, her eyes red and puffy. She was still beautiful, even tear soaked and jagged.

"Yeah?" I ran my knuckles down her cheek.

"Will it always hurt?"

"I don't know, Peach."

She leaned her head on my shoulder, her hand coming to my heart like she could feel it twisting. "I think yes."

Yes. It would probably always hurt. But she wouldn't be hurting alone, not anymore.

We stayed against that tree for hours, just holding on to each other. Finally, when Vera shifted to stand, we climbed to our feet and made our way back to camp.

Every tent, including ours, had been packed up. Jasper was putting the last cooler in his rig before slamming the tailgate shut. The other vehicles were loaded, and my parents' fifth wheel was hooked to their truck.

The moment Dad spotted us, he walked over with the keys to my truck in his hand. "Allie is riding with us. We're moving campgrounds."

Thank fuck. Not a chance I was making Vera stay by this lake. "Where to?"

He reached out and ran a thumb across Vera's cheek, giving her a smile. A father's smile. "The Eden Ranch."

CHAPTER 34

VERA

The alarm clock on Mateo's nightstand glowed blue. Five twenty-three in the morning. I'd been watching him sleep for over an hour.

It was an effort not to touch him. Not to run my fingertip down the straight line of his nose. Not to put my palm on his chiseled jaw to feel the coarse hair against my skin. Not to brush his soft lips with my own.

His hair was a mess, dark and disheveled against the white pillow. His chest rose and fell with each slumbering breath. His arm was outstretched and draped across my waist to keep me close.

Every morning this week I'd woken up before dawn and had spent my early morning hours memorizing his face. Sleep had been sporadic, at best, since the camping trip. My brain couldn't seem to shut down. Confiding in Mateo had been a relief and a torment.

The box down deep was empty now. The lid had sprung open and everything I'd worked so hard to keep locked away was free to fly away. Except those memories hadn't flittered into the ether. They hovered close, buzzing in my ear. No amount of swatting seemed to chase them away.

At least I wasn't swatting alone.

Mateo was now the keeper of my truths. As hard as I'd tried to hold everything inside, it felt right that he knew. We hadn't talked about it again. I wasn't ready. The cuts were still too fresh. But if—when—that time came, he'd be there.

The Edens, Harrison especially, felt awful about the camping trip. No one had realized it would be a lake to trigger those memories.

Not Mateo.

Not Vance or Lyla.

Not even me.

In the years Dad and I had spent in hiding, we'd never gone to a lake. Not once. When I'd needed to bathe, it had been in streams or rivers. For four years, Dad had kept me away from lakes.

Either because he knew I couldn't handle it.

Or because he couldn't.

But seeing Allie in that water...

It had been the catalyst. Or maybe time had simply run out, and whether we'd been by a lake or a pool or in downtown Quincy without a drop of water in sight, that was always going to be the moment when I broke apart.

At least I'd been around people who loved me.

That first night camping, after we'd moved sites to the ranch, had been awkward. Everyone had tried to move forward, to wear bright smiles for my benefit, but I'd been too raw and embarrassed to appreciate them. So I'd just cuddled with Allie in a camp chair until she'd fallen asleep and we'd retreated to our tent.

But the next morning, after sleeping in Mateo's arms in our sleeping bag, I'd snuck out early.

Anne had been up already, sipping coffee alone. She'd pulled me into her arms and kissed my hair. She'd told me she loved me. And she'd hugged me tight.

It was a mother's hug.

Mine was gone. So I was keeping Mateo's for myself.

With the dawn of a new day, camping had actually been fun. We'd played cornhole and horseshoes. We'd hiked with the kids and let Allie pick wildflowers. We'd laughed around the campfire, telling stories for hours.

Then we'd come home. We'd gone back to normal.

A new normal.

A weight had been lifted from my heart. It wasn't gone, but it was lighter because Mateo was carrying part of it now.

I should be able to sleep. I should be able to rest. Except something kept plaguing me. Something that felt unfinished. And it wasn't until this morning, watching Mateo sleep, that I finally realized what I had to do.

It took twenty more minutes before he stirred. His eyes opened slowly and when he met my gaze, a lazy grin spread across his face. The arm draped over me hauled me close so our bodies were pressed together.

"Morning, Peach." He buried his nose in my hair and slid his hand down my side, lifting my thigh over his until we were tangled together beneath the sheets.

I snuggled into his chest, breathing in the spicy scent of his skin. "Mateo?"

He hummed.

"I need to do something today."

He leaned back to stare down at me. "What?"

I sucked in a fortifying breath because he wasn't going to like this. "Hike Sable Peak."

He blinked, surprised for a moment, then that jaw set in a hard line. "No."

"Wait." I clutched his neck when he shifted to get out of bed. "Please, hear me out."

"Vera," he growled but stopped moving.

"Dad and I never talked about it. I couldn't. But now... there are things to say. Things I want to tell him and I can't find him. I don't know if I'll ever find him again. But I want to try. One last time."

Mateo's eyes softened as he sighed. "He doesn't want to be found."

"Maybe not. But if I quit now, I'll always wonder." This hike was more for my heart than anything.

"He blames himself," I told Mateo. "When I was eavesdropping on Dad and Vance and Lyla, he blamed himself for not noticing she was spiraling and using and drinking. I think a part of me blamed him too, I don't know."

Should Dad have noticed? I had as much guilt for not telling him about her drinking as he did for loving her blindly.

"It's not his fault," I whispered. "It's not mine either."

"No, it's not." Mateo's hand came to my face, pushing the hair off my temple.

"In my head, I know it wasn't my fault. But I'll always feel guilty. I'll always wish it had ended differently. It helped, talking to you. He doesn't have anyone."

"Darlin', we have looked and looked."

"We didn't go to that lake."

Mateo propped up on an elbow. "You think that's where he's been?"

"Maybe? I don't know. But in all our years in the mountains, he never took me to a lake. I didn't even realize it. Looking back… he avoided them completely, like he knew it could set me off."

"Huh." He fell back onto his pillow, staring at the ceiling as he rubbed his jaw.

I didn't need Mateo's permission. But I loved him enough to let him be a part of my decision.

"And if he's not there?" he asked.

"Then it's done." For my heart, for Mateo's sanity, this had to be done.

He wore a frown as he whipped the sheets from his legs

and got out of bed, swiping his phone from his nightstand. He swiped across the screen, then pressed it to his ear. "Hey, Mom. Any chance you could babysit Allie today?"

I hadn't asked him to come along, but I'd known he would anyway.

When he glanced to the bed, I sat up and mouthed, "I love you."

He winked. Then he got dressed so we could get an early start.

With Mateo on my heels, I set a fast pace up the ten-mile Sable Peak trail. We were sticking to the path today, and without having to wade through underbrush and weave around trees, we'd make good time to the lake.

My muscles were warm, and with every breath of clean air I pulled into my lungs, I felt more and more at peace with this decision.

Today was the last day I'd come to Sable Peak. Whether we found Dad or not, I wouldn't come up here again.

Mateo and I would find new places to explore. We'd hike the mountains around the cabin or discover places on the ranch. But I was saying goodbye to Sable Peak. And I wouldn't return to the spot where Dad and I had lived either.

It was time to move on. With Mateo and Allie.

"Vera?"

I turned, finding him close. "Yeah?"

"What were they like? Your sisters?"

"Hadley and Elsie." It still felt strange to speak their names. It still caused a jolt of pain. But I didn't want to hide them, not anymore. Especially from Mateo.

"They were beautiful. Their hair was a shade darker than

mine, but we had the same eyes. They looked so much alike it was hard to tell them apart unless you knew them. They played tricks on people sometimes, just to mess with them. After Vance became Dad's new partner, he came over for dinner a few times. They messed with him for months until he finally realized who was Hadley and who was Elsie."

"How'd he figure it out?"

"Their nicknames." I slowed, glancing back at Mateo. "Dad went along with the ruse except he always called them by their correct nicknames. He called Elsie Sprout. And he called Hadley—"

"Jellybean."

I nodded.

"Vera." He stopped moving. "You didn't tell me about the nicknames. I would have picked another one."

"I know." I gave him a sad smile. "But I like that you call Allie Sprout. And I thought it was fitting that I could call her Jellybean."

He closed the distance between us, staring down at me from beneath the brim of his baseball hat. He'd dressed in a plain gray T-shirt today, the cotton stretched across his wide chest.

I wrapped my arms around his waist and tucked my hands into the back pockets of his jeans. "My sisters would have loved you. They were witty and loud and sweet and snarky. Elsie would have wanted to have a big belt buckle just like yours and a pair of boots so she could call herself a cowgirl. Hadley would have asked you to teach her how to ride. They both would have begged Dad to get them horses."

Mateo tugged on the end of my ponytail. "What else?"

"Hadley wanted to become an actress. Elsie wanted to write a book about dragon riders. They had these huge imaginations. Everything was over-the-top drama. They were always together. And they never learned how to knock. It used to drive me crazy. I'd close the door to my room, and two seconds later, they'd burst into my room to tell me a story or gossip or raid my closet for their latest costume."

I could still see their faces in my mind, but I couldn't hear their voices anymore.

"I miss their noise."

"I'm sorry."

My nose started to sting, but I sniffed it and any threat of tears away. "We went too long without talking about them."

"I'm here," Mateo said. "Anytime."

Maybe if I talked about my sisters enough, I'd hear their voices, their laughter, again. Maybe if I stopped avoiding their memories, they'd get brighter, not fade away.

"Vance had them cremated. He scattered their ashes in a meadow. When we went back to Idaho after I left Dad, it was too snowy, so we didn't visit. But I think... I think I'd like to." I already knew his answer, but I asked anyway. "Would you go with me?"

"Yes."

"Thank you."

"You don't have to thank me, Peach. We go together. From here to Idaho to the ends of the earth."

How did he always know the right thing to say? We weren't going to the ends of the earth today. Just to a lake. So I took his hand, laced our fingers together and climbed the trail.

It took two hours for us to make it to the top of the mountain. The lake was another mile on a narrow path that wound through the woods.

The trail wasn't as worn this far up and in one place, a tree had fallen, forcing us to go around. But then the scents of pine and earth changed to something lighter. Fresher.

The track led us straight to the water's edge. The lake was only as big as a football field, three times longer than it was wide. It was crystal clear and as smooth as glass. A breeze kicked up a tiny ripple on the surface.

It was breathtaking. Terrifying, but beautiful.

My pulse quickened as fear began to take hold, but then Mateo's hand clamped around my elbow.

I sagged into his side, stealing some of his strength. "I'm okay."

"Vera." The edge to his voice made me stand tall.

"What?" I followed his gaze across the water.

To the man standing on the opposite shore.

Dad.

I gasped.

Was that really him? If not for Mateo's grip, I would have thought I'd conjured him from a dream.

But it hadn't been my imagination all those weeks ago. His beard was that unruly, scraggly red.

We'd found him. Finally. I'd found him.

He was alive.

Dad stood, shocked, staring back. Even from this distance, I watched the color drain from his face. His scar looked too pink. His hair too gray. His frame too thin. Exactly how it had been that day I'd spotted him weeks ago.

He'd known I'd been searching. He'd watched me come for him.

And he'd left anyway.

I took a step forward, toward the water.

My movement seemed to jerk him out of his stupor. He pressed a hand to his heart, his face falling.

He was going to leave me. Again.

"No." My voice, loud and strong, carried across the lake. "Don't you run from me."

"Go, Vera. Forget about me." There was a crack in his voice, but God, it felt good to hear him. To see him.

He was alive. Two years, and the fears I'd refused to acknowledge faded. He was alive.

And he was leaving me. Again.

Dad turned toward the forest.

"Stop!"

His shoulders fell. His feet stopped. But he didn't turn back.

I'd spent four years following him through the wilderness, and he'd always been wearing his pack. It was strange to see him without it. It made him seem vulnerable. Smaller. Weaker.

But still strong enough to walk away.

"Don't go," I yelled. "Please, Dad."

He turned his profile to us with a sad, hopeless smile and shouted, "Live your life, Vera. Stop trying to find me."

"Never."

He twisted enough to take me in, head to toe.

A long, final look at his daughter.

There was no way we'd catch him. If he bolted into those trees, I'd never see him again. He'd outpace us no matter how fast we were. By the time we rounded the end of the lake, he'd be long gone.

And even if I could convince Mateo to come out here again, it would be pointless. Dad would leave Montana forever.

I took a step toward the water. Then another.

"Vera." Mateo was at my side, that grip on my elbow holding firm.

"He's leaving me."

The look on Mateo's face was devastating. It was full of anguish and pain, my pain. Because he knew Dad was leaving me. And he knew this was our last goodbye.

Unless...

I didn't let myself think. I didn't let the fear take hold. If Dad did run, there was only one way to catch up.

With a quick shrug, I slipped out of Mateo's grip and dropped my backpack to the ground. Water splashed onto the hem of my jeans as I took that first step into the frigid water. The second brought it to my knees.

The cold. God, it was so cold.

"Vera!" Dad's panicked voice boomed off the trees.

I locked my gaze with his, seeing the same fear on his face that I probably wore on mine.

Maybe he'd kept me away from lakes. Maybe he could stand them if he was alone.

But to see his daughter in this water?

He froze.

Tears filled my eyes and streaked down my cheeks. My heart pounded so hard and fast against my sternum it was impossible to breathe, but I managed to suck down an inhale.

Then I dove.

The water was like ice. It soaked my clothes and the weight began to pull me down to the shallows.

I kicked my legs, taking two hard strokes with my arms.

Swim, Vera. Swim.

It was that night all over again. I kicked my legs harder, pulled my arms faster.

Swim. Swim. Swim.

There were no waves. There was no boat. The lake wasn't deep and there was no storm. But the panic was crippling. It clawed at my throat, refusing to let any air come inside. I slipped, sinking a little, and choked on a gulp of water.

I kicked harder, thrashing as the panic took hold of my movements, making them frantic and wild. Oh, God. What was I thinking? I couldn't swim. I couldn't be in this lake.

"Swim, Vera."

It wasn't my voice. It was Mateo's.

His arm clamped around my bicep, hauling me up as he swam at my side.

I dragged in a breath, forcing air to my lungs. Then I gripped his forearm, using him to steady my strokes.

"Swim," he ordered.

So I swam. We swam together to my father, standing waist-deep on the opposite shore, ready to dive into this lake and rescue his daughter.

The second I found my footing on the slippery rocks, he rushed to catch me, hauling me out of the water.

"Vera." He pushed the wet hair off my face. "Oh, God, Vera. What were you thinking?"

I let the tears fall and the sobs choke loose. "Don't leave me."

He hauled me into his chest, hugging me so tightly it was hard to breathe. "This isn't what I want."

"But it's what she wants." Mateo was breathing hard as he stood by our sides, his hands planted on his dripping jeans. "And that's all that matters."

Dad shifted me to the side but didn't let me go.

Mateo held out a hand. "Mateo Eden."

Dad glanced down at me, looking between the two of us. Then he blew out a long breath, a breath that seemed like two years in the making, and shook Mateo's hand. "Cormac Gallagher."

CHAPTER 35

MATEO

"What are you doing with all this lumber?" Griffin asked as he stared at the back of my truck. It was loaded with the two-by-fours and treated posts I'd just picked up from the hardware store in town after lunch.

"Building." Had I known Griffin would be waiting for me when I got home, I would have come up with a better lie.

"No shit," he deadpanned. "*What* are you building?"

"A firepit. Vera likes s'mores."

His gaze narrowed. "Thought you finished that firepit."

Yeah, I'd finished it last week. But he didn't need to know that. "Had an idea for some enhancements."

"Enhancements." My brother narrowed his gaze. Like Mom, Griffin had always been good at sniffing out bullshit.

"Enhancements." If enhancements for the firepit meant a shelter built three miles up the mountain for Vera's father.

It had been a month since we'd found Cormac at Sable Peak, and not a soul knew he was currently living on Eden Ranch property.

And as risky as this arrangement was, it was what Vera wanted. She needed to see her father. Cormac needed to see his daughter.

He'd looked like hell when we'd found him by the lake.

Too thin. Too frazzled. Too hopeless. But just a month of being closer to Vera, he'd put on some weight and even shaved that nasty beard with a razor she'd put in a box of supplies.

If it made her worry less about him, then we'd chance this secret.

Griffin might run the ranch and own a sizeable chunk of the land, but we'd decided the fewer people who knew the truth, the better. We weren't even telling Vance and Lyla.

Besides, Cormac was on my property. The acreage around this cabin was mine to do with as I pleased, including hide a fugitive.

"Thought you were working on the treehouse today?" I asked, changing the subject.

"I am," he grumbled. "But that project is turning into a nightmare."

"It was your idea."

His mouth pursed into a flat line. "Now you sound like Winn."

I chuckled. "Would you like some help? Is that why you came up here?"

He kicked a rock with his boot. "Yes. Are you busy?"

"Not today." I smacked him on the shoulder. "Let me call Mom and make sure she's good to keep Allie for a few more hours."

"She is." Griffin smirked. "I already called her."

I rolled my eyes and, with a smile, grabbed my phone and gloves from the truck. I left the keys on the console before climbing in Griffin's truck to ride down the mountain to his place.

We spent five hours on the treehouse, finishing the deck's railings and stairs. By the time we were done, it actually looked like a treehouse.

It had been Griff's idea to build it for Hudson and Emma. He wanted the kids to have a spot to escape, and what better hideaway than a treehouse in a small evergreen grove off their backyard?

But when the Edens did construction, we didn't fuck around. He'd spent countless hours researching tabs and braces for the structure, something that would allow the trees to grow and the house to float between them on windy days.

The house had a tin shed roof and the siding was reclaimed barnwood, giving it a rustic look as it blended in with the surroundings.

"Maybe I'll build one of these for Allie," I told him as we stood on the ground, surveying our handiwork.

"Good idea. Whenever that is, consider me busy. Ask Knox for help if you need it," he teased.

I laughed and dug my phone from my pocket when it buzzed.

Picked up Allie & we're heading home xo

"Vera?" Griff asked.

"Yeah. She's on her way home."

"Want to stick around for a beer? Winn mentioned something about grilling burgers. I think Eloise and Jasper were going to come out. Have Vera come here instead."

"All right. Want me to text Lyla and Talia?"

"Sure. I'll call Knox."

That was how all of the impromptu barbeques started with our family. Someone offered a beer. There were usually cheeseburgers. And we were more than family. We were friends.

Mom and Dad declined, wanting a night alone. So my siblings and I invaded Griffin's house.

Years ago, not long after he'd met Winn, these gatherings would last all night with at least one of us crashing in a guest bed. But now that we all had kids, we were waving good night by eight to head home.

"Did Eloise really date a guy who shoved a cucumber down

his pants at the grocery store?" Vera asked as we drove home.

"Yep." It was one of many stories we'd shared tonight, and I wanted Vera to learn them all. To fit so completely into our family that it filled her heart.

She'd always miss her sisters. But maybe with time, it wouldn't cut so deep.

She glanced through the rearview mirror at Allie buckled in her car seat.

My daughter's yawn was loud and long.

"She's totally going to fall asleep before we get home." Vera frowned. "But she really needs a bath before bed."

The kids had all played in the sandbox tonight after dinner. There was dirt streaked on Allie's face and her legs were dusty.

"Maybe she'll make it," I said.

"Not a chance." Vera was right. When we parked outside of the cabin beside my truck, Allie was sleeping with her head hung forward and her mouth open, her body only upright because of her car seat's harness. "I hate waking her up."

"I'll bring her in. You get the bath started." I leaned across the cab, dropping a quick kiss on the corner of her mouth, then unbuckled.

Allie whined the minute I hauled her from the car, and when she tried to fall asleep on my shoulder, I jostled her to stay awake.

"Time for a bath."

"No." She kicked and squirmed, but I pulled off her shoes as we walked, dropping them on the floor when we were inside. The sound of running water echoed from the bathroom.

Vera was kneeling by the tub when we made it to the door.

Allie reached for her. "Ve-wa."

"Mommy," I corrected, my voice low enough that Vera couldn't hear with the water sloshing. The days of *Ve-wa* were gone. "That's Mommy."

Allie rested her head against my shoulder, her dark little

eyebrows coming together. "Mommy."

It clicked, faster than I thought it would. Probably because my girl, even at two, was smart. She knew how lucky we were to have Vera in our lives.

Someday, I'd tell her about Madison. When she was older and I knew what to say, I'd explain that Vera wasn't her biological mother. But in every other way, in every way that mattered, Vera was her mother.

With a kiss on Allie's forehead, I set her down and started stripping off her clothes.

"Ready?" Vera opened her arms, picking up Allie to set her in the tub. The water was still running, bubbles still building.

Allie was groggy, her eyes heavy. When Vera picked up the cup to fill it with water for her hair, Allie simply tilted her head back and closed her eyes.

I leaned against the doorframe and dug my phone from my pocket, taking a quick picture of them together. Then I found a towel and got the lotion from the counter, both at the ready when bath time was over. Vera had Allie washed and the drain pulled when I brought in a clean diaper and pajamas.

"I'll take her," I said after Allie's hair was combed.

"Okay." Vera stood on her toes to kiss my cheek, then slipped past us for the living room while I carried our daughter to her bed.

Five minutes later, with Allie already asleep, Vera was standing in the open front door, staring into the night.

"Your truck is gone."

I wrapped my arms around her, resting my chin on her head. "He'll bring it back."

"Tonight's note." She held up a slip of paper that had been folded in half. It was the receipt from my lumber order. "It's for you."

I snagged it. My name was scratched on the front. When

I flipped it open, in the upper corner was a single word.

Good.

I grinned and crumpled the paper.

These notes were how we communicated with Cormac. Vera would leave a note for him every day beneath a rock tucked under the front porch with a pen. He'd slip in at night beneath the cover of darkness, read it and write her back.

Sometimes he missed a day or two. But for the most part, she was able to communicate with her father every day. And if he needed something, he'd leave a list.

Last week, it had been for lumber.

Tonight, he'd drive my truck to the end of a two-lane, dead-end road that no one had used for years. From there, he'd unload the boards and carry each piece over two miles to the small hut he was building.

The location was remote enough that a random hiker wouldn't stumble upon his place. The spot he'd chosen was backed up against a rock cliff, and the only way to access the land was from the ranch.

Since I had no intention of letting anyone on my private property, Cormac should be safe. At least for the time being.

The arrangement was new. Nerves were running high and he'd refused to let Vera or myself come to his shelter more than once. That visit had been simply so we'd know where to find him, but he'd given explicit instructions for us to stay away.

Beyond that, he'd only seen Vera once since we'd found him at the lake. He'd snuck down in the dead of night a couple weeks ago, and they'd sat at the firepit and talked for an hour.

Cormac had told her about Yosemite. He'd gone there right after Vera had left with Vance. He'd planned to get away and give her some distance, knowing the media and authorities would be in a frenzy for a girl believed dead but found alive.

He'd wanted to be as far away from Idaho and Montana as he could manage in a short time, so rather than risk crossing the border to Canada, he'd headed south. As I'd guessed, he'd left the pack behind intentionally, hoping someone would find it, presume he was dead and give him a break.

Maybe that ploy would have worked on the former FBI agent assigned to Cormac's case. Unfortunately for us all, Swenson was a serious pain in the ass.

When Vera had told Cormac about Swenson, it had spooked Cormac enough that he insisted on limited contact. Notes only.

Hopefully in time, we could all relax. Not entirely. But a little.

Agent Swenson had left Montana after he'd ambushed Vera in the hotel lobby. With luck, we'd never see him again, but I had a hunch he'd be back.

My theory was that Swenson would poke around every so often, breezing in and out of Quincy like he owned the town, simply to ruffle Vera's feathers—the asshole.

So far, his visits had been tame. But I suspected if she gave him even an inkling that she was in contact with Cormac, Swenson would become more diligent. Maybe he'd start coming to the house. Following her around.

We were going to do our best not to give him that inkling.

Even if that meant Vera communicated with her father in scribbles.

"I don't understand this note," Vera said. "What did you write him?"

"That I was going to marry you."

She jerked in my arms, her head whipping up to mine. "W-what?"

I shifted to dig in my pocket and pull out the ring I'd hidden in Allie's toy box. Taking her hand in mine, I slipped it on her ring finger. "It was Mom's."

Vera's hand trembled as she stared at the solitaire diamond. It wasn't big. It wasn't flashy. Just a simple jewel on a golden band.

"Dad upgraded her ring for their ten-year anniversary. When I told her I was marrying you, she gave me this. She won't be offended if you don't like—"

"I love it." She twisted in my arms.

"I love you." I framed her face in my hands, dropping a kiss to her mouth.

"You're really asking me to marry you?"

"There's no question here, Peach. We're getting married."

"And you call me stubborn."

I winked. "Would it make you feel better if you said yes?"

"Does it mean something when you wink?"

I'd been winking at Vera for years. It meant something. It always had. "What do you think?"

The light danced in those pretty eyes as she launched herself into my arms. Then she leaned in close, her mouth hovering over mine with a smile. "I think yes."

CHAPTER 36

VERA

FIVE YEARS LATER...

"Got your flashlight?" Dad asked.

I held it up. "Yep."

"Better get back to camp. It's already dark."

"Okay." I threw my arms around his shoulders, hugging him as tight as possible with my massive belly between us. At eight months pregnant, hugs were becoming tricky. "Love you, Daddy."

"I love you, Vera." He kissed my hair. "Never forget how much I love you."

"Never." I held him for another moment, then let go.

In the five years since Mateo and I had found Dad on Sable Peak, it hadn't gotten easier to walk away. There was always a lingering fear that something would ruin the peace we'd found.

Maybe Agent Swenson. He came to town every year, sometimes twice. He'd ask questions and be a general nuisance, but otherwise, his visits felt like a huge waste of time. Luckily, he usually found me at Eden Coffee. Only twice had he visited our home. But with each unannounced ambush, it would put us on alert.

Dad would stay close to his home in the mountains—his "chalet" as he referred to it because that sounded fancier than shanty. And I'd spend weeks looking over my shoulder.

But the nerves would eventually pass, and we'd settle into our routine again, and Dad would visit me at home late at night.

Tonight, home was the camper Mateo and I had bought before this year's annual Eden family camping trip, because not a chance I was sleeping on the ground while I was this pregnant. The spot we'd chosen for this year's campout was close to the cabin, in case something happened with the baby, so Dad had snuck down to meet me for a hug.

He met me a lot these days, at least three times a week. Last week, he'd come every day. His visits had increased with the size of my belly.

We usually sat on a swing at the firepit, talking for an hour. I'd tell him about Mateo and Allie. He'd ask questions about my college classes. When I'd finished my last course this spring, he'd whittled a graduation cap out of wood as my gift. The night of my baby shower, he'd brought me a set of woodland creatures, each intricately carved, to put in the nursery.

It was rare that we talked about my sisters. Even rarer that we talked about my mother, though he shared the story of how they'd really met. I knew it already, but I'd let him tell me anyway. He'd confessed about her struggles with addiction and explained her upbringing with abusive, alcoholic parents.

Only once had we discussed that night. I told him exactly what I'd shared with Mateo. I cried hard, reliving that nightmare. For each tear I'd shed, Dad had wept two.

It had been important to me that he know I didn't blame him for that night. But no matter what I said, he'd always carry that guilt. So we stuck to safe topics about school, the future and the Edens.

I was an Eden now. Two months after we'd gotten engaged, we'd married in a small ceremony in a fall meadow on the ranch. My wedding ring was a bit tight on my swollen fingers, but I hadn't taken it off since Mateo had given it to me.

Vance had walked me down an aisle of wild grasses to an archway wreathed in flowers. My dress had a lace bodice with long sleeves. The back had dipped low, revealing my spine and shoulder blades before the skirt flared out in a swish of silk.

Allie had been my flower girl, dressed in a burnt orange fluffy tulle skirt and white lace shirt. She'd done remarkably well at dropping petals on the path, soaking in the attention of her grandparents, aunts and uncles.

She'd turned around at the end of the aisle and yelled, "You go, Mommy."

Three months after the wedding, the final paperwork to approve my adoption had come through.

There were days when it still didn't feel real, but then I'd kiss Mateo and send up a silent thanks to the angels who'd kept me going. Who'd kept me alive. All so I could be here, walking along a forest trail with my flashlight illuminating the way to a campground brimming with laughter.

Everyone thought I'd snuck away to rest. Though I was sure Vance knew what I was actually doing.

He'd spotted Dad on an autumn hike a couple years ago. Or rather, Dad had let Vance spot him. We didn't talk much about it. Secrecy had kept Dad's whereabouts safe, so we'd agreed the less we said the better. But sometimes, I'd come home and find Vance's truck parked at the cabin and Vance nowhere in sight.

When I reached the clearing cramped with seven campers—every couple had upgraded from tents—I glanced over my shoulder.

Dad stood in the shadows, twenty feet away, always keeping watch to make sure I made it home.

I blew him a kiss, then waddled toward our camper.

Mateo shoved off the side where he'd been waiting since I went to say hello to Dad. "Hey, Peach."

"Hi." I walked straight into his arms, burying my nose in his T-shirt. The flannel he'd been wearing over it was so warm that I'd stolen it earlier. The sleeves were rolled up three times and the hem fell nearly to my knees.

I leaned away, my chin on his sternum as I stared into the sky. "What did I miss?"

"Foster and Jasper are sharing old UFC stories. Remind me never to pick a fight with either of them."

I laughed. "Because you fight so often."

"For you, I'd fight them all."

I tipped my head back farther. "I love you."

"Love you too. Want to go back to the fire?"

As our family's laughter and stories filled the night air, I smiled up at the heavens. Out here, with no city lights to interfere, the Milky Way swirled through twinkling diamond stars.

"Let's hide out here for a few more minutes. Make a wish on a shooting star."

"You get the wishes."

"You don't have any?"

"They already came true." He spun me so my back was pressed against his chest, his hands splayed on my belly.

We were having a boy. Mateo had wanted to name him Jake, but I'd dug my heels in and insisted he was Mateo Jr.

Matty.

Allie was practically vibrating with excitement to be a big sister. She'd been helping me get everything ready by folding onesies and baby blankets. Now that school was over, I was nesting.

I'd graduated with my bachelor's degree in social work this spring. The online offerings had only gotten me so far, and for the past three years, I'd been taking classes at the university in Missoula.

The four-hour-round-trip drive from Quincy would have been impossible had I needed to make it every day. Luckily, my husband was a damn good pilot.

I'd been able to limit my classes to two or three days a week, and on those days, Mateo would fly me to Missoula, drop me off for school, then return every afternoon to bring me home.

On the days when the weather was bad, we either drove or I stayed home. Every one of my professors had been understanding, and since I'd worked my tail off to get good grades, they'd accommodated my absences.

The job hunt would start when I was ready, but for now, I was enjoying the last month of my pregnancy. Besides, with Mateo's schedule getting busier, I wanted to stay home and spend more time with the kids.

Mateo's flight school had been more popular than either of us could have imagined. He flew almost every day with at least one student, sometimes more. He was in the process of building another hangar at the airfield for the Cessna he'd bought, a less complicated plane than his Cirrus and more affordable for his younger students.

Three Quincy High kids were becoming pilots, two seniors and one junior.

The hangar was his second big construction project of the year. We'd added on two bedrooms to the cabin and a bathroom.

It was exciting and busy and... normal.

"It's more than I expected."

"What? Camping?"

"A normal life."

Mateo's arms tightened as he leaned down for a kiss. Then he stood tall again, both of us staring up at the stars.

They offered light. Hope.

They stared down at us without a cloud in sight.

Maybe my sisters were up there. Allie knew about them. So did Mateo. Whenever a memory crossed my mind, I gave it voice. Five years, and I saw them the way I saw Mateo and Allie.

Not a cloud in sight.

This life of ours was clear and a million.

EPILOGUE

MATEO

TEN YEARS LATER...

"**M**om." Alaina rushed to Vera's side, eyes as wide as her smile as she bent to whisper something in her mother's ear.

Vera stood straighter at whatever Allie said, then searched through the crowd beneath the massive white tent.

"Who are we looking at?"

They both ignored me, having one of their silent conversations with a thousand words passing between them.

And whatever was happening went right over my head.

Allie gave Vera a pleading look.

Vera nodded. It was that insistent nod that said I wasn't going to like what Allie was about to tell me.

Hell. It was probably about a boy.

"Daddy, I, um, sort of invited a date."

Was she trying to ruin the party? "A date."

"Yeah." She chewed on her lower lip.

"Who?" I crossed my arms over my chest, scanning faces.

Vera had warned me that Allie had a new crush. Apparently some kid she'd met weeks ago at Eden Coffee.

Allie worked for Lyla every summer and this guy had come

in one morning, new to Quincy, for breakfast. According to my wife, he stopped in to see Allie a few times a week. But if he was at my parents' anniversary party as a *date*, then we were way past some flirting at the coffee shop.

"He's standing beside Papa. Light blue shirt. Jeans."

The boy was easy to spot. Though "boy" wasn't the right term. Young man. "No. Absolutely not. He's way too old."

"Mateo." Vera elbowed me in the ribs as she smiled at Allie. A conspirator's smile. "He's cute."

"Peach," I scoffed. I didn't give a shit if the kid was cute. I cared about his birthday. That was not a boy from Quincy High.

"Give him some credit," Vera said. "Coming to this party is the equivalent to walking into the lion's den." Not only was I here, but so was every one of Allie's uncles.

"Fair point," I muttered.

"Dad, please be nice." Allie looked up at me with those pleading blue eyes. "I invited him here for a reason. If he isn't man enough to handle our family, then he's not the guy for me."

I was proud of my daughter every day. But some days, I had so much pride it hurt.

Damn it. I was going to have to be nice. "How old is he?"

Allie gave me an exaggerated frown. "Twenty."

And she was seventeen.

"For fuck's sake." I pinched the bridge of my nose.

Vera tucked her hand into the back pocket of my jeans. "We'll be over to meet him in a bit."

"Okay." Allie kissed Vera's cheek. "Thanks, Mom."

"Alaina." I stopped her before she could disappear. "Don't sneak off. I don't trust him."

That earned me an eye roll from both mother and daughter.

Vera and I watched as she made her way to the boy.

When he spotted her, the smile he gave Allie was blinding.

He was totally hooked on my daughter, wasn't he? Probably a good thing that there were three hundred people separating us at the moment. I had the urge to throw him out of this tent.

I groaned. "And I was having such a good night."

Vera giggled, leaning into my side. "It's going to be okay."

"I hate this."

"I know you do."

My little girl wasn't a little girl anymore. This wasn't her first date, but something about this felt different. Like that twenty-year-old was pulling her farther and farther out of my grasp.

"Hey, Vera." A woman she worked with came over, giving her a hug.

It had taken Vera years to get her master's degree and become a licensed social worker, but she said that every new case, every new struggling person to help, especially kids, made the long hours and late nights studying at the dining room table worth it.

Maybe if her mother had had help earlier in life, Norah Gallagher's story would have had a different ending. Maybe if someone had recognized the signs that her parents were abusing her, they could have helped her find a different path.

Every now and then, Vera would bring up her mother, but she tried hard not to go too far down the road of *what if.* She focused on helping other families. Giving back to Quincy.

"Mateo." A group of guys I knew from high school waved me over to join their conversation. We reminisced for a few minutes, then talked about the ranch, and when I glanced over my shoulder to find Vera, she was gone.

Wait. Did she go meet the boy without me?

"Better go find my wife," I said. "Thanks for coming out tonight."

With a nod, I weaved through the crush, seeking out that pretty red hair.

Nearly the entire town had come out to the ranch for the evening. Mom and Dad's anniversary was the party of the year.

The tent spanned the parking area in front of the barn and stables. The live band was playing country music from the stage at the opposite end of the tent. The caterer had cleared away the buffet, but the bar was surrounded by adults and the cake table mobbed with kids.

Two boys were getting what had to be their third piece of cake.

Matty turned, carrying a piece of double chocolate. When he spotted me, his smile dropped. He leaned in to say something in his little brother's ear. Probably a warning that Dad was coming.

When Braydon turned and spotted me, he just giggled. There was frosting on the tip of his nose.

They loved wedding cake. They were my sons, after all.

"This is your last piece," I said when I made it to the table.

"Okay." Matty nodded.

Braydon chased after him to a nearby table filled with their cousins. At least the pieces were small. I snatched a plate of my own, shoving the whole slice in my mouth in a single bite. Good thing they didn't know it was my fourth.

Matty was nine and Braydon was seven. Where one went, the other was never far behind. They were more than brothers. They were best friends.

Braydon, we'd named after my uncle. We'd used Briggs's middle name.

When Vera was pregnant, we'd told Uncle Briggs about the namesake on one of his lucid days. Anymore, the dementia kept him from recognizing anyone but Dad. Regardless, I tried to visit him every other week. Usually I went alone, but sometimes Vera would tag along. Other days, Allie would go.

She had one more year of high school left, then she'd be

going to Embry-Riddle in Arizona. Allie had her heart set on becoming an aerospace engineer and had already completed her certification as a private pilot.

I'd taught her to fly.

The hole that she'd leave behind when she left for college was already too big. I was ignoring it for now. We had another year.

And that boy she'd invited to the party had better not break her heart and fuck it all up.

Where the hell were they?

It took a minute, but I finally found them talking to a group of Allie's high school friends. But no Vera.

I was just about to change direction, head toward the dance floor, when a swish of red caught my eye.

Vera had a hand to her mouth, covering a yawn, as she slipped past the tent's open walls and into the night.

If we were at home, she'd be going outside to visit Cormac at the firepit. But tonight, she was probably going to get caffeine.

It was midnight and we'd been here since seven this morning getting everything set up. The party showed no signs of stopping—the band was playing until one. She probably wanted a cup of coffee.

The bar was not serving coffee.

I rushed toward the nearest opening, then jogged to catch Vera, wrapping my arms around her before she reached the porch stairs at Mom and Dad's. "Where do you think you're going?"

"Sneaking out. I need coffee if I'm going to make it all night."

"Want company?"

"Always." She leaned up and kissed the underside of my jaw, then took my hand and tugged me into the house.

I'd expected it to be empty, but voices drifted from inside.

"Guess we weren't the only ones ready to ditch the party."

When we walked down the hallway, we found our family in the kitchen.

The coffee pot was brewing.

"Seems we all had the same idea." Knox grabbed another mug from the cupboard. "Coffee?"

"Please." Vera yawned again, and I pulled out a stool for her to sit beside Lyla.

"Who's the guy with Allie?" Vance asked. "He's a little old for her, isn't he?"

"Yes," I muttered.

Knox slid Vera's mug across the island just as Mom and Dad, walking hand in hand, found their children in the kitchen.

"So none of us are at the party?" Anne laughed. "We're terrible hosts."

"The kids are still out there," I said.

The next generation of Edens could handle it.

"Ugh." Griffin dragged a hand over his face. "I don't trust Hudson to stay away from the bar. We should probably go back out there and supervise."

"Probably." Harrison sighed.

No one moved. Because here, inside this house, in this kitchen, was our party.

Mom and Dad.

Griffin and Winn.

Knox and Memphis.

Foster and Talia.

Jasper and Eloise.

Vance and Lyla.

Vera and me.

Some of us hadn't started with the last name Eden. Some of us had changed it with marriage. But every person in this house claimed it.

We were the Edens.

BONUS EPILOGUE

Harrison

"Congratulations." Covie, our retired mayor and Winn's grandfather, clapped me on the shoulder.

"Thanks for coming." I shook his hand, then waved as he escorted his wife, Janice, toward the exit.

I stifled a yawn, checking my watch. Midnight.

Tonight was an anniversary party for Anne and me. The kids had wanted to celebrate and do something special this year, so we'd gone all out, inviting most of Quincy out to the ranch.

Sure, this party was fun. It was good to see folks, like Covie, who I didn't meet as often for lunch at Knuckles as I used to. But I didn't need a big gathering to celebrate my marriage.

Just sharing life with Anne was reward enough.

The tent was crammed with laughing, happy guests. The band was playing my favorite classic country. Songs I'd loved since the eighties. There was too much food and plenty of cake.

But up until midnight, it had just been a party.

Now it was our anniversary. And it was time to find my girl.

I searched the crowd of faces for the prettiest.

Anne was laughing with a group of ladies from her book club. She'd always loved books, but lately, she'd been reading voraciously and rarely left the house without her Kindle. Lucky for me, whatever she was reading was damn spicy.

Not that we hadn't had a lot of fun in the bedroom throughout our marriage. But this year, it felt like we were kids again. Like we were in our twenties, desperate to make love and babies. Or maybe we were both simply taking advantage of the years we had left, not wanting to waste a moment together. My dick still worked. My wife still liked it.

I strode to Anne, slipping an arm around her shoulders. "Ladies, mind if I steal my beautiful bride?"

As they nodded, I eased her away, bending to kiss her temple. "Having fun?"

"Yes." Anne looked up at me, her bright blue eyes twinkling. "You?"

"Yep. But I was thinking we could sneak away for a minute." I wagged my eyebrows. "Let's go have a quickie."

Her cheeks flushed as she checked over her shoulder. "Harrison, this is our party. We can't leave."

"We're not leaving. We're just going to fool around for a few minutes. Then we'll be right back." Maybe. A few minutes might not be enough.

She worried her lip between her teeth. "You can't mess up my hair."

"Deal." I let go of her shoulders to clamp my hand over hers. Then I dragged my wife to our house.

Familiar voices greeted us as we stepped through the front door. My children and grandchildren were my pride and joy. But this wasn't the first time I'd hoped to give my wife an orgasm only to be blocked by my progeny.

"So much for foolin' around," I muttered. "Maybe we need to start locking the door."

"Stop." Anne smacked me in the gut with her free hand,

then tugged me down the hall.

All six kids were in the kitchen. And all six stood beside the loves of their lives. My other six kids.

They might not have been born Edens, but they were mine all the same.

"So none of us are at the party?" Anne laughed. "We're terrible hosts."

"The kids are still out there," Mateo said.

"Ugh." Griffin dragged a hand over his face. "I don't trust Hudson to stay away from the bar. We should probably go back out there and supervise."

"Probably." I sighed.

Did we have to go back to the party? Now that I was inside, I kind of wanted to stay.

I wasn't alone in that.

No one in the kitchen moved.

So I tucked Anne into my side, letting the love in this room fill my heart.

God, we were lucky. To have these kids. To know that they'd found the love I shared with Anne.

"This is better than a party," Anne said, quiet enough for only me to hear. "Don't you think?"

"Yes, it is." I bent to give her a kiss. "Happy anniversary, darlin'."

EXCLUSIVE BONUS CONTENT

MATEO

Mom rapped her knuckles on the open door to my child-hood bedroom. "Can I come in?"

"Of course." I finished adjusting the sleeves of my shirt beneath my charcoal jacket. The clothes weren't too tight but they felt too tight. No matter how much air I sucked into my lungs, it was hard to breathe.

"Here's your boutonniere." Mom popped the lid on a small plastic box, taking out a peach rose adorned with greenery. With quick fingers, she slid the pearl-head pin through the stem and fitted it to my lapel. Then she stepped away, surveying me head to toe, her face softening when she was finished. "You look so handsome."

"Thanks." I bent to kiss her cheek. "You look beautiful."

"Thank you." She swished the skirt of her maroon dress, her embroidered boots peeking out from beneath the hem. "Nervous?"

So nervous I couldn't see straight. "No."

"Liar." She laughed. "It's normal to be nervous on your wedding day."

"Well, then mission accomplished."

It wasn't that I worried Vera would get cold feet. I wasn't anxious about the logistics of the ceremony or scared to

have an audience while we exchanged vows. I was just...
fucking nervous.

"How was everything at the cabin?" I asked.

"Good. Chaotic. They were just finishing up Vera's hair
when I left."

Mom had spent the day at my house with Vera, Allie
and my sisters. They'd brought in a couple stylists from the
salon in town to do hair and makeup this morning.

I'd left shortly after breakfast to meet Dad and go for a
ride. It was tradition, something he'd done with his father
before his wedding. Something he'd done with Griffin and
Knox.

After our ride, we'd met my brothers in the meadow
where Vera and I were getting married today. We'd spent
a few hours setting up folding chairs and a floral archway.
After everything was in place and I'd said countless prayers
that it wouldn't rain—there wasn't a cloud in sight, but I
wasn't taking chances—I'd come to Mom and Dad's to
shower and get dressed.

With every passing second, the jitters in my stomach
seemed to double. My hands had been shaking so badly
while I'd shaved it was a miracle I didn't have nicks and
cuts all over my jaw.

"Is Vera doing okay?"

"She's fine, Mateo." Mom patted my arm, then reached
into a pocket of her dress, taking out a small envelope.

"What's this?" I took it from her, about to pop the seal,
but she held up a hand.

"Read it later. When you have a quiet moment."

"All right." I tucked it inside my coat, then checked the
time. "We'd better get going."

Going was good. Moving was good. The longer we
waited, the more I felt like puking.

"Rings?" Mom asked.

I patted the pocket of my slacks for the thousandth time. "Got 'em."

She led the way through the house, meeting Dad in the kitchen.

"Looking sharp, son." He clapped me on the shoulder. "Ready?"

"Yeah." More than ready. I suspected these nerves wouldn't quit until Vera was my wife.

Following my parents outside, I let Mom ride shotgun and took the backseat. As Dad drove us to the meadow, I slipped the envelope Mom had given me from my pocket and took out the letter inside.

Dear Mateo,

Did I ever tell you the story about Gary? He was this old tabby cat who moved out of the barn to live under our porch. That little bastard was the bane of my existence. Every time I came down the stairs, he'd hiss and swat at my ankles. But he loved your dad.

Gary would rub against Harrison's jeans and let him scratch his ears. He was an entirely different animal if your dad was around. But if I was alone, he was a terror.

I don't know how many times I told your dad we needed to get rid of that cat. That I was tired of rushing down the stairs because I didn't want to get scratched. But he never believed me. He never saw Gary act like demon spawn. Months and months we argued about that cat. Until one day, your dad told me I was overreacting. (Maybe I was overreacting. In my defense, I was eight months pregnant with Griffin and the hormones were raging.)

I got so mad that he'd side with an asshole cat over his wife that I packed a bag and went to stay at your grandma and grandpa's house. Never in my life have I been so pissed at your father. It took two hours before he came to bring me home, but I told him the only way I was coming back was if that cat was gone.

Gary must have sensed your dad's allegiance had changed. It took a week to trap him. Then he gave that cat to Briggs, and for three years, I refused to visit the cabin. Not until that cat was dead and buried. You've probably seen the tree Briggs marked over Gary's grave. He loved that cat.

Your dad and I have had plenty of arguments in our marriage. You'll have that with Vera too. But that fight over Gary was the worst. We came out of it together. Stronger. And we laugh about it these days.

If there's one thing I could wish for you and Vera, it's stupid fights. Maybe that seems strange, but I want you to have the fights that you survive together. The fights that make you stronger. The fights that you'll laugh about one day.

I love you. I'm proud of you. And I'm happy for you.
I see the way you look at Vera and it fills my heart.
Congratulations. To you both.
xoxo
Mom

I stared at the paper, reading it for a second time. Then a third. It was on my fourth pass that a laugh bubbled free.

What the hell? Mom had written me a letter about an old barn cat. On my wedding day. Seriously?

The truck came to a stop and I glanced out my window. The archway was still standing in the meadow. The chairs hadn't blown away. There was no rain.

And those crippling nerves were… gone. Vanished, like they hadn't been there in the first place.

Because Mom had written me a letter about an old barn cat, and somehow, it was exactly what I'd needed.

"Mom?"

"Yeah?" She twisted in her seat.

I held up the letter. "Thanks."

She winked. "You're welcome."

I refolded the letter, carefully putting it in my pocket so Vera could read it later, then climbed out of the truck. And thirty minutes later, beneath a *clear and a million* Montana sky, I married the love of my life.

For Allie's sixth birthday, we bought her a kitten. Vera named him Gary.

ACKNOWLEDGMENTS

Thank you for reading *Sable Peak*. It doesn't quite seem real that my time with the Edens is over. This series will always hold a special place in my heart.

Massive thanks to Elizabeth Nover. To Georgana Grinstead, who I couldn't live without. To Logan Chisholm and Vicki Valente. Thank you to Julie Deaton and Judy Zweifel. To Sarah Hansen. To Bill, Will and Nash. Each of you contributes something special to these books, and I am so very, very grateful.

Lastly, thanks to everyone who has come with me on this incredible journey. To everyone who has fallen in love with this fictional family. Thank you!

*Don't miss the exciting new books
Entangled has to offer.*

Follow us!

f @EntangledPublishing

⊙ @Entangled_Publishing

𝕏 @EntangledPub

♪ @EntangledPub

an imprint of Entangled Publishing LLC